The Golden Princess

Brian L. Braden

For Beth Ann, my true princess.

TABLE OF CONTENTS

ACKNOWLEDGMENTS

Workshopped by Katie French

Edited by Katrina Monroe

Cover by Hanna Elizabeth

Part One: Afternoon

"The Age of Gilded Darkness rose and fell thousands of years before Yu the Great built his capital upon the Yellow River, before the Silk Road, or the Pharaohs laid the first stone of the first pyramid. That age came crashing down when the Emperor of Heaven turned his face from the unspeakable evil of men and gods, and pronounced a terrible judgement on both. He buried their empires, and cursed them to be forgotten for eternity. Millennia passed before men dared to stack stone once again, or remembered what it was to read and write.

"In the twilight of that forgotten age, one city stood above the rest in splendor and wickedness. Hur-ar, City of Gold, reigned at the edge of the Caucus Mountains, and challenged the Scythian Empire for domination of the steppe surrounding what men would one day call the Black Sea. Yet, even in that dark place an ember of hope was born. Here, a princess fell from a golden throne, and transformed by grace, became a flame of hope for a lost people."

- Emperor Fu Xi, First Sovereign of China

1. Shadow at the Gates of Gold

Hur-ar wasn't so much a city as a lair.

Surrounded by jagged mountains and nestled deep in a three-sided canyon, the city resembled the gaping jaws of a ravenous beast. The weak would find themselves consumed by her power, the foolish crushed under her might. This city would one day devour the world, of that the trader was certain. Here, a cautious man might survive, but a cunning man could make himself a prince…

…Or a king.

He walked between the worlds of steppe and city, lord of neither. Behind him lay the endless grassland ruled by terrible horsemen, the Scythians, masters of the west. Ahead rose Hur-ar, the rising power in the east. The trader found himself trapped between two princes, each determined to conquer the world, each sworn to kill the other. Only one could emerge victor, and, at this moment, both needed his services. One slip, one misspoken word, and either would tear him apart. If he played his hand wisely, he would find himself on the winning side, not to mention considerably wealthier.

Half a dozen iron chains draped over his shoulder gently clinked with each step. Forged by his personal blacksmith, he relished the metal's weight pressing against his heavy fox fur cloak. Only truly powerful men possessed iron. Most displayed it on their hip in the form of a blade, but not this trader. His personal bodyguards could carry their swords for all to see. He, however, kept his Scythian dagger sharp and hidden. The chains dangling over his shoulder spoke adequately regarding his power and status.

The trader had almost reached the wall when his men, following a few paces behind, began to laugh.

He turned and scowled. "You jabber like a bunch of hags. What do you find so amusing?"

"Itch'n for some wine and whoring, m'lord," Wadim, the one Virag considered the most intelligent of the bunch, replied. "Been a long, dusty road, know what I mean, eh?"

The mercenaries exchanged knowing glances and lusty laughter. All except the fearsome looking giant of a man they called Spako. The overgrown idiot was too enthralled with a butterfly on a blade of grass to pay attention to the ongoing conversation.

The trader looked beyond them toward the west. "Have any of you fools considered glancing behind us from time to time?"

The six Sammujad bodyguards halted and considered their master. With slack expressions, they turned around and looked west from whence they came. The King's Road cut straight through the wheat fields on either side, toward the Hur River. A few miles away, the sun began to dip behind the two massive towers that supported the Kupar Bridge.

"Are we being followed?" Spako asked.

The trader shook his head.

Mountainous men, shaggy black manes, and grizzled beards blended with their filthy furs, giving his men the appearance of spear-wielding bears. To enemies, they may appear fearsome, but the trader knew how stupid his bodyguards truly were.

Stupid is easier to control, he thought.

"Do you see dust rising above the fields?"

"No, my lord." No hint of understanding graced Spako's face. For a moment the trader considered trying to explain it to the oaf, but it would be a waste.

"Come here," he crooked his finger at them as if they were children.

The men crowded around the trader, towering over the little man. Not the least bit intimidated, he rubbed his bald head impatiently. "Listen carefully. Where is our caravan?"

The warriors frowned at one another, and then at their lord.

"*Where* is our caravan?" he repeated.

Bolian shrugged and rubbed his scar-covered head and cheeks. "Back at camp where we left 'em, m'lord."

The trader leaned in. "Why do we enter Hur-ar?"

They shook their heads.

"Because you wanna trade?" Spako replied timidly. The trader reached up and slapped him hard.

Cowed, the giant of a man dropped his gaze.

"Because I am *buying*, not selling." He jingled the heavy purse tied firmly to his waist. "Having no caravan marks us as carrying gold, and that marks me for a knife across the throat.

"I don't give a damn about the Festival. In and out by tomorrow night. We deliver the goods to base camp before Prince Tuma and his warriors arrive. And you know what happens when the Scythian prince is disappointed, don't you?"

The mercenaries exchanged uneasy glances.

"No whoring. No wine. Stay close to me, don't let anyone within arm's reach. If you have doubts, kill first, talk later. I'll pay any fines for bloodshed. This time tomorrow, we march out of these gates with our treasures, or face death under Scythian hooves."

Without another word, he turned and resumed the march, his shadow, stark and crisp, led the way.

The sunset swept across the unbroken steppe and bathed the city wall and the mountains beyond in glittering glory.

Only at sunset did Hur-ar live up to its name, *the City of Gold*. Nestled at the bottom of a box canyon, sheer cliffs and rugged mountains protected three of its sides, but cursed the city to almost permanent shadow. Its only wall sealed its western access overlooking the Hur River, and beyond that, the steppe.

Thick crowds milled before the closed gates, beseeching the captain for entrance to join the Festival of Gold. The annual celebration of the yellow metal, with its unrestrained debauchery and decadence, drew threefold the number of traders from the steppe and beyond.

The trader gestured his warriors forward. With shoves and threats, they cleared a path through the riffraff who could not afford entrance into the city. He strolled casually forward, hands on hips, savoring the way his shadow towered against the giant gates, an omen that one day he would become a giant, a force to be reckoned with.

Flanked by two warriors, the gate captain crossed his arms and glanced the trader up and down. Resplendent in gleaming bronze armor and richly embroidered ochre waist wrap, golden ringlets laced his thin, oiled beard. The trader didn't recognize this particular officer, likely a minor prince from a family in the King's good graces.

The captain stalely recited the challenge he'd likely uttered thousands of times before, "State your name and purpose. But be warned: All who enter must pay the King's tax. All who enter must come to trade."

The trader bowed low. "I am Virag, Lord of the Marshes that surround the Great Sea, Master of the *Limita,* and friend of Hur-ar." From somewhere in the folds of his tunic, the trader produced a gleaming gold coin bearing the likeness of the city's king and held it out to the captain. "Of course, I can pay the tax."

The captain eyed Virag suspiciously and then reached for the coin. Virag quickly closed his hand, before slowly reopening his fingers, palm up, revealing not one, but two thick coins.

"I can pay the kings tax, *and then some,*" Virag purred.

The captain took them both. He tested each with a small bite, and grinned. He craned around Virag, perhaps to see if any wagons or carts followed behind. "Welcome, Virag. Do you come to buy or sell?"

Virag grinned and shook the rusty chains on his shoulder until the manacles clanged together.

"Buy."

2. Sarah

Sarah burst from the enormous gilded doors, just as she had done on the first day of Festival every year since she could remember. Excitement vibrated through her body, invigorated by the late afternoon sunshine. Rosewater and jasmine floated on the air as she dashed down the stairs and across the crowded courtyard. Brushing by the central fountain, she didn't care if the spouting lions splashed her with icy water. Sarah *had* to see the wagon, to touch it before it departed to join the parade assembling just outside the palace gates. As with every Festival, Sarah pretended she would be a participant in the glorious event, and not just another distant spectator.

She glimpsed the beautiful wagon through the milling crowd. Between the wagon and the palace gates, she spied Asul barking orders at his warriors as they struggled to assemble the House Azubehl's contribution to the Parade of Princes. Behind them, drummers and trumpeters warmed up, filling the palace grounds with music. Soldiers herded gayly dressed dancers, acrobats, fire breathers, and plumed horses to the head of the line. Behind them milled a bedraggled pack of chained slaves, her Father's slice of the booty from Hurar's many wars against the steppe tribes. All of these would precede her father's wagon, announcing the power of the House Azubehl.

She ducked low to avoid Asul's eyes, and weaved amid the crush of Hur-ar's high ranking warriors and royalty chosen to follow the Prince's wagon. By following the prince's wagon in the annual parade, they announced their fealty to the ancient and powerful House Azubehl.

Tended by a small army of slaves, the nobles clucked excitedly to one another. Broad silver trays piled high with exotic delicacies from across Hur-ar's vast trading empire twirled and danced through the crowd. The struggling slaves beneath their shadows remained invisible to privileged eyes.

Sarah, however, was not invisible. Noblemen occasionally ogled her despite her golden veil, but Sarah knew her status as First Daughter and betrothed to the Crown Prince kept her safe.

Her father had arranged for his guests' every appetite. Scantily-clad slave girls and boys, rented from the city's finest brothels, prowled the lush gardens at the courtyard's edges. As her mother had taught her many times, Sarah averted her eyes from the goings-on in the shadows. While Sarah had no illusions what the men did with the slave girls behind the garden's thick foliage, she felt uncomfortable at the thought some of the girls were younger than her.

The enormous parade wagon resting before the sealed palace gates commanded her attention. Slaves hurriedly put the final touches on the family's contribution to the Parade of Princes, the Festival's opening event. Long ago, it had been a heavy wagon used for hauling trade goods and ore up and down the steep Cliff Road to the Black Fortress. Standing almost twice as high as a man, her grandfather had ordered it rebuilt decades ago. Ornately carved stairs replaced the mundane wooden loading ramp on its side. Silk bunting draped over polished wooden slats and interwoven with silver and golden threads, bore images of the House Azubehl's great deeds. Wooden wheels were replaced with gilded bronze spokes encrusted with glittering jewels. Atop it all, two gold and ivory thrones sparkled in the sun.

This is where her father and mother would sit as two snow-white oxen pulled the wagon up the Avenue of Kings. Only the wagons of the King and Prince Hector, first in line for the throne, would proceed them. The rest of Hur-ar's nobility would follow in order of their Court status. All the great houses were expected to participate, each displaying their wealth and might. The parade would terminate at sunset at the King's Palace in the city center. There, a gala feast would rage until dawn, marking the official opening of the Festival of Gold.

Sarah looked about, making sure Asul wasn't watching. The High Prince and his First Wife, her mother and father, had yet to make their appearance. Noblemen drank and laughed around her, ignoring the High Prince's daughter lingering in the wagon's shadow. The slaves tending the oxen paid her no mind, nor did those tasked with shoveling manure from the cobblestones.

Sarah reached up and caressed the silky bunting, still as crisp and bright as she remembered it as a young child. The wagon held a special magic for her. In her imagination, she pictured it one day transporting her beyond the palace's gilded prison. She could count on her fingers the number of times she'd been beyond the palace walls. In those times, she had been concealed behind thick curtains in a wagon, on her way to and from the family's country villa.

Impulse overrode good sense, and she scurried up the stairs.

Perched on her Mother's throne, Sarah straightened her white silk and chiffon dress, pushed up her golden bracelets, and firmly set her gaze on the closed courtyard gates. If the force of her stare could open the gates, it would. She imagined what it would feel like to ride down the Avenue of Kings with the entire city's eyes upon her. Sarah wanted to see the people, to experience Hur-ar's vibrant sights and sounds.

Her mother would have none of it.

Laughter shook Sarah from her trance. Afraid Mother or Asul might have spied her, Sarah slunk down and peered around. The crowd paid her no attention, everyone focused on the party's latest arrivals.

A court page cleared his throat and shouted above the chattering crowd, "Announcing Her Highness, Ashtoreth, Eighth Princess of the House of Azubelh, and her son Prince Bal-eeb."

With disarming smiles and leering eyes, the freemen flocked to Ashtoreth's side. The women of court fell back, whispering to one another jealously.

"Witch," Sarah heard several of the women hiss under their breath.

Hiding behind her mother's throne, Sarah could not tear her eyes away from the woman who had arrived into their lives like a whirlwind only a few months ago. Her father's latest, and eighth wife, Ashtoreth had become a powerful force in court.

Fully in control, Ashtoreth waded into the crowd, goblet in one hand. Her dress looked as if it were spun from black spider web, originating from her full left breast and radiating across her body. Golden silk beneath the black strands afforded minimal modesty and accentuated each dangerous curve. Diamonds woven into the thin strands gave the illusion of morning dew clinging to the black webs. Long ebony hair fell down her right shoulder, glistening in the sun and barely concealing her right breast.

Beautiful, Sarah thought. And then, with a hint of unease, *Powerful.* She watched the way Ashtoreth drew men to her, and manipulated them with a look, or a word. Sarah frowned, considering her own body, wondering if men would ever look at her that way.

Then she caught the gaze of another. From behind his mother, Bal-eeb grinned at Sarah.

She blushed and turned away, slumping deeper into the wagon, back pressed against the chair.

Her heart thumped wildly. She slowly snuck a peek, but he no longer looked at her and mingled with the crowd.

People said Bal-eeb had already distinguished himself in battle against the Scythians. Broad shouldered and bare-chested, he wore only military sandals and the traditional ocher waist wrap of a Royal officer. Tall, with a bushy black mane of hair and thick oiled beard, he resembled his cognomen, *The Lion*. Her father's younger officers flocked about him, as did many of her step-sisters. The handsome prince had caused a great stir among Prince Azubehl's many daughters since his arrival. Many of her half-sisters openly wondered if marrying their stepbrother would be permissible.

Sarah hated to admit it to herself, but she thought of it, too. Though she never publicly showed it, her mother had been furious when Prince Azubehl had taken a new wife who already had a son, and one so old. Everyone knew this presented an immediate threat to Ezra, the First Son. Sarah wanted to hate Bal-eeb, but kept finding herself stealing glances at the handsome Sammujad.

Brash, arrogant and savage, Bal-eeb represented everything Mother taught her was wrong, everything the ancient teachings of the Narim, the god-men of the Black Fortress, rejected. To Sarah, Bal-eeb was like spring thunder in the mountains. She knew he should be feared, but she couldn't pull her attention away from his power.

"All Hail Prince Azubehl and his beloved First Wife, the High Princess Meribeph!"

A flurry of activity in front of the palace's great doors foreshadowed the imminent arrival of Mother and Father. Sarah knew she must leave the courtyard before Mother spotted her. Backing down the stairs and staying low, she tried to blend in with the crowd. Then, her right sandal caught a stair, sending her tumbling backwards. She grabbed at the wagon's edge, but only snatched air. She closed her eyes and braced herself.

Corded muscles caught her. Sarah's arms naturally fell across an iron neck.

When she dared open her eyes Bal-eeb smiled down at her. "You must be more careful, princess."

Sarah's face turned bright red behind the veil. Her mind battled between the desire to crawl beneath the wagon and curl up and die, or perhaps, to stay right here in Bal-eeb's arms.

"P-put me down." She added, "Please," and then cursed herself.

"Of course." He set her down, but inched closer, trapping her between the wagon and his broad chest. He snagged a goblet from a nearby tray, eyes twinkling playfully. He smelled of wind and steel and smoke and every fantasy she'd ever imagined of life outside Hur-ar.

She smoothed her gown and hair, struggling to regain composure.

Sarah struggled to think of something, anything, to say. Her years of training under the stern matriarchs of Hur-ar's oldest families did little to prepare her for the likes of Bal-eeb.

"Are you enjoying the party?" She asked voice cracking.

Bal-eeb emptied the goblet in one deep swig, and tossed it to the ground. He stepped even closer, further invading her space. "You talk much. All of you city dwellers love to talk."

"Yes. I guess we do."

Ironically, Sarah realized this was the most they had said to one another since his arrival at the palace.

He placed a palm against the wagon, blocking her escape, and leaned even closer. "You're different from your sisters."

"Oh, really?" Sarah swallowed. "How?"

"A man might find you desirable."

Sarah held her breath; her heart pounded. *Desirable?*

He playfully fingered her hair and toyed with the delicate knot holding her veil in place. "Your hair. Your eyes. There are no women like you beyond the wall."

Sarah glanced around, but no one in the crowd seemed to take notice of them. Unexpected excitement washed over Sarah as his warm breath caressed her cheek.

"Princess, you should not be here." A stern voice came from beside them.

Sarah turned to find Asul locked eye-to-eye with Bal-eeb.

"Hello, Captain Asul," she exhaled, simultaneously relieved and disappointed.

"Be gone, guard," Bal-eeb gave Asul a dismissive glance.

"Princess Sarah isn't supposed to be here."

"Go away," Bal-eeb glanced at Asul the way a mad dog does before it snaps.

"She's coming with me."

Bal-eeb drew himself up and turned to face Captain Asul. "When does a commoner give orders to a prince?"

Those who took no notice before now turned and watched the two warriors face off. Bal-eeb hovered over her like a predator protecting its kill, Asul the unyielding interloper.

Asul's tone never changed, his face impassive. "I am under orders from High Princess Meribeph. Take it up with her."

Even though she seemed forgotten, Sarah tried to flatten herself as much as possible against the wagon.

Bal-eeb laughed and stepped back. "Who am I to oppose the will of the High Princess?"

The tension broke as Asul grasped Sarah's wrist and pulled her away.

The crowd began to chatter again like crickets after a passing storm. Asul led Sarah behind the columns at the courtyard's edge.

"Sneaking about again, my princess?" Asul said gruffly once they were out of earshot.

"*A proper princess doesn't sneak*, isn't that what you tell me?"

"Yes."

"Then I guess I wasn't sneaking."

3. The Iron Captain

Once they were well within the cool shadows of the gardens surrounding the courtyard, Asul stopped and sighed. "Every year, it's the same. I catch you trying to climb on the wagon against your mother's wishes. She won't be happy if she finds out."

"She won't find out, because you won't tell her." Sarah grinned.

He grunted and crossed his arms. "I should. I should also tell her about your conversation with Bal-eeb."

Her smile fell. "So? We were just talking."

Asul opened his mouth to speak, but the crier's voice interrupted from the courtyard. "All Hail Prince Azubehl and his beloved First Wife, the High Princess Meribeph!"

Sarah peered around Asul and saw the palace's great doors began to swing open. Mother and Father stepped into the sunshine. Sarah gasped.

Last night, for the first time, Mother had asked Sarah's opinion regarding what gown to wear. Mother never took Sarah's, or anyone's council save Asul's or Rashka's. Shocked, but excited, Sarah made a recommendation, but never truly expected Mother to wear it.

Yet, here Mother stood, regal as always, with practiced smile and head held high adorned in the very dress Sarah had selected.

The floor length gown accentuated Mother's hourglass figure. Cut from luxurious midnight blue silk, it flowed around Princess Meribeph like the night breeze. It crisscrossed over her front with high, yet appropriately modest slits down each thigh, held in place by a delicate golden girdle below her breasts and a thin golden belt around her waist. Silver pins held honey colored hair piled high, and revealed a graceful neck bearing a silver necklace, upon which hung a plain, unadorned golden cylinder with a small knob on one end.

In Hur-ar, a man could have as many wives as he could afford, but only the First Wife had the honor of producing legitimate heirs. *The Golden Scepter,* the symbol of a nobleman's power, represented a First Wife's exclusive right to bear royal children with a direct line to the throne.

To everyone else, it appeared as if Mother lightly held Father's hand out of affection, but Sarah knew better. Mother supported her doddering husband, his fat quaking beneath the heavy folds of his golden robes, as he lurched down the steps, sloshing wine from his goblet onto the steps.

He's drunk already, Sarah thought, disgusted, though unsurprised.

Heavy lidded and dull with wine, Father stared straight ahead with a cow-like expression, sweat trickling down his bald head.

Sarah glanced up at Asul. Whatever scolding he was about to deliver now obviously forgotten as he followed her mother's every graceful step down the stairs. "Come," he said absently. "You've seen the wagon, now it's time to leave."

Sarah permitted him to lead her into the columned shaded walkway along the courtyard's edge.

Asul glanced to their left, where a young nobleman grunted with a slave girl behind a potted date tree. "This is no place for the virtuous."

"It's obviously fine for Mother and Father," she snapped.

"Your mother is here because it is her duty."

"If all this is so wrong, why does Father arrange this party every year?"

"Because it's expected of him."

She pulled away putting exaggerated distance between them. "By the Narim, Asul, I'll be married in a year. Why does everyone try to shield me so much?"

The Iron Captain halted in front of the servant's entrance to the courtyard, and placed his hands on his hips. He considered her sternly. Hands behind her back, she fearlessly returned the expression.

"Because," he spoke in slow, measured words, "there are many in this household who care for you and Ezra."

Mother had once remarked Asul hailed from a long vanished tribe far to the east, one of the first victims of the Scythian invasions. He could not be mistaken for a *Hur-po*, a city native. He had served the House Azubehl as Captain of the Palace Guard long before Sarah's birth. He'd earned his cognomen, *the Iron Captain*, not only for his excellent reputation in battle, but because he shunned the Hur tradition of wearing gold.

My scars speak for me, he once told Sarah.

Taller than most, his short silver-peppered hair, gray eyes and pale complexion accentuated his nickname and added to his mystique. Asul sported a short goatee, as if in defiance of the traditional thick Hur beard. While he proudly wore the ochre waist wrap of a Royal captain, he shunned the common bronze breastplate in favor of dull chainmail and a simple conical helmet. In lieu of a stubby Hur short sword, Asul wielded a longer, thinner blade. Covered in nicks and gouges from countless battles, it was the only blade she'd ever seen him carry.

Sarah lowered her gaze and sighed. "I know you care about us, Asul. The other wives will celebrate all week, as will my half-sisters, while Ezra and I piddle around the villa."

"I thought you enjoyed the summer villa? Aren't you and Ezra going to explore the foothills?"

She shrugged. "We can't be shielded from the world forever. If I am going to rule as queen, I need to see the world as it is."

He offered her no council. How could she expect him to? "You wouldn't understand."

Asul stared down at her. His stern gaze softened as he lifted her chin. "So much like your mother. You have a restless spirit, but a good one." Armor clinking, he knelt on one knee and took her hands in his, just as he had done since she was a little girl. His strong, calloused hands gently rubbed her palms. If any other soldier in her Father's garrison so much as touched her, he would have died before the sun fell. By Mother's decree, Asul had always had special privileges.

Asul had been like an uncle to her and Ezra, a protector and mentor. She would have liked to say she loved him like a father, but her father barely acknowledged her existence. No, she loved Asul because she knew he loved her and Ezra the way their father should have.

An odd expression clouded Asul's granite face.

"Captain, what's wrong?"

He sighed. "Have I ever told you how I came to possess my sword and armor?"

She shook her head, intrigued she might finally learn something new about this mysterious man.

"I grew up in a tiny village at the edge of a mountain of ice, far to the north."

"Did the Scythians...?"

He nodded. "I escaped. The rest is not important. What is important was how my parents loved me. It was that love which fashioned three of the four instruments that assured my survival."

17

Brian L. Braden

He tapped his sword hilt. "My father forged this blade from ore gathered in boulder fields beneath the glacier's shadow. It has drank the blood of many foes." He touched his chest. "My mother spent long hours twisting hundreds of ringlets into this armor. It has turned many a blade. Together, they gave me the third gift." He tapped his chest. "This beating heart, which knows good from evil. It has kept my feet on the righteous path." He chuckled. "Mostly kept…

"You see, my princess, a good heart must be protected from evil when it is young. It must learn what it is to be tender, for only a good heart can carry love and hope into a dark world."

She stood spellbound by the old warrior's words. "Asul, I've never heard you speak this way before."

He frowned and avoided her gaze. "Just the ramblings of an old soldier."

"Please, Asul, tell me. What was the fourth gift?"

The sparkle in his eye and the warmth in his smile returned. "My scars, bestowed not by my parents, but by Fate. A sick heart surrenders to pain. It permits the scars to twists its spirit to tortured purposes. A good heart remembers the times before the wounds, and the scars become its servants; they become armor."

She looked down at the kneeling soldier and felt her heart breaking, and she didn't know why.

Asul placed a finger lightly over her heart. "Let your heart laugh and be young for a little longer, my beloved princess. Let an old soldier protect you one last time before you become a woman."

A horn blared across the courtyard and the crier shouted again, breaking the spell. "Assemble the parade!"

With goblets raised high, the crowd roared. From the surrounding garden, pleasure slaves and noblemen emerged, adjusting their tunics and robes.

Asul stood, cleared his throat, and addressed her in a more formal tone. "The moment this rabble follows the wagon out of the gates, I will begin assembling the caravan for

18

tomorrow's journey. Morning will come quickly, so get a good night's sleep. Rashka will wake you and Ezra shortly before dawn. You will eat breakfast and then be ready to depart before sun up. We have many miles to travel before we arrive at the villa."

Sarah frowned. "You're leading the Legion in the parade?"

"Someone else can strut down the Avenue of Kings like a peacock this year. I have too much to attend to."

As with every Festival, Mother would take Sarah and her little brother to visit the family summer villa in the nearby foothills. The caravan would not only include an escort of her father's warriors, but a supply wagon bearing food, cooks, servants and all the creature comforts her mother demanded for several days of pleasant distractions far from the festival she loathed.

"Why are we leaving so early? We've never left at dawn before."

Not looking at Sarah, Asul's eyes narrowed on the crowd and seemed to focus on Ashtoreth. "Your mother wants a larger staff this year," he said absently. "So the caravan will be significantly larger. I don't want wagons strung along after dark, so we're leaving early."

His expression darkened, but in a different way. She knew he could only be thinking of one person. "Have you seen Ezra lately?"

She shook her head.

"Hmm." He rubbed his beard. "Well, if you do, tell him not to be late, or he will have to deal with his mother's wrath, not just mine." His eyes narrowed. "I don't suppose you know where he's been disappearing off to?"

She shook her head again. He would know she was lying is she opened her mouth.

Asul folded his arms. "Tomorrow. Sunrise. Understand?"

"Yes, Captain."

"Good. And stay away from Bal-eeb."

With that, The Iron Captain turned and rejoined the crowd.

19

As Sarah watched him go, the young nobleman she had spied earlier fell out onto the walkway from behind the date palms. He pulled himself up on a column, and then staggered out to take his place in the assembly. What she had thought was a slave girl, stepped calmly out from behind him. She instantly recognized her half-sister, Tazrech. The thin faced daughter of the Second Wife adjusted her dress over a breast, and wiped her mouth.

Sarah flushed, but caught Tazrech's eye before she could turn away and pretend not to see her.

The girl, only a year older, flashed Sarah a wickedly defiant grin. "Have fun running around the wilderness this week." She giggled and ran into the courtyard to join the line already filing out the palace gates.

In a cloud of conflicting and confusing emotions, Sarah turned and quickly departed, knowing exactly where to find her brother.

4. The Tiles

Sarah felt shame spying on the lovers below, but neither could she look away. She tightly gripped the roof's low wall, and her breath came in short, heavy bursts.

From the palace roof, Sarah and Ezra had been watching the March of Princes snake its way down the Avenue of Kings. The din of celebration echoed over the rooftops. Drums thundered and bells clanged, as the excited throngs danced and shouted from the King's Palace to the Grand Market. House Azubehl's contingent had long ago slipped out of sight beyond the endless expanse of flat roofs, where other noble families gathered to watch the proceedings. Sarah caught a glimpse of a couple ducking into the alley just over the palace's eastern wall. Intrigued, she remained standing even after Ezra sat down behind the parapet to resume their game of Tiles.

The alley lay in shadow, and the stragglers thought they were alone and unseen. The man, dressed like a court fool in white silken trousers and a small golden mask, pressed his lover against the wall. Also wearing a small mask, she eagerly wrapped her legs around his waist. Consumed by passion, they submerged themselves in each other's flesh.

The woman moaned so loudly it echoed above the parade noise.

"What was *that?*" Ezra, a year her junior, sat on the brick roof, mixing the palm-sized clay tiles.

Sarah glanced guiltily at her brother. "Nothing."

"That's a loud nothing." He stood.

The man began thrusting faster, harder, and the woman responded in kind.

"Oh." Ezra wrinkled his nose in disgust. "You shouldn't be watching this. Mother would not approve. This is why she drags us out of the city every Festival.

"Come sit down; I'm almost finished sorting. You can go first since you lost the last game."

Sarah noticed he didn't bother to look away, either.

"Do you think it hurts her?" She asked

"What hurts?"

"You know, when he…"

Ezra rolled his eyes. "Don't be disgusting. Are we going to play Tiles or are you going to watch people boff?"

"*Boff?*" She giggled. "I've never heard that before. What does that mean?"

Ezra sputtered, "It means…" he shook his finger at the copulating couple, "…*that!*"

"Who calls it that?"

"I don't know, it's just something I heard once." Ezra blushed. "We can see you!"

Sarah yanked Ezra below the wall and hit him hard on the arm. "By the Narim, you're embarrassing me!" A momentary wave of shame washed over Sarah for using the name of the gods in vain.

"Me?" Ezra laughed. "You're the one spying on people boffing."

"Look at you, acting worldly."

"I don't want to talk about this with my sister." Ezra settled into a crosslegged position, and began to sort the tiles.

22

She studied him while he sorted. Both possessing gray eyes as sharp as cut glass, they looked so much alike, as little children the household staff once called them the Gray Twins. Mother always called Ezra her restless child, and Sarah her curious one. At the dawn of their adulthood, the brother and sister had begun to diverge outwardly, as well as inwardly.

Ezra had begun to display a man's leanness, but Sarah thought he'd changed in other ways, too. He'd become moody and sullen, vanishing for hours at a time. Today, however, he acted like his old carefree self.

Almost.

"It would be nice to see at least one parade from street level. This is the one we're supposed to be in."

"*Father* is supposed to be in it." Ezra didn't look up from the tiles. "And he is, and so is Mother, but only because she has to."

Sarah sighed and picked up her four tiles: Queen, Horseman, Priest, Slave.

Ezra always beat her in Tiles. *Sneaky little brat.*

"Ezra, don't you ever grow tired of never leaving the city?"

"We leave plenty." Ezra peered at his tiles, each hidden from her sight. He screwed up his face, as if deeply disturbed by his draw. Likely a ruse, she knew not to trust his expression.

"You leave plenty. Asul takes you to the royal barracks all the time for training. I never get to leave."

"We're leaving tomorrow, aren't we?" Without looking at her, he laid down a tile. The Spearman.

"That's different. We always go to the villa during Festival."

Only her Horseman could match the Spearman. Both would be left on the field, taking the game to another level.

If she played the Queen, she could take the Spearman, or he could play an equal or greater tile on his next turn and win the game. Only the King or Fate tiles trumped the Queen, and chances were he didn't have them.

She laid down the Queen.

He grunted.

She crossed her arms smugly. "Did I finally win?"

He laughed. "Of course not," and casually set down the King.

"You're impossible!" She tossed down the rest of her tablets.

"Sarah, you cracked one!"

A thin line ran through The Queen's chest, right over her heart.

"Sorry. She's still good. Losing is just getting old."

Shooting his sister an aggravated look, Ezra snatched up the tiles and began to mix them again. "One more game." He looked her up and down. "I have a question."

She raised her eyebrow, concerned. "Yes?"

"Why do you even bother getting dressed up when you know she's not going to let you out of the palace?" Ezra never bothered dressing up for Festival, and wore his everyday white tunic and sandals.

"Because I like to," she said defensively and smoothed her fine Festival dress.

Ezra shrugged and began to sort the tiles. "It seems completely wasted on an afternoon of playing Tiles with your little brother."

"I like feeling beautiful."

He stifled a laugh. "My sister isn't allowed to feel beautiful. It's against the rules."

"Shut up and give me my tiles." She stuck out her tongue.

He slid them over and they sat in silence for a long moment, each considering their hand.

"I'm stirring the tiles next time," she said, chewing her lip. "I think you're cheating."

"Quit making excuses and play."

She laid down The Slave. Draw him out, she thought. He won't waste a powerful tile on my weak one.

Ezra didn't respond as quickly as she hoped. After each round, they both drew a tile from the common stack.

"Asul said you better be ready on time tomorrow," she began casually. "He wants to know where you've been disappearing to, lately." She paused and looked up from her tiles. "And so do I."

"I haven't been disappearing. I've been laying low." He scowled. "And where I lay low is none of your business."

He laid down The Merchant on top of her Slave and pushed them both to the side. His tile immobilized hers, and up to three additional slaves she might place on the field.

This made her next choice easy, and she placed The Priest on the field. The Merchant could not touch it, but neither could the Priest harm the Merchant. Both tiles could, depending on what lay in their hands, serve as catalysts to radically alter the game.

"Brother, you're laying so low no one can find you. Asul isn't happy about it. Neither is Mother."

"Good. I like it that way." His voice took on a cold edge, and the old, easy going Ezra began to slip away. The closed, elusive Ezra took hold again. She'd probed too far.

Might as well go all the way, she thought. "Why are you so angry?"

"I'm not angry. Are we going to play or not?" He tossed down another Merchant.

He has no good tiles, she thought. Or he's setting me up. His attack had stalled, but the field became further charged. One right tile could set off a chain of events resulting in quick victory or defeat. If she could defeat his Merchant, she'd free whatever slaves he held and quickly use them against him. To make that happen, however, she needed to draw a Prince or higher.

She laid down another Slave and drew a Spearman.

Damn.

A long trumpet rang out, answered by the gleeful roar of thousands. The thundering shouts erupted from the street, killing all traces of merry singing and gongs.

The game tiles rattled as slight tremors shook the rooftop.

Ezra and Sarah looked at one another.

25

"The Army is marching," she said. "The parade is almost over. Do you want to watch?"

He glanced solemnly at the parapet. "No," and returned his attention to the tiles.

Goosebumps stirred across Sarah's skin as the roof trembled under the weight of thousands of sandaled feet pounding as one. Drums and trumpets blared in unison. Neither of them moved, nor did they immediately resume their game. The deafening roar made it too difficult to hear one another. She craned to peak over the parapet.

The Army dominated the last half of the March of Princes. Led by the King's Guard and commanded by her fiancé, Prince Hector Vadaz.

His armor looks too big, she thought in disgust. Rumors of Hector's cowardice and disposition for pretty little boys circulated as an open secret among the royalty, no matter how the High Advisors in court tried to cover it up. The familiar panic seized Sarah again as she thought of their fast-approaching wedding. The thought of Hector touching her, of planting a baby inside her, made her guts churn, and angry at her mother for arranging the wedding in the first place.

Hector and the King's personal bodyguards soon passed, and Sarah was able to push the revulsion from her mind, but knew there would come a day she could not ignore her fate. Next came the chariot ridden by the Army's Supreme Commander, the general who answered only to the King and held imperium over all the divisions to follow. He was followed by Hur-ar's five main battle cohorts, each bearing the standard of one of the five great royal houses.

Sarah knew each of the Five Families had openly sworn oaths to support the King, but in secret they schemed to the take the throne. Mother had versed her children in the current political hierarchy. House Vadaz held the King's highest favor. Since the old King had produced no male heir, and likely never would due to impotence, the first born of House Vadaz would inherit the Golden Throne.

The largest contributor of gold and men to the King's legions, House Vadaz led the Five Families in the parade. They marched under the banner of the Hunter and were led by Gylikos, Hector's infirm old father. Once a powerful warrior, now two soldiers supported Gylikos on either side on the chariot.

As legions of Vadaz marched by, Sarah lifted an ear, waiting for the unique ram's horn cadence which would signal the arrival of the Legion Azubehl.

She didn't have to wait long. The crowd roared as their family's contribution to Hur-ar's war machine passed in review. She found it hard to believe Asul wasn't leading the soldiers this year. She found it harder to believe her little brother would command next year, albeit surrounded by a host of battle-hardened advisors like Asul.

Only her fiancé's heartbeat stood between her brother and the crown. Mother had ensured that when the king died, at least one of the Gray Twins would occupy the grand Palace at the end of the Avenue of Kings. For him, it meant mastery of the world. For her, it meant a grander cage.

She caught Ezra staring off into the distance, as if he could see the army through the parapet.

"Something is bothering you. I know you better than anyone, even Mother, so don't lie to me."

Ezra didn't answer, and returned his stare to the tiles fielded between them. A moment later, he placed The Swordsman beside his other tiles.

"We have quite the standoff here," she said.

"I guess so."

She put down her tiles. "I'm not playing anymore until you talk to me."

Ezra closed his eyes and took a deep breath. "Do you remember when Mother once told us that hell was a life spent without passion?"

"Yes," she said slowly.

A look of peace washed over her brother's face, as if he'd come to a decision, further piquing her curiosity. "I didn't ask

27

you to meet me up here just for a game of Tiles. You must not repeat what I'm about to tell you."

She leaned forward. "I promise." Relief swept over her. Finally, her brother, closer to her than anyone else in the world, would open up. "Is it a girl?"

He almost laughed. "I wish. It's about our life here, and my future. I know you hate how Mother shields you, but it's because you count for something. You are the Golden Princess, destined to be queen. You'll be the mother to a future king. She's shielding me because I'm a liability. Do you understand?"

Sarah opened her mouth, but a thought held her tongue. "No."

"Play your hand," he said. "And give me a moment to collect my thoughts."

She had lost all interest in the game, and impatiently laid down a third Slave. Ezra raised an eyebrow and slid the tile next to his Merchant. "If you lose on purpose I won't tell you anything."

"Oh, whatever." Sarah drew a tile.

The King.

She glanced up, hoping he didn't see her reaction, but Ezra's eyes still rested on his tiles, one of which had a thin crack.

He can't stop me this time, even with the Queen, she thought.

He paused and took a deep breath. "I have no future. That's it, nothing more, nothing less."

"Ezra, don't be stupid. You're a prince of Hur-ar. Self-pity doesn't become you."

"That's not what I'm saying!" he snapped. "If I were a minor prince, I'd serve in the army and live out my days in anonymity. But only Hector's heartbeat separates me from the Golden Throne. And since Father brought that woman into our house, I have a target on my back."

"You worry too much. Bal-eeb isn't that way."

"Naivety doesn't become *you*. You don't worry enough. Do you know what one of the servant's overheard Ashtoreth say to several of the other wives?"

She shook her head.

"She said, 'If Ezra doesn't have the guts to have Hector killed, he isn't worthy of the throne.'"

"She's just talking." She made her hand look like a duck's bill. "Cluck cluck cluck, that's what our stepmothers do." She suddenly didn't want to hear what her brother had to say.

"Bal-eeb *will* try to kill me. That's how it works, you know it. If Father gave a damn about us, he would have never married her. Father won't protect me, and Mother can't." Ezra partially opened his tunic, revealing an unadorned dagger, the kind she saw common soldiers wear.

"When did you start wearing that?"

"Since the first time I saw Bal-eeb."

She put her hand over her mouth. "Are you going to...?"

"I'm not going to kill him. If I cared about being king, or at least keeping my birthright, I would have slit his throat already."

He laid down a Slave, which did nothing to hurt her and continued the stalemate, and drew another tile. "I can see it and I think Mother knows it, too. Ashtoreth and her son hail from the steppe. Asul says if you want to conquer the steppe, you have to think like those of the steppe." He leaned in, his voice barely audible above the marching legions. "They're savages."

Sarah shook her head. "Even if it's true, Asul will protect you."

"Asul is one man, and he serves Father. I can't rely on him or anyone, especially Father. Anyway, I think he knows. That's why he's been training me so hard lately."

His words carried sadness and anger, the same feelings she'd experienced when thinking of their father.

Sarah looked at her hand, the horrible feeling in her stomach stripping away all joy from her imminent victory.

"Well, then you'll have to be extra careful. After I'm queen, I'll have Ashtoreth and her son exiled."

Finding no reason to continue, she laid down the King.

"I win."

His look of shock slowly turned to a grin. "Maybe, maybe not."

"You don't..."

"I do."

He slowly turned around one of his tiles.

The Narim...the Fate Tile.

Fist clenched, Sarah let out a stifled scream of frustration. "You always do this. Always!"

When the Narim tile enters the field, all players' tiles are eliminated, even the King. No further tiles could be drawn. The game's outcome hinged on each player turning over a single tile, the best one they held in their hand. Fate now determined the victor.

"Wipe the field." Obviously enjoying tormenting his big sister, Ezra swept the carefully arranged tiles to the side like a vengeful god.

Sarah considered her meager hand...The Slave and The Lover, the game's lowest tiles. The cracked tile remained in her brother's hand.

Ezra slowly laid his tiles facedown and stood. She looked up at him, trying to read his expression. "Aren't we going to finish the game?"

"I'm going to finish the game, but not on the Tiles' terms." He squinted against the lowering sun.

The tremors lessened as the Army's last legion passed by.

"Do you have any idea how much suffering there is out there?" He didn't wait for her to answer. "I do. Suffering grows in this city the way wheat grows in the fields beyond the wall. People die forgotten in the streets, their rotting corpses not even worthy of being collected and buried. They let the dogs and rats feast on them." Rage clouded her brother's face. "Out there, starving children play among the dead the way we once played among the courtyard's silver fountains. And it's all because of us, Sarah."

"What are you talking about?"

"The nobility are no better than the Scythians. The plainsmen may kill the weak, but Hur-ar bleeds them dry a little at a time. The poor don't have a chance to walk away and start all over, but I do."

Sarah's tiles fell to the wayside as she stood. "What are you saying? You're scaring me."

"I hate this place. I hate this city. And I hate Father. I don't want to spend my life playing Tiles, waiting for Hector to die, or for Bal-eeb's knife in my back." He shook his head. "But if it were only that, I could deal with it. My real fear is waking up one day finding myself like Father, another decrepit Prince the Golden Throne has passed by. Such a fate tempts me to plant a knife in Hector's back, but then I'd be no different than Bal-eeb.

"Murdered, murderer, or a soddened degenerate. I'd rather die than accept either fate. A single tear trickled down Ezra's cheek. "I don't want the throne."

"But as King you can change it!"

"Do you remember what Mother once said about the Narim?" He pointed to the Black Fortress on the cliff high above the city. "She said they tried to turn the city from wickedness. They failed, and walled themselves in the Black Fortress out of revulsion. If gods could not turn nobility from evil, I harbor no illusions I can."

She searched his expression for any sign this might be a joke, but saw only sadness and steel.

Ezra put his arms around her and held Sarah tight.

"I love you, Sarah. You and Mother are the only reasons I have to stay, but I must be free."

No," Sarah squeezed him tighter, as if she could hold him here forever. "Please, Ezra. You can't."

"I must."

"Don't leave me. I'll be alone!"

"You will never be alone. You will be Queen. Be a merciful ruler, even if Hector is not, and the people will love you. When you see the poor in the streets, remember me."

"Where, Ezra? Tell me where you will go, I beg of you."

Ezra gently supported Sarah as she collapsed in sobs, crushed by the imminent reality she may never see her beloved brother again.

"I found a way out. I'm leaving the city tonight. Tell Mother not to look for me; she'll never find me, anyway."

"Where are you going? I am your sister. You owe me that."

Through her tears she saw conflict raging below the surface. After a moment's hesitation he spoke, "I'm going south into the mountains. I plan to sell my sword arm for passage to Havilah."

"A mercenary? You're going to be a mercenary? You're supposed to be a king! You're being stupid. You're betraying the family." She pounded his chest. "You're betraying Mother!"

He tenderly kissed Sarah on the forehead, and released her. "The time has come to wipe the field," he whispered. "I must become master of my own fate."

Sarah wiped her tears and felt a dull throb in her palm. Blood trickled from her hand. Beside her rested The Queen, the thin ceramic tile now fully cracked in two, stained with her blood. She looked up, but Ezra had vanished.

The sound of the parade had completely faded as sunset shadows once again began to claim the City of Gold.

Sarah lifted Ezra's other tile and turned it over.

The Thief.

5. The Grand Market

The slave girl stood between the black dragon statue's hind legs, a living sacrifice to the city's insatiable lusts. With oily smoke pouring from its jaws, the enormous statue's fiery eyes glared down as if poised to devour her at any moment. Behind the woman-child, the auctioneer paced back and forth, barking at the crowd to open bidding. Along the platform's edges, black robed priests waited as patiently as vultures for the auction's conclusion.

Virag ignored the theatrics and coldly assessed the merchandise.

Some in the crowd shouted for the auctioneer, the Master of the Block, to parade the slave so they could better see her. He complied, and prodded her with his whip handle. "An exquisite specimen of Sammujad beauty. She'll clean your tent and keep your bed warm. Look how healthy she is. Why, she'll breed her master a whole army of slaves!"

"I don't think so," Virag muttered to himself.

Perhaps twelve summers old, her ankle chains jingled as she shuffled back and forth, her lifeless gaze plastered to the floor.

"She's fat," someone in the crowd remarked.

"I'd work the fat off her," Bolian, Virag's guard closest to the auction platform, licked his lips.

Amused, Virag bit deeply into the succulent fruit for which he had no name. Yellow juice dribbled down his cheek, which he didn't bother to wipe off. Safe within the spacious perimeter formed by his bodyguards, Virag enjoyed the auction with plenty of elbow room in the otherwise packed market.

"Some of her softness is baby fat," Virag commented to no one in particular. "But some of it isn't."

"Virag, you old dog. When the hell did you give a damn about them being too young?" Wine skin in hand, a roly-poly merchant swayed just outside Virag's line of bodyguards.

"Bilbus, if you were a slaver, you'd know narrow hips die too easily in childbirth."

"Good. Who needs kids?" The metal trader belched and raised his finger. "Quarter Kingsman."

The auctioneer grinned and pointed at Bilbus. "There is a gentleman who knows quality. Bidding opens at a Quarter!"

"Suit yourself," Virag shrugged. *There is a man who knows how to eat and shit, and that's about it,* he thought. He despised the soft Hur-po, especially those like Bilbus, who had inherited their trades and fortunes. He wanted to say that only an idiot would come to the auction with gold and wine, but he held his tongue. *It's always best to let a fool impale himself.*

Still, Bilbus ignited a small bidding war, and soon the girl's price had risen to two full golden Kingsman.

"Let me see her face!" Virag shouted, feigning interest and wondering if anyone else would notice what he had from the outset.

The auctioneer momentarily hesitated, but then lifted her chin with his whip handle, before quickly letting her resume staring blankly at her feet.

I knew it, Virag thought and grinned inwardly.

A few prospective merchants, mostly outlanders like himself, quickly drifted away. Bilbus and several other locals paid no attention to the obvious warning signs.

Wanting to have some fun, Virag waved his hand casually. "Four Kingsman."

Bilbus huffed.

Excited whispers rippled through the crowd. If the notorious Virag had committed so forcefully a bid, she must be worth buying.

"Four and a quarter!" The fat merchant countered.

Virag knew flesh, how to buy it, who to sell it to, and how to twist it to his purposes. Slaves were a resource, no different than copper or livestock. It didn't matter that slaves could talk or feel or cry or give pleasure. Slavery was business, and he knew it better than any. He also knew the auction was no place for emotional bidding, a lesson Bilbus obviously hadn't learned. Virag had often done business with Bilbus's father, a notable city merchant in the iron and bronze trade. After the elder's passing, Virag soon discovered the man's son a drunkard and a thief. He also knew that Bilbus possessed dark appetites.

Such men were easy to manipulate.

Virag's guards looked at one another questionably.

"I thought we're weren't buying today?" Wadim whispered.

"Shut up," Virag said. "Don't spoil my fun."

A silk merchant drove the price to five Kingsman.

He better stick to silk, Virag thought and raise his hand. "Five and a quarter."

The girl raised her head and squinted against the setting sun.

The silk merchant spat and stomped away, taking his entourage with him.

Virag raised his voice toward Bilbus. "If I owned her, I'd make her a tent slave, under the care of the older slave women. They would teach her the arts of pleasure and then, in a year or two, I'd put her on the block for three times the price."

"You're just trying to steal her away." Bilbus raised his hand like a child and shouted, "SIX!"

Virag rolled his eyes.

"Six!" The auctioneer pointed to Virag, "Do you bid again?"

He shook his head and bowed to Bilbus. "Too rich for me. I'm out."

"The slave goes to Bilbus of Hur-ar for six Golden Kingsman."

A smattering of clapping, and a few laughs, accompanied the announcement.

Virag finally allowed himself a laugh. With that much money, he could have bought ten good slaves.

Bilbus's eyes bulged in anger. "What do you find so funny, you Sammujad dung heap? Are you upset another of your women will be bed by their betters?" Bilbus looked about and raised his voice in a gloating tone. "You know, we have a new word for slave here in Hur-ar, it is *Sammujad.*"

Other than Bilbus's bodyguards, only a few of the other merchants laughed. Most knew Bilbus, but they also knew Virag.

Virag slipped between his towering bodyguards and calmly considered Bilbus. "My blood is Sammujad, which makes me uniquely qualified to buy and sell my own. You, however, should stick with trading copper and tin, and send an agent to buy your slaves." He leaned forward like a confident and winked. "I tell you what, the next time I'm in the city I would be glad to do so, for a small commission of course."

A soldier appeared among them and addressed Bilbus. "Your merchandise awaits. Come to the Royal Block and settle your debt."

Bilbus turned up his nose and began to follow the soldier.

"Oh, and about your slave," Virag called to him. "They fattened her up to hide her swollen neck, but I'm sure you saw that."

Bilbus spun about.

"Likely gut worms." Virag shook his head with a mock sympathy. "She'll be dead in a week. Enjoy her while she lasts."

The crowd burst into laughter. Bilbus turned red and opened his mouth as if to say something, but instead stumbled off after the soldier, muttering to himself.

"The day isn't a waste, after all." Virag took a cleansing breath, as if inhaling the sweet aroma of marsh lilies, and returned to the safety of his bodyguards to watch the remainder of the auction.

On the platform, the Master of the Block conferred with several of his aides as they prepared for the afternoon's last sale. Virag covered his face and looked up at the sun, which had begun to touch the rooftops along the Grand Market's southwestern rim. Soon, the Market would close and the evening's festivities would begin. He leisurely looked about, taking in the sights and sounds.

While a few slaves had caught his eye, he wasn't serious about buying, at least not until tomorrow. He needed to be seen here, to make his rivals think he'd come intent on buying.

Virag commanded a dozen camps nestled along the *Limita*, the narrow strip of thin forest between the steppe and the nearly impenetrable marshes along the Great Sea's north coast. Accustomed to life alternating between the steppe's windswept dryness, and the marsh's insufferable humidity, he found the dizzying mix of human scents in the city almost overwhelming.

Then, the reek of goat hair, and goat piss dominated all others. He glanced right and saw a pack of Aryan traders settle into Bilbus's old spot. He despised Aryans slightly more than most people, which, in Virag's mind, they barely qualified as.

Dressed in goatskin from head to foot, they stood on their toes, struggling to peer over heads. The short, dark-skinned plainsmen, who hailed from the southeastern fringes of the steppe, babbled incessantly. They, like his tribe the Sammujad, had almost vanished from the grasslands beneath the Scythian onslaught. Where most of the Sammujad had perished, or fell into a life of bondage behind Hur-ar's walls, the Aryans escaped to the mountains beyond the reach of the dreaded horsemen.

Disgusted, he returned his attention to the auction, where the number of priests at the platform's edges doubled. Some of them had begun to circulate through the crowd.

"The Dragon is hungry," he said.

His bodyguards briefly turned to him, and then to each other with questioning looks.

Virag allowed himself a moment of magnanimity, and answered their unspoken question. "They're going to bid on the last slave, which means no one will win the next auction."

It made sense, as this was the final auction of the afternoon. "The priests occasionally purchase a slave, albeit for a significant discount. They'll use it for the Gleaning, the morning sacrifice opening the Market. There is a giant iron pit on the block between the dragon's legs. They'll line them up starting at dawn, sometimes up to a hundred slaves. Sometime before noon, they begin to burn them alive."

"They buy a slave just to kill him?" Wadim, his head bodyguard, asked.

Virag shrugged and crossed his arms. "It's none of my affair." He didn't want to waste his breath explaining it to an underling, but Virag understood the uses of fear to gain power, even if he found this particular method distasteful.

Several black robed servants of Ba'al had begun to circulate through the crowd. Sunken eyes shot the traders warning glances. The crowd quickly thinned.

Absolutely no one challenged the Temple over a slave. Those who dared to outbid the priests often vanished. Some say they took the slave's place at the Gleaning.

"Shall we leave, my lord?" Wadim asked nervously.

"No. This will go quickly. Let's find out who the unlucky bastard will be." Virag tossed what was left of the fruit to the ground and wondered what piece of garbage would be offered up on the block.

Slavers often bribed the Master of the Block not to draw the last auction of the day. If they did draw the last auction, they never offered their best wares. When the priests made it known they wanted a victim, they would stop at nothing to secure it for the Dragon God.

Virag looked up at the enormous black dragon statue looming over the market and took another bite. "Religion is an expensive hobby."

He didn't believe in Ba'al, or in any gods, at least none you could pray to. Power had to be cultivated, not worshipped.

He lifted his head and glanced at the cliff boxing in the city's eastern flank. Brilliant sunlight reflected off the granite, starkly revealing the Cliff Road zig-zagging all the way up to the Black Fortress, the realm of Hur-ar's other gods.

He didn't understand why the Hur-po chose to worship such a dark and useless god like Ba'al, and practically ignore the real gods living for centuries at their back door. The cult of Ba'al had grown in power and influence since arriving only a few years ago, especially in court. Yet, no one worshipped the gods that gave Hur-ar the source of its true power - *gold*.

Only the poorest of the Hur-po made the arduous trek to the Black Fortress to lay flowers at the mighty wall that had sealed in the mysterious god-men for centuries. Well, that wasn't entirely true. The Royal Trader made weekly visits to the Black Fortress, but not for worship.

No one ever saw the Narim, but legend said they were immortal giants with silver hair. Legend also said they founded the city, built the great Kupar Bridge, and taught the arts of agriculture and civilization to mortals. After witnessing the evil of men, they walled themselves inside the Black Fortress, never to emerge again.

He'd never witnessed a trade expedition to the Black Fortress, but everyone knew how they worked. Before dawn, a caravan of ox-drawn heavy wagons, laden with basic trade goods like blankets and grain, would depart in the dead of night from the Royal Trader's palace. After spending hours climbing the Cliff Road, the caravan would arrive at the Black

Wall. At dawn the Royal Trader would ring a bell outside the gates. In response, the outer gate would open, and the delegation would roll the wagons into a holding area between the gates, vacate and ring the bell again. The outer gate would close and, sometime later, reopen. The trade goods would be gone, and the wagons would be filled with gold ore.

The Master of the Block interrupted Virag's thoughts. "And now for the final auction of this first day of Festival!"

To the hiss of the crowd, two musclebound warriors prodded a chained young man onto the platform.

Bowed legs. Olive skin. Bald except for his black hair tied into a long top knot.

A Scythian.

Naked, like all slaves sold on the block, the horseman strode into the platform's center with all the dignity he could muster. Battle wounds, some still oozing, criss-crossed his chest.

"Here is a strong buck recently taken in battle by Prince Sammura's forces in the northlands."

Strong, but his wounds are septic, Virag observed.

"Savage!" someone shouted, followed by boos and calls of "Murderer!" and "Animal!"

"Is he one of Tuma's?" Wadim asked. "Perhaps we could curry the Scythian's favor by returning him."

Virag shook his head. "Not this one. See how his top knot is cut? And look at his tattoo, it's a bear. Tuma's clan is the Horse. It doesn't matter if he was Tuma's, he dishonored his tribe by being captured. They would kill him if he returned. If he had the chance, he would kill himself."

Scythian captives were rare, healthy ones even rarer.

"A quarter Silver Queen," one of the priests said.

"I have a quarter Queen, do I hear a half?"

The crowd remained still, no one daring being mistaken for issuing a bid.

Resigned, the Master of the Block nodded to the priest. "He's yours."

The priest wasted no time, and dropped a velvet bag into the auctioneer's palm. A dozen of Ba'al's servants mobbed the Scythian. Deep drums thundered unseen from below the statue and auction platform. The slave's eyes widened and, as if sensing their dark purposes, he began to struggle against their clawing hands.

Virag hated the Scythians, but admired their fearlessness. He saw terror in the unfortunate warrior's eyes, and knew the man summoned all his bravery not to scream.

Moments later, he vanished down the stairs between the dragon's legs and into darkness. The drums ceased as a tongue of flame, accompanied by black smoke reeking of sulfur, rolled from the dragon's mouth.

Virag saw no further purpose in lingering. "Let's go to the City Wall. I need a drink."

A shadow darted from the crowd so quickly Virag barely had time to react. Instinct propelled his arm just in time to clothesline the thief before the boy had a chance at his purse. In a flash, he had the thief's neck firmly locked in the crook of his arm, dagger at the boy's throat.

"I am sorry master; I didn't see him!" Spako stumbled about dumbfounded, as if looking for more mice scurrying between his feet.

Virag grunted, struggling against the surprisingly strong boy. "Shut up, or I'll cut you ear to ear." He glanced at Wadim. "Take him."

Virag brushed off his hands and shot the towering Spako a vile look. "I should gut you for letting him through."

Bolian quickly snatched the boy's other arm, and the two bodyguards pulled until the thief's wrists and shoulders cracked.

"Let me go! I wasn't doing nothing."

"Don't hurt him," Virag warned his men and considered his catch.

The boy squirmed, almost wiggling from Wadim's grasp. "Let go or I'll slice your balls off, you piece'a maggot dung."

"He's got fight, I'll give him that," Virag remarked.

Not much more than skin and ribs, the young teenage boy wore only a loincloth, a scrap of cloth that might have once been an over shirt, and a filthy turban. Unusually delicate facial features provided a thin veneer for boiling rage below the surface.

What was left of the crowd gathered about, eager to see how the outlander would deal with the thief. A nearby market guard glanced over, whistling a tune, at the events unfolding a few paces away.

"You almost had my purse," Virag chuckled and rubbed his bald head. "I got complacent. My men," he pointed at the bodyguards, "are fine for places like the steppe, but are a bit overwhelmed by the city. If you were brave enough to try for my purse, then you must be either a fool or an excellent thief."

The boy glared at Virag like a cornered beast. "I told you already, I wasn't snatching nothin. Just strolling by, dat's all. Heading to Market, looking fo a bit to chew on."

"And what will you purchase this feast with?"

"I got my own. Now bugger off and let me go, or you'll get what's comin'!"

"Got your own? I'm sure." Virag tapped his chin for a moment, and then snatched off the thief's turban. Black hair, filthy and matted, fell about the boy's shoulder's. Silver and gold clattered on the cobblestones.

"That will buy a fine supper, and then some."

" 'Dat's mine!" The thief's boldness almost summoned a glimmer of admiration in Virag.

"You're good. Not good enough, but good." Virag stretched out his foot and separated the coins with the toe of his sandal. "As an excellent thief, you are likely an intelligent thief. Tell me, have you ever been outside the city?"

The boy, perhaps thirteen, only glared.

"Beyond the walls, this metal is almost worthless. Gold can be turned into pretty things without a forge, but silver, well, I haven't found a good use for it. Copper is worth more than slaves on the steppe. Why the Hur-po waste something so precious as copper to make these discs, I'll never know."

Virag spoke casually, as if bartering over the price of a pig, while he separated the dozen or so coins into two piles.

"I'm not ashamed to say I once stole to survive. I learned that an excellent thief usually works with other thieves. I wager we're being watched by your accomplices right now. They're probably wondering what I'm going to do with you." He glanced up, eyes darting around the bazaar. "There, by the carpet trader…and there, just behind that potter. Urchins all." Virag leaned forward and sniffed the thief. "Sewers, I knew it. You're from an underworld gang, aren't you?"

The boy dropped his eyes to the ground and began to tremble. Virag grabbed his chin and lifted it. "It makes sense, with that much money, that you should be fatter. You're turning most of it over to a boss, aren't you? No matter. Your friends can watch all they want." He turned his face left to right, studying the boy. "Hmm… a good thief always carries a good knife. Let's have a look."

He reached down and ripped off the loin cloth. A rusty soldier's knife clattered to the ground.

Bolian grinned.

Virag picked up the knife and turned it over in his hands. Smirking, he considered the naked thief. "As I thought, you got a good knife hidden between your legs, but not much else."

"She's a girl!" Spako exclaimed.

The thief lifted her chin defiantly, but her trembling jaw betrayed the terror squirming within. "Whach you gunna to do wid me?"

Virag considered her appreciatively. "I wish I could take you as a slave, but I can't and that's too bad. You see, the King's law states no one except the King can take a prisoner as a slave inside the city. As a practical man, this would cause only trouble for me and my men." He shook his head sadly. "What does that mean for you? If you were a poor thief, and not beholden to a guild boss, I could bribe you. I always need good informants. But if you have a boss, that means I can't trust you." He sighed, "So, my hands are tied, so to say."

The girl began to squirm between the bodyguards. "I didn't do nothin! I was just walking by."

He raised a finger and shushed her. "Don't worry, you still have value." Virag picked up the pile with two gold Kingsman, and five copper Dragons. His face turned impassive as stone, his word's sharp as a dagger. "This is now mine."

He pointed to the other pile still on the ground. "Tell me, my pretty little thief, how much money is that?"

Silence, and then her eyes grew wide in horror. He watched with satisfaction as her face turned pale.

"Oh, come now! Just answer my question, how much money is that?"

He flashed a cunning smile. "Yes, you *do* know, don't you? Smart girl. It's the current rate for the death tax, the price I must pay to slay a criminal and save the city magistrate the trouble. You know, it's funny, but on the steppe, slaughter is a way of life. In Hur-ar, it's a luxury."

Despite the girl's obvious terror, her eyes still burned with defiance.

Too tough to cry, too proud to beg, Virag thought.

He hefted her weapon. "It's a good knife, a sharp knife. I can trade this for a profit." He reached out and caressed her cheek, and then pressed the knife to her throat. "I'm going to kill you with it while your friends watch, as an example of course. No one steals from Virag."

Then, a kettle-hollow voice stayed Virag's hand. "I will buy her from you."

He turned to face a crow of a man. With a hatchet beak nose and shadow eyes, Virag instantly recognized Shellbaz, High Priest of Ba'al.

Virag bowed slightly to one of the most powerful men in Hur-ar. "I wish I could, but she's not mine to sell."

"The temple is permitted certain indulgences in regards to Hur law." Shellbaz stepped forward and produced a silver coin, stamped with the dragon. "Take this and all the thief's death tax as a token of Ba'al's blessings."

The girl screamed as if suddenly on fire and tried to yank free. "Don't let 'em feed me to the Beast!"

Something about the High Priest made him uncomfortable and, for a fleeting moment Virag considered killing her anyway. Then he remembered himself and the feeling quickly passed. Good business was always better than unnecessary mercy.

The silver felt like ice in his palm, and he quickly dropped it in his purse.

Several of Shellbaz's henchmen slipped among Virag's men, who seemed to recoil. They surrounded the girl and she vanished behind black cloaks. The priests and the girl's screams slipped away like a receding fog, leaving Virag and his men in discomforting quiet.

Virag scooped the rest of the coins off the ground. He looked up at the dragon statue, and then to the Black Fortress overlooking the city. "Gods, gods everywhere, and not a shred of salvation to be found. Let's go. I'm thirsty." Virag and his men climbed the stairs out of the Grand Market, making their way to the tavern called The City Wall.

6. Over the Wall

Lies.

The last words he would ever speak to his beloved sister were lies. It soiled the moment, a foul morsel corrupting the taste of freedom waiting beyond the palace wall. Ezra had made peace with the decisions that led him to this pivotal moment, all except that one.

The moment had come. If he went over the wall tonight, there would be no turning back. Ezra had never been more afraid, or more alive.

Only the household servants had any business in this dark corner of the palace compound. Ezra had business beyond the perimeter wall, a ten foot leap from where he knelt inches from the stable roof edge. Only the gap lay between him and anonymous freedom in Hur-ar's raucous streets. He'd leapt farther before, but if he missed the lip, the wall's smooth plaster offered no purchase, and he'd drop to the hard cobblestones below.

"I've seen Sarah leap farther," he whispered to himself. "If she can do it, so can I."

He wore only a rag, stolen from the kitchens months ago, and fashioned into a loincloth. He tightened the knot securing a makeshift linen bag over his shoulder, bunched up his legs like a rabbit, and prepared to jump.

Below him, a horse neighed, followed by metal clanging on stone. Startled, he flattened onto his belly and peeked over the side until he looked directly below the overhang.

"Sijeva! My precious Sijeva, you be good. I will brush you soon." The stable master's gravelly voice drifted up from below. Wearing no more than a waist wrap and a slave's brand, Leonus looked like an ancient scrap of sinew left too long in the sun. The stable master stroked the mare's nose, whispering sweet words to the horse Ezra could not fully hear, nor understand.

"Leonus!" someone shouted, and Ezra slowly slid back over the edge, and out of sight.

"Captain Asul, you've come for a horse?"

"No, stable master, I require a young prince. Have you by chance seen one?"

Fearful that Asul saw him, Ezra rolled onto his back, closed his eyes and held his breath.

"He is late for sparring practice...*again*. I can't find him anywhere. I know he often spends time here with you."

The old man coughed a laugh. "I have not seen the boy all day."

Ezra heard the scuffle of the Captain's sandals, and tried not to breathe. Asul stood immediately below him.

"Captain, you do not join the Festival tonight?"

"Too many duties."

"Me and the horses, we like to listen to the music beyond the wall." Ezra heard clattering iron and shuffling jars, and then liquid being shaken in a clay vessel. "You celebrate with us, eh?"

"You old Scythian dog."

Ezra sensed mirth in the warrior's voice.

"Leonus has just what the Captain needs. Drink."

"That's...powerful," the Captain sputtered after a pause. "Good."

Ezra covered his mouth and suppressed laughter.

"What is that?"

"They make it from grain. It dulls the aches in my old bones." Leonus chuckled softly. "My heart hurts even more, though it makes that pain worse. Sweet Rashka never visits me."

"What do you Scythians say? 'Women and the sword will both kill you, but only the sword will do it mercifully.'"

Taken captive long before Ezra's birth, the venerable Scythian warrior shared a jug and laughter with the Hur soldier as if they were old comrades. Torn between the desire to listen and the urgency of escape, Ezra found it hard to lay still as the clay tiles dug into his back.

He heard the jug repeatedly slosh, and the men's voices took on a relaxed tone.

"My master is a great man, a busy man. You teach the boy for him. I can tell you care. The Horsemen say, 'All the clan's warriors teach the chieftain's son, so the next chieftain is a good chieftain.'"

"The boy must learn he is a prince," Asul said in a grave tone. "Soon, he will have great responsibilities."

"The boy, he is good with the blade, no?"

"Yes," Asul said reluctantly. "Exceptionally good, even by a man's standard. He fights instinctively. The other princes won't spar with him anymore, and even my men are wary of crossing blades." He heard the captain take another swig. "But none of them would ever admit it."

Ezra grinned at the praise the Captain never paid him in person.

"He fights good in close. In the past few years, he's become instinctive with a knife, and isn't afraid to get a little bloody. He likes to fight dirty, like a street fighter, and not above using his fist or leg. He needs more work with the spear, though. He shies away from it for some reason."

"Hmm," Leonus grunted. "A Hur warrior must know the spear. It was a Hur spear that brought down my horse all those years ago. Ezra, he is smart."

"Yes," Asul said. "And reckless. He vanishes for hours on end, and no one can find him. I think he's hiding something. The house slaves tell me his clothes often stink. And I've seen fresh scars on his arms. He blames them on sparring practice, but I know better." Azul took a long swig. "He has secrets."

Ezra's stomach tightened.

"Young boys have secrets, though not as many as young girls."

"His secrets *are* likely young girls." He could almost hear Asul's teeth grit together. "I've told him again and again a prince bound for the throne shouldn't slum for whores in the Pottery District. Bastards and a rotting crotch can overly complicate a king's reign."

After a long pause, Leonus spoke in a hushed, almost playful tone. "I bet you were once reckless too, eh? Ezra needs to feel free before he picks up his father's burdens, before he takes his first wife. We both had our chance to run free, to be reckless before collar and oath bound us to Lord Azubehl. The boy's chains will be heavier than ours."

"You see much for a stable slave," Asul said. "But Ezra has a decent chance at the throne. That means he's a target, and will not live to see manhood if he continues his foolishness."

"I am only a slave and do not envy your burdens, Captain, but I am glad it is you who bears them. Prince Ezra is in good hands."

The two men shared the silence for what seemed an eternity. Pride filled Ezra when hearing his teacher speak of him with such fondness. Asul had become a relentless and stern teacher, especially in the past few months, almost to the point of making Ezra hate him. Seeing Asul unmasked sent creepers of regret burrowing into his thoughts.

Street music floated on the night and beckoned Ezra once more.

"I see you harnessed all the remaining horses for the journey tomorrow. Good."

"All except Sijeva, I assume she will be your steed."

"Of course. She's the finest in the stable."

"We barely had enough. Many more wagons than the Princess's holiday last year."

"Her Highness decided a larger villa staff would be required this year," Asul said quickly. "That horse…the black mare, I've never seen her before. When did Lord Azubehl get it?"

Leonus's voice darkened. "It's not the master's. It belongs to that Sammujad woman's son."

It didn't escape Ezra that the slave didn't call Bal-eeb by his new title, prince. Nor did he speak Ashtoreth's name.

"Captain Asul!" a voice called from somewhere near the palace. "The kitchen steward requests your presence in the cellars."

"What the hell does old Potbelly want?" Asul shouted back.

"It's regarding provisions for tomorrow's journey. He says it can't wait, muttering something about not enough room in the supply wagon." Ezra recognized the voice as Zrula, Asul's second-in-command.

Ezra heard Asul curse under his breath. Ceramic scraped against brick as someone set down the jug.

"Thank you, stable master." The edge returned to Asul's voice. "If you see Ezra, tell him to prepare for tomorrow's excursion. His mother will expect him to be ready at dawn, and so do I. It is absolutely imperative he is not late," he added with unexpected urgency.

"Yes, Captain."

Without another word, he heard Asul's footsteps fade toward the palace. Ezra chanced raising himself back into a crouch and taking a peek over the edge.

In the gathering twilight, he saw Leonus standing with his back to him a few paces away, hands on hips, watching the Captain return to the main palace.

Ezra tried to will the old man to keep walking, to leave so he could attempt the leap. Yet, something about Asul's last words lingered in his mind.

"Your sister could make that jump," Leonus called without turning around.

How did he know?

"And she wouldn't have taken so long making up her mind. Nor would she have enjoyed eavesdropping like a thief."

The old man turned around. "Decide, boy. Either way, you're leaving something behind."

Ezra grinned and leapt, grabbed the top of the wall with both hands, and scurried over the top to a new life.

Part Two: Nightfall

7. The Cellar

The cellar smelled of herbs and grain and countless other things domestic. The quarters were too cramped, the oil lamps too dim. Asul's scabbard scraped against the earthen wall as he dipped his head below the cellar ceiling and shouted to the shadows, "Potbelly! Where the hell are you?"

"Here." A timid voice responded from below. Asul peered down among the larder's ample rows of jars and shelves heaped with dried meats, and other staples, but couldn't see the High Princess's personal kitchen steward.

"I'm busy. This better be important."

The slave cleared his throat. "You were the one who ordered all the additional provisions, not me. We're running out of room on the wagons and decisions must be made."

Asul took a deep breath and reluctantly descended the stairs. "The disposition of provisions is your job. I don't give a horse's ass if you load grain or shit, just get…"

He stopped cold at the bottom of the stairs. Potbelly stood stiffly on the far side of the cellar between two tall shelves. Unconsciously, Asul's hand found his sword hilt.

It took only a moment for him to notice the steward's tall cap rested akimbo, his legs spread unnaturally beneath his ankle-length robe. His usually sloped shoulders appeared too high, as if caught in mid-shrug; his round belly poked out too far, as if pissing in a pot.

"Potbelly?"

"I'm sorry." A weak smile trembled beneath the steward's thin gray beard.

The cellar door slammed from above. Asul glanced up to see Zrula staring impassively down upon him, sword in hand.

Before Asul could react, Bal-eeb emerged from behind Potbelly. The Captain registered pressure in his chest the same time he saw Bal-eeb dropping the short bow.

The old warrior didn't look down at the arrow he knew protruded from his chest. He didn't ponder that he'd just fallen into a well-set trap, or calculate the odds of survival. Asul simply drew his sword, snapped off the arrow with his free hand and spun about to rush up the stairs.

Bal-eeb's sword found him first.

The world ebbed away down a dark tunnel as Asul felt himself being dragged across the dusty cellar floor.

"What shall we do with the body?" he heard Zrula ask before all went dark.

"Leave him here, by the time he begins to stink it will all be over."

8. The Horse and the Wolf

Sitting on the window ledge overlooking the torch-lit courtyard, Sarah rested her chin in her hands while her body slave brushed her long, wheat colored hair. She watched as Asul's men busily assembled the caravan for tomorrow's journey to the mountain villa. Sarah's thoughts wandered to Ezra, where he had gone, and if he would ever return. Loneliness, heavy and constricting, smothered her. She didn't think she could ever feel happiness again.

Sarah wanted to confess all that had happened to Rashka, but knew better. Even if she ordered her beloved slave to keep Ezra's departure a secret, it would eventually find its way to Mother before dawn.

Out of love for her brother, she would have to carry the secret alone.

Trying to let the brush work its soothing magic, Sarah leaned against the window sill. Sounds of celebration rising from beyond the palace gates teased her. Tonight, the Festival of Gold began in earnest. The streets would be crowded both day and night with drunken revelers. As she'd seen from the rooftop, nothing was taboo during the holiday.

"Do you think Bal-eeb is a good man?"

The brush hesitated for a moment and then resumed. "It isn't the place of a slave to comment on the qualities of a prince."

"Oh, Rashka, it's just me. You see and hear everything in the palace. I want to know what you think."

"It's why you want to know that frightens me."

"My sisters think he is handsome."

The brushing stopped and Sarah could sense it shaking behind her like a reproachful finger. "*Half-sisters,* and the gods didn't bestow a single one with a shred of sense. I keep telling you not to listen to that ugly, jealous gaggle."

"My half-sisters are already courting men they love, men they chose."

The brushing resumed, but with increased speed and severity, as had Rashka's voice. "They're just spares. You are not just the First Daughter and High Princess, you are the Golden Princess."

Sarah rolled her eyes. "Please don't remind me." Hector's pasty face flashed into her mind and she shuddered. She thought of the rumors circulating around court about her fiancé', the King's only son - rumors about his poor health and close calls with death, and about his dark desires for young boys.

Despite all her brother said, she thought again of the tall, bronze skinned son of Ashtoreth.

"They all want to court Bal-eeb. I know he is our step brother, but would it be so wrong?"

The brushing stopped again. Rashka asked in measured tones, "Tell me dear, what is going through that pretty head of yours?"

"What is going through my head?" Sarah trailed off, desperately wanting, but not daring, to utter her thoughts. My brother and only friend has run away, she thought. I am doomed to marry a despicable man, and until then I shall be locked up in this palace.

Her heart cried for something else, the right to throw off her invisible chains and follow Ezra's reckless example.

Perhaps it was the music in the air, and feeling of glorious abandon that infected the city that opened her lips to speak the next words.

"I think Bal-eeb is beautiful," she whispered to the night.

Rashka threw the comb across the room, where it clattered on the marble floor, before snatching Sarah's chin toward her. The beloved hag's ancient face, usually soft and understanding, twisted into an unyielding scowl. "The young are incapable of reason, especially in the spring. Let me tell you something right now, young lady. Bal-eeb is a usurper, a filthy Sammujad vagrant. *And dangerous.* Almost as dangerous as his mother. Don't let that handsome face deceive you. Do not concern yourself with the son of that Sammujad whore. She is your father's latest infatuation, nothing more. Once he grows bored of mounting her, she will end up as a kitchen wife just like all the rest. In a few more months, she'll be servicing soldiers for scraps."

Sarah knew it best to be quiet when Rashka started into one of her tirades. She would rather suffer a tongue lashing from her beloved nanny than from her mother. This time, however, Rashka's scolding truly stung.

"I've been your faithful servant since the day you were born, so listen to me!" Rashka continued. "He's not of noble blood, that's for certain, so get any thoughts of romance out of your head." Rashka's expression softened as she looked away. "Don't go off and start acting foolish on me. This palace is full of foolish girls, don't be one of them. I raised you better than that."

Like the spring winds rushing unexpectedly down the slopes before a storm, the pain and anger in Sarah's heart burst forth and spilled over in a rain of tears. She sobbed into Rashka's lap.

Rashka patted Sarah's back and softly shushed. Soon, she quietly hummed a sweet tune she often sang when Sarah was a child. As always, the haunting melody's magic slowly melted away the pain.

"I know I'm being stupid," Sarah finally whispered. "But I can't help it. I'm so alone."

"I know, my sweet, but you *are* being stupid."

Sarah shot up off the window sill and crossed her arms. "You wouldn't understand. You've probably never been in love."

The old woman in the plain gray wool wrap, slightly plump from years of palace life, slid off the sill and turned slowly, one eyebrow raised. "Of course not. I sprang from the earth an old woman, made by the gods from mud and misery just to serve you."

The slave and princess locked determined stares, neither one flinching, until Sarah covered her mouth and giggled. The old woman's stern expression evaporated.

"I don't know what to do. Why do I have all of these feelings? Does it ever get easier?"

Rashka kissed her on the forehead. "No, but the callouses grow thicker. We earn our scars in our youth, and, if we're lucky, the gods grant us the wisdom to keep them few in number."

Sarah pouted. "You sound like Asul."

Rashka wiped Sarah's tears and then nudged her toward the wardrobe. "Forget Bal-eeb. Forget Hector. Forget all that troubles you and go to sleep. Tomorrow we have a long journey."

"You're right, of course." Sarah removed her gown and handed it to Rashka, who hung it in the wardrobe among the other priceless clothes.

"Yes, I am right, and you're just telling me that to shut me up."

Sarah grinned.

A loud knock at the chamber door interrupted them. Rashka moved with surprising speed between Sarah and the door.

"What is it?" Rashka barked.

"It is Zrula, of the Palace Guard. We're looking for Prince Ezra. No one can find him. Is he in there?"

"No," Rashka responded.

"Has the Princess seen His Highness?" he called through the door.

Rashka looked to Sarah, who shook her head quickly.

"No, now go away. The Princess is preparing for bed."

They heard the rattle of armor and metal fade beyond the heavy wooden door.

Sarah didn't think she would ever be able to sleep again. The urge to confess all to Rashka boiled up again, but passed in a torrent of guilt and fear.

Rashka eyed her suspiciously, but said nothing. She lit a long spool of incense from the hearth and strolled around the chamber, igniting the oil lamps affixed to the walls as twilight surrender to a silky nightfall. Every so often, Sarah caught her glancing in her direction with a questioning expression.

"It is not a slave's place to tell a prince his business, but..." Rashka shrugged. "That boy is going to get himself killed if he keeps running off to who knows where."

Sarah turned her back to Rashka as she fought to maintain control. She slipped off half a dozen jingling gold bracelets and necklaces and placed them in the small chest atop her vanity. A moment later, she stepped into a thin silk slip and flopped into bed.

Sarah suddenly wanted to be alone, but knew Rashka would linger until she had answers. She also knew by morning Mother would want answers, too.

Sarah was a princess, so everyone insisted on reminding her. She had every right to command Rashka to leave. But she knew better. The old slave had a power all her own. Magic, almost. She had a will that could make the strongest warrior turn away. If she couldn't bring herself to make the slave leave, she would change the subject.

"I think Leonus loves you," Sarah said casually, examining her fingernails. "He won't let me pass the stables without asking about you. He complains you won't visit him."

Rashka straightened up and spun toward Sarah with a shocked expression. "Bah! He's Scythian. I'm too good for the likes of him."

Sarah could have sworn Rashka blushed, and some of the pall lifted from her heart. "But you're Scythian, too, aren't you Rashka?"

"Of course, which means I know better. The older horsemen get, the crazier," she cackled. "And that bastard is almost as old as me."

"He says you won't say his name, and it makes him sad."

"Among the Scythian, if a woman speaks a man's name, and that man has feelings for her, it means she shares those feelings. That is why I call him 'Little Old Man', and nothing more."

Sarah frowned. "That explains much."

"What does it explain?"

"Why he calls you 'Little Old Woman.'"

Rashka thrust her hands on her hips and harrumphed. "He does, does he? That good for nothing…"

Troubles momentarily forgotten, Sarah burst into cleansing laughter, rolling back and forth on the bed.

"It's not wise to toy with an old woman's heart." Rashka smiled.

Sarah rolled onto her stomach, suddenly serious. "Rashka, what does it feel like to *really* be in love?"

The slave hesitated, and then reached up on her tiptoes to light the last oil lamp. She lightly touched the punk to the oil cup, birthing the smoky flame before blowing out the stick.

With her back to Sarah, the old woman sat on the edge of the bed and folded her hands on her lap. She stared out the balcony window at the City of Gold, or perhaps beyond it. Rashka remained silent too long for Sarah's comfort.

Nurse, nanny, playmate, and surrogate mother all in one, Rashka had raised Sarah since birth. The Princess thought she had seen all the woman's faces, experienced all her moods. Yet this melancholy, so full of longing, caught her off guard. This wasn't Rashka's face anymore, this was a *woman's* face, one who had known passion and loss that Sarah's young heart could only guess at, and dream of.

Concern for her beloved nanny banished all thoughts of Ezra and her own sadness. On her knees, Sarah walked across the bed and laid down beside Rashka, laying her head in the old woman's lap. "Have I said something to upset you? If I have, I'm sorry."

Rashka ran her fingers through Sarah's hair and clucked softly. "What a splendid queen you will make!"

Sarah cuddled closer. "You have been more of a mother to me than my real mother."

"Do not speak ill of your mother," she tenderly chastised. "Being First Wife to nobility is difficult enough. Your mother is First Wife of a High Prince of Hur-ar, and *that* is a dangerous position. She toils tirelessly to please your father and, in turn, assure her children's future. *Your* future. Blessed is the day she bought me, most blessed still the day I helped deliver you and your brother."

"I did not mean it that way."

"I know child, I know," Rashka sighed and patted her cheek. "What you feel for Bal-eeb is a girl's infatuation. You have already known love, like the love you feel for your mother and your brother."

Sarah rolled her eyes again. "Everyone feels *that* kind of love."

"No!"

Sarah almost jumped at Rashka's bark.

"Most of the poor souls who live and suffer in this world do not know love, even from their family. Beyond the palace walls life is brutal and short. Beyond the city walls, its even worse. Not everyone is given the gift of this kind of love. It is rare. Rarer and more precious than gold. You are blessed with riches beyond the King himself."

"I meant," Sarah whispered, "What does a man's love feel like? And what is it like when he loves you back?"

Rashka exhaled. "I knew what you meant. Let me tell you a story.

"There was once a Scythian princess, not much older than you, who lingered at the edge of camp every day and evening. From behind the pickets' safety, she would watch the wild horses by day, and by night listen to the howling wolves.

"*'Come to me,* called the Horse, 'and be my wife. I am strong, and upon my back you can lay all your burdens. I will carry you far from danger, or into battle. If need be, I will shield you from the arrows of your enemies, even if it means my life. Together, we will become one and, in the doing, become greater than the two. Come, and be my wife.'

"She believed the Horse, and knew he was good, but the princess turned away nevertheless, and waited for night and the wolf.

"*'Come to me,'* the wolf called. 'You are young and beautiful, worthy of my passions. I will let you touch me, and I *shall* touch you. I am strong, and will devour your enemies. Run wild with me across the steppe, let us plunge into the night and know unimaginable pleasures. Come, and be my lover.'"

Rashka's voice trailed off, her gaze fixed at the deepening night.

"Well? What happened? Does it end there?"

"What do you think she did?"

"I think she went with the horse."

"I am glad you believe that," Rashka exhaled, shoulders sagging. "Now, it's time for bed. You have a busy day tomorrow."

She slowly rose and made her way to the hearth. Rashka threw several split logs onto the fire and stirred the coals until the fire flamed anew. Sarah suspected she had disappointed her nanny. "I'm sorry, Rashka. You're the only one I can talk to."

Rashka turned from her chores and gave Sarah a smile that spoke in the language of the heart. A soothing silence grew between them as Rashka went about preparing the Princess's chamber for the evening.

Sarah curled up in bed and stared up at the mosaics decorating the chamber ceiling. They depicted scenes from

Hur-ar's glorious past, such as its founding by the Narim, the god-men who dwelt in the Black Fortress overlooking the city.

After several long moments Sarah turned her gaze to find Rashka standing over her. "You still look troubled."

Sarah puffed out her cheeks and exhaled. "I dreamt of the Golden Woman again last night."

Rashka remained silent, examining the back of her liver spotted hands. Then, she shivered and rubbed her arms. "The night chill is here already."

Rashka stepped around the bed and closed the curtains over the balcony. Outside, a horn blared and the crowds laughed at some unseen amusement in the alley beyond the courtyard wall.

"Was the dream any different?" she asked, not looking at Sarah.

"No. She wore the gown with the embroidered golden dragon, just as before." Sarah ran her hands through her hair, as if imagining herself as the woman who haunted her dreams. "Her hair was so black. And her eyes, Rashka, her eyes! They look like those of the Silk People beyond the mountains, but they burned with blue fire."

Rashka sat down on the bed beside Sarah. "And how many nights has she returned?"

"Six. Tell me, what does it mean?"

"I am not a seer, my princess, and even they cannot fully understand the meaning of dreams."

"Should I tell Mother? Do you think she will take me to the priests?"

Rashka frowned. "If this is a vision from the gods, it is for you alone. Let it unveil itself in its own time."

Frustrated, Sarah returned her stare to the ceiling. "Do you think she is a Narim? Could they be sending me a message?"

"Perhaps, but I would think that if the Narim wanted to send a message, they would open the Black Gates and simply tell the Royal Trader himself."

Sarah's eyes focused beyond the ceiling, imagining the stars unfurled in the night sky. "She never speaks, but her eyes are like stars." Sarah turned to Rashka and held her hand. "Like yours, Rashka."

The old woman placed her hand on her bosom. "Like mine? Oh dear, you flatter me."

Sarah smiled. "I mean, she seems kind, but sad, like you are when you think no one is looking."

Rashka leaned over and embraced Sarah. "The gods and the old have one thing in common - We know that for every smile, there is a tear."

Rashka stood and made her way to the chamber door, and stepped through. "No more talk. I'll wake you before dawn."

"Rashka?"

"Yes, my princess?" the slave asked wearily, closing the door until only a crack remained.

"Which did she choose?"

"Who?"

"The princess...in the story. Did she choose the horse or the wolf?"

"The wolf," Rashka whispered, and closed the door.

Somewhere in the night, a woman screamed and the crowd cheered.

9. Left Hand

Ezra let the pack of revelers vanish around the corner before dropping the last few feet to the cobblestone alley. He landed as light as a cat and knelt close to the ground.

Laughter echoed from both directions, but the narrow alley remained empty. Over the low, flat roofs, sunset's afterglow painted the west in melting strips of purple, crimson and gold. Deep in this alley, only darkness reigned. Slinking into the shadows while glancing left and right, he stepped lightly downhill toward the Avenue of Kings. Sticking close to the wall, he eventually came to a filthy puddle and knelt beside it. He scooped up large handfuls of stinking mud and smeared them over his body.

Asul and Leonus's conversation reverberated in his mind. Regret began to gnaw at him once again as he thought about all he was leaving behind. He chanced a glance over his shoulder at the compound wall. In the dingy alley light, it reminded him of prison, not a palace.

"More mud, or you will only look like a pig, and not a proper thief," a voice called from behind.

Ezra whirled about, knife at the ready.

A few paces away, a wiry boy about his age, with big ears and eyes older than his years, casually considered him.

Ezra sheathed the knife in his loincloth. "Left Hand, why do you do that?"

"What?"

"Sneak up on me."

Left Hand shrugged. "I dunno, 'cause I can." He peered with anticipation at the bag tied over Ezra's back.

"You're the only one in this city who can still sneak up on me." Ezra removed the bag and tossed it to Left Hand.

"If you say so." The thief rummaged through the bag's contents. He removed a flat loaf and tore it into quarters, quickly devoured one section, before stuffing the rest in the bag. He did the same to a small chunk of goat cheese.

Left Hand unslung the skin from his side and tossed it to Ezra, who took a deep swig of the surprisingly good wine.

The outlaw shook his head sorrowfully as Ezra drank. "No matter how hard I try, I still can't teach you how to look like a real thief."

"Why do you insult me?" Ezra said with mock disappointment. "Am I not filthy enough?" Ezra tugged at the old rag he had stolen from the kitchens, now tied around his waist with several crude knots.

Covered in grime so thick Ezra didn't know what was skin and what was filth, Left Hand's eyes shone brightly in the dark, reminding Ezra of a mischievous alley cat. "The cloth is poor, the skin is rich. You're 'bout as pretty as a temple whore."

"A temple whore, you say?" Ezra tossed him the wine skin. "I didn't know you thought so highly of me."

"I don't." Left Hand winked, took a gulp, and wiped his mouth. He suddenly looked serious, and leaned to the side and peered over Ezra's shoulder. "Sure you want to do this? It's not too late to turn around."

Ezra shook his head. It felt like he was about to plunge into a cold mountain lake, knowing the painful shock would pass quickly if he just jumped.

"Okay, but remember, from here on, its *Blade* not Ezra."

Ezra nodded. Tonight, he would cast aside his given name forever, and embrace a name bestowed by the streets.

Left Hand looked over at the palace walls and shook his head in dismay. "No in-between. There are no half-thieves in the Narrow and Wide, only good ones or dead ones. Think about it - Let go or go home."

Let go or go home. Ezra glanced up at the wall and swallowed hard. "Let's go. No regrets."

"Only the rich can afford regrets." Left Hand grinned with that strange, bubbling energy Ezra had come to expect; always in motion, always moving. "Ezra is dead, long live Blade!" Left Hand turned and sped up the alley.

Ezra raced to catch him. "Where are we going?"

"To celebrate your new life!"

Together, they raced up the alley and into the City of Gold. Excitement kindled anew, Ezra followed his heart and his only true friend to a new destiny.

***

Two years earlier, while playing in the palace cellars, Ezra spied an impish face poking absurdly above the cellar floor. While attempting to steal food, a brazen thief had overestimated the drain pipe's diameter. Ezra curiously considered the boy as he writhed futilely among the grain jars and wine casks.

Large ears poked through uneven shocks of filth-matted hair. Trickster's eyes, as sharp and gray as Ezra's, twinkled in crystal contrast to a face as grimy as pitch.

"Where did you come from?" Ezra had asked.

"Chasing supper down the Narrow. Don't s'pose you spied a fat rat 'round here, eh?"

Ezra slowly shook his head, mesmerized at how odd the boy's head and partial shoulder jutted from the pipe, like a weed springing unexpectedly from the dirt floor.

The boy sighed. "No supper then. I'll be wiggling down and out. Mind giving me a push back down? Sorta in a bind."

The boy spoke in a broken mix of Hur and Sammujad, like some of the palace slaves. One day Ezra would come to learn Scratch, the dialect of the streets.

"I should retrieve the guards. They will cut your head off, and mount it on a spear, and then throw your body over the wall as a warning to others."

Left Hand nodded at a jug. "It'da be better if you snatched dat jug of slick n'stead, and pour some around dis pipe."

"That's wine, not oil," Ezra had replied. He remembered how the boy seemed so calm, so self-assured; more like a man.

"Well, then pour that sweetness down my mouth, and then go fetch some slick. Hurry, I have places to be, women to boff, ping-ping to be grabbing."

"Rats to eat?"

Left Hand looked around sheepishly. "That, too, I guess."

"Why shouldn't I fetch the guards instead?"

He grinned devilishly. "Maybe first you pull me out, so I can scratch my balls and all. Maybe swig the sweet before they gut ol'Left Hand."

"'Left Hand,' that's a silly name." Ezra puffed up. "Do you know who I am?"

Left Hand rested his chin in his free hand and rolled his eyes absurdly, as if examining the rafters for the answer. "I dunno, a boy playing in his daddy's cellar."

"I am the son of High Prince Azubehl, second in line for the Golden Throne. Who do you think you are, *Left Hand?*"

The thief looked hurt. "I'm a prince just like you."

Ezra laughed and folded his arms. "Ha! Prince of what, rats?"

Left Hand's voice deepened, his sly grin transformed to something darker, interwoven with hints of secrets and promises of adventure. What he spoke next, he did so perfectly, without a trace of the street. "I am the Left Hand of the Legless King, who rules the Narrows and the Wide where warriors fear to go. His palace is Darkness, Silence his cloak.

He is Master of the Night, ruler of the Untouchables, Lord of the Underworld."

"Well, well, the thief can speak with a proper tongue. Impressive."

"The girls like it when I talk like a snooty princeling."

"The only girls around here are my sisters."

"Are they pretty?"

"I wouldn't know. They're my sisters."

"I boff the ugly ones, too. You know, out of mercy and all."

"What's 'boff'?"

"You know, when you take a woman."

"Take her where?"

Left Hand frowned. "You really don't know what I'm talking about, do you?" He looked about the cellar. "Do they let you out much?"

"No, not really."

"I tell you what, let me out and I'll tell you all about the boff-boff and women and a thousand other things I bet you never heard of or done."

Heart pounding, Ezra looked about to make sure no one was watching. "If I free you, how do I know you won't try to kill me?"

Left Hand laughed. "You don't." He pointed at the pipe. "Honor is kinda like cloth, it rots quickly down there. But gratitude is as valuable as gold, and I know the value of friends, especially those with money, wine and lots of pretty sisters."

Ezra thought for a moment. "Most of them aren't very pretty."

Left Hand's voice darkened. "Be my friend, princeling, and I will show you what it is to be truly free."

Freedom. The word seized Ezra's imagination and never let go. Visions of the world beyond the palace's stifling confines, and the Court's crushing burdens, filled his mind. As with boys on the edge of manhood, the decision came with an impulsive rush, unfettered by consequence.

"One day, I will be king. If I release you, you must make me an oath. An oath of gratitude."

"Lesson one, prince..." Left Hand slipped back into street talk. "Ain't no promisin', ain't no oath'n down there. But Left Hand knows The Good Thing. Down there, in the Narrow and the Wide, we never turn the back on The Good Thing."

"I'll take that as a yes. Fine, show me your world. Teach me to be a thief, and you will live. Perhaps, one day, you will have the favor of the King."

"Agreed. But first you make me a promise."

"I thought you said there were no oaths or promises down there?"

"We ain't down there yet," Left Hand said with a twinkle in his eye.

"You are not in a position to be asking for anything, but..." Ezra had said, astonished at the boy's brazenness. "Okay, what is it you ask?"

"Trust me, and do what I say. If you do not..." his eyes flicked downward," ...the Underworld will kill you."

10. Wilding

Ezra basked in freedom's glorious abandon. Only the wind mattered, and the feel of baked brick under his feet, and the breath burning in his lungs.

Darkness robbed him of any reference points as they hurtled recklessly across Hur-ar's flat rooftops. Left Hand led the way, leaping like a gazelle across narrow alleys and not breaking stride on the other side. Left Hand knew this city far better than he did. Ezra trusted his friend, and didn't stray so much as a hair from Left Hand's path.

Left Hand somersaulted over low walls, often ending up in a roll before springing back up in full run. If he could not spring over a wall, he would bound up its side in two or three long strides, and then scramble over the top. Ezra followed behind like a clumsy shadow, able to keep pace only by sheer will, and yet utterly failing to match Left Hand's fluid grace. Years of training in the Royal gymnasiums paled compared to what the streets had taught this wiry thief.

Thieves called the nightly scramble across Hur-ar's skyline "The Wilding." Exploiting Hur-ar's flat and terraced skyline, great distances could be covered quickly. Otherwise, it would take a thief hours to traverse the sewers or, worse, the streets.

Families often slept on the roofs, therefore only a narrow window of opportunity existed between sunset and when people migrated to the skyline for the evening. The thieving guilds knew which wealthy families posted watchmen on the rooftops, and gave them a wide berth. Regardless, when smudgy twinkles blossomed across the skyline, a good thief knew The Wilding had passed.

They ran east as nightfall took dominion of the city. Other than knowing they were circumventing south of the city's center, Ezra had no idea where Left Hand led him. Lanterns and torches, held high by thousands of revelers, turned the streets around the Market Square to their left into rivers of light.

Left Hand paused atop a low parapet on a two-story building. Chest heaving, Ezra caught up with him. Left Hand didn't seem to be sweating.

"You're fat."

"Am not!" Ezra shot back between breaths.

"Look at this view! I wager the King himself never sees the city like we do."

"I suppose," Ezra heaved, hands on knees and not paying attention to the sweeping view of the glittering city. "When are you going to tell me where we're going?"

"We're going to see Ezmoria." Left Hand laughed and darted off again.

"Ezmoria?" Ezra followed. "Why the hell are we going to see her?"

"Because she made me promise to bring you by if you were in the neighborhood again." He laughed. "She says she has something for you."

"What?" Ezra regretted asking the moment he said it.

"She thinks you're cute. I think she must be blind."

Ezra suddenly flushed. He hadn't expected that.

They approached the Pottery District, the city's oldest quarter. Known as much for its brothels as for it numerous pottery vendors, its twisting, tight alleys made it a favorite haunt for thieves. They proceeded cautiously now, slowly darting from shadow to shadow. Silhouettes began to stir on the adjacent rooftops. Mothers herded giggling children to stuffed mats spread under the stars, while men gathered around smoky braziers. The daily routine of life went on, even during Festival.

In the flickering shadows Ezra caught glimpses of smiles, and bread being passed from hand-to-hand among family members. He could not resist thinking of his mother and sister.

"Blade," Left Hand's voice pulled him back to the present.

The thief crouched behind a low wall and nodded to the alley below, where Ezra heard deep voices. He peeked over the edge at a sliver of an alley. Two guards stood directly below; a tall, thin fellow leaned against the wall while a short, fat guard squatted on a rickety crate. Across the alley, a lazy-eyed beauty reclined against a doorsill, arms folded, with the air of utmost boredom.

"It looks like Ezmoria has a few customers tonight," Left Hand whispered and winked. "I guess she'll have to give you her surprise some other time."

Ezra was relieved, but took care to look disappointed.

"A copper dragon for the both of us." The tall soldier licked his lips, shifting his spear nervously from palm to palm.

"Two copper each," Ezmoria yawned, and began to brush her luxurious, raven hair. Ezra eyed the whore appreciatively. Left Hand knew everyone in Hur-ar's backstreets, and introduced him to Ezmoria early in their friendship. He would have liked to say he hadn't fantasized about the older woman, and she made no secret of her attraction to Ezra.

"You come by sometime without your little monkey and I'll give you a free sample," she had told Ezra the first day they had met.

"I'm not little, and you never gave me free samples!" Left Hand had protested.

He'd instantly liked her.

Tonight, Ezmoria wore more gold than clothes, and even those were thin, gauzy strips that left little to the imagination.

"It's Festival. What's between my legs is at a premium. So pay or leave, because I'm tired," she said in that mysterious, almost musical accent of hers.

The fat one stood quickly. "Careful, wench. We can take you anytime we want, copper or no copper."

She threw her head back and laughed. "Your watch officer might think otherwise." She placed a hand on her hip, her lazy gaze replaced by a stare sharp as obsidian. "Margus is one of my best customers, you know."

Left Hand grinned and pointed straight down. Ezra followed his finger and saw a bulging purse dangling off the fat guard's belt.

"You're crazy," Ezra whispered.

"Yes," Left Hand elbowed his ribs. "Hold my ankles."

Before he could protest, Left Hand slipped over the side, Ezra barely snatching his ankles in time.

"Wait!" Ezra whisper-shouted, frantically glancing about the barren rooftop. "I have nothing to wrap my legs around."

"Quit whining. I'll be quick." Left Hand arched backwards, back against the wall, and let go.

As pebbles and clay shards dug into his knees, Ezra grunted and strained to hold on.

Hair dangling, Left Hand signaled with his palm for Ezra to lower him more. Ezra leaned farther forward, and struggled not to fall or let go.

Ezmoria didn't so much as raise an eyebrow at the sight of Left Hand slipping silently down the wall in the narrow space behind the guards. Left Hand gave her a little wave and blew a kiss.

Ezra's biceps began to quake. *Hurry up,* he thought.

She struck a sultry, welcoming pose. "Maybe I haven't been fair to you boys. It is, after all, Festival."

The guards took an eager step forward.

Ezmoria held up her hand. "Easy. One at a time." She placed a finger on her lips and seductively licked the tip before narrowing her eyes at the two men. "Hmm. I know, two coppers for the first, one for the second." She smugly folded her arms again and leaned against the doorframe, revealing a long, smooth thigh. "Well, who is it going to be?"

"That's decided then." The thin one shoved the fat guard back and lunged forward.

The rotund guard stumbled backwards, almost trapping Left Hand's head between his ample posterior and the wall, before snatching the thin one's chainmail skirt and yanking him back. "Not so fast!"

Ezra snatched Left Hand higher just in time.

The thin guard tapped his own chest. "I am senior, therefore I will go first." He never felt Left Hand liberate his purse.

Ezra's fingers began to cramp and his biceps burned.

The fat one licked his palm and smoothed back his thick, greasy hair. "I am better looking. She can have me, then close her eyes and imagine my face while you're sweating and grunting."

Ezmoria snorted, obviously enjoying this. Ezra would have enjoyed it, too, if he hadn't been straining with all his might not to drop his friend.

As Left Hand reached for the fat soldier's purse, the guard released an explosive, wet-sounding fart directly into his face.

Ezmoria bit her lip and stifled a laugh.

As the two guards argued, Left Hand managed to cut the other purse free without being noticed.

Ezra summoned the last of his strength and pulled him up before collapsing against the low parapet.

"Give me that wine!" Left Hand hissed. He gulped several large mouthfuls and then spat. "That was disgusting , I could taste it."

Left Hand craned back over the wall, where the guards had resorted to shoving one another.

Left Hand caught Ezmoria's eye and held up two fingers. She gave a barely noticeable head shake.

Left Hand rolled his eyes, and held up three fingers. She winked.

He handed Ezra one of the purses, and then sifted through the other.

The boys peeked over the wall, where the soldiers now stood toe-to-toe, hands resting on hilts.

"I am first, and that's it!" The thinner shouted.

Ezra raised three coins where Ezmoria could see them, and placed them on top of the wall for her to retrieve later.

She nodded and returned her attention to the squabbling customers, and then donned her bored mask again. "Enough, enough. I'll settle this myself before you buffoons kill each other." She pointed to the thin one. "You're first."

He began to step forward before she stopped him with a finger jab to the chest. "First, show me the money."

The boys stuck around only long enough to enjoy the initial shocked expressions, the frantic scramble around the alley, and Ezmoria's dismissive theatrics. She slipped back into the doorway, and the thieves returned to the shadows.

They made their way cautiously a few blocks from Ezmoria's brothel before settling cross legged on a deserted rooftop to count their spoils.

"Look at all the gold!" Left Hand exclaimed. "The bastards must have been busy shaking down a lot of poor souls tonight. I bet they haven't even given their watch captain his cut yet."

Ezra found his purse equally full of gold, with a liberal smattering of silver and copper. He would have never told Left Hand how paltry these few coins, most of them shaved, were compared to the true wealth behind Hur-ar's highest walls. Nor would he have confessed to Left Hand all that gold paled compared to the feeling he had right now.

"You don't have to set me up, you know."

"Yes I do. You're getting laid tonight."

"I can get myself laid anytime I want," Ezra lied. Until tonight, his sex life would have been determined by arranged betrothal. He had no idea how to talk to women, especially commoners.

"Of course you can," Left Hand said, "But Ezmoria is crazy about you, almost as much as she likes me." He shrugged. "But they all like me."

"Of course."

"Of course."

Ezra grinned. "Do you have any idea how close I came to dropping you?"

"You wouldn't have dropped me. You're going to let go tonight, but not that way."

Ezra opened his mouth to protest, but thought better of it. "You're heavier than you look."

"Are you calling me fat?"

"Thick, especially your skull."

Left Hand punched him in the shoulder, and they finished counting their booty. Left Hand transferred most of the money to one purse, and placed several of the thickest gold pieces in the other purse and tossed it to Ezra.

"That's Slug's cut, so don't lose it."

"How will he know?" Ezra asked.

"He'll know," Left Hand replied coolly. "He always knows."

Ezra tucked the purse under the fold of his loincloth and tied it off with what remained of its leather drawstring. "What next?"

"We celebrate. It's Festival and now we have money."

"I'm game. Where?"

"Wherever I can get you boffed." He put his hand on his chin and considered Ezra thoughtfully, once again shedding his street accent. "That will be tough, because you're so damn ugly. I better have a back-up plan, and that plan better include wine, and women and lots of trouble."

Ezra rolled his eyes.

"You're not afraid, are you?"

"Of course not." Ezra shook his head.

"You gotta let go, Blade."

"Alright, let's go. Someone has to keep you out of trouble, and I guess that's me."

"No, someone has to get you in trouble, and I guess that's me."

11. The Kings of Hur-ar

Courtesy of two passed out Aryan traders they found behind a trash heap along the way, the two thieves had new disguises to complement their gold.

"*This* is the place you want to celebrate?" Ezra tried to grab Left Hand's shoulder and pull him away, but the thief shrugged him off and pressed deeper into the throng.

"What's wrong, are you scared?"

"No," Ezra lied. The press of humanity and canyon-like atmosphere made him uneasy. "But it's the City Wall! Every off duty warrior in the city will be there tonight." Ezra spoke in a forced whisper as they waded through the packed Perimeter Alley. Almost as wide as the Avenue of Kings, Ezra had no idea why they called it an alley. Roaring braziers hung from iron chains on high poles lining the street, bathing the sea of sweaty faces in an orange pall and casting ghoulish shadows on mud-brick walls. Low-slung buildings lined one side, the city's wall lined the other. Soldiers wandered the parapets high above the street, occasionally glancing down, likely wishing their shift completed.

"They're drunk and loaded with coin. They'll be looking for women, not thieves. The oafs could never imagine a thief foolish enough to wander into their favorite tavern." Left Hand said.

Unlike the Market Square, this part of Hur-ar never went to sleep, Festival or no Festival. Here, the heart of Hur-ar's black market thrived under the army's ever watchful eyes; an open secret conveniently ignored by the King's tax collectors. The only taxes paid here were to off-duty soldiers, most of which were funneled to senior commanders. Like warlords, they divided the spoils to feather their own personal fiefdoms.

Ezra and Left Hand could barely move, shoulder-to-shoulder with those drifting in from Festival's tamer venues. Barkers and pimps shouted to passersby; hawking wares delicious and exotic.

The soldiers' proximity made Ezra uneasy. "We should go somewhere else to celebrate."

"Fine, you go somewhere else. I'm going in." Left Hand tugged his goat hair vest away from Ezra's grasp and pressed ahead.

"There will be nobility and soldiers in there that know me. I'll be recognized."

"We're in disguise."

"We don't come close to passing as Aryans," Ezra said.

Left Hand whiffed his goat hair vest, which hung over him like a tent. "The smell is convincing." He guzzled the last of the wine from the skin and tossed it to the ground. "Now stop whining! Let's get something to drink."

Ezra relented and followed, trapped between excitement and a nagging caution he could not shake. He scratched his head beneath the itchy conical wool cap. The wickedly curved Aryan blade felt alien on his hip. "Have you been in here before?"

"Never inside. I thought this might be a good time to check it out."

Ezra had often heard Asul and the palace guards speak of the City Wall, and many times yearned to see it.

Asul would have none of it.

Its a place for fools to get drunk, lose their money, and die, Asul had said. *Soon enough, duty will require you to be seen there, but not until you have led men in battle.*

Left Hand plowed their way through the revelers across the alley to the place where the southern cliff intersected the city's western wall. A gaping hole, five men high, had been hacked from the limestone. Huge iron braziers mounted on either side of crudely carved columns blazed so brightly Ezra could feel their heat from at least forty paces. They pushed their way through the crowd until they stood before roughhewn stairs carved from the living rock. To their right, the city wall stretched north for over a mile until it found the northern cliff and sealed the city into the box canyon.

"They say this cave was carved when the wall was built," Ezra said. "There is a tunnel that cuts right into the wall's core, and runs the entire length to allow soldiers to move freely in case the top of the wall is under siege."

"You don't say? I just heard it was a place soldiers get drunk when they aren't hunting down thieves. Now shut up and let me do all the talking."

Two bare-chested guards flanked either side of the entrance. Both carried spiked clubs as wide as Ezra's chest. Either looked like they could crush the boys with their bare hands.

"Three copper," the sentinel on the right barked as they approached. "One for the glorious King, one for the Commander, and one for the common soldier by whose blood the Markets are made safe."

"That's reasonable," Ezra murmured.

"Each," the guard on the left added forcefully.

Left Hand bowed slightly and handed over a silver coin they had lifted off the drunk Aryans. "And here are a few extra for you two."

One of the guards bit into the coin, but didn't seem impressed. For a moment, Ezra feared (and hoped) he wouldn't let them in. Then, with a curt jerk of his head he bid them entrance.

"I love being generous with other people's money," Left Hand whispered as they passed between the impassive sentinels and entered a smoky tunnel.

Raucous laughter spilled past them, blasting around the tunnel so loudly Ezra fought the urge to cover his ears. A common guard, not much older than them and wearing the bright, gaudy colors of the House Kvar, stumbled by.

"Air…" he croaked before keeling over in the middle of the tunnel and vomiting.

A barrel-chested man shoved Ezra and Left Hand aside and, whip in hand, flogged the young drunkard violently across the back of the neck, driving him into the street.

"If ye can't handle the wine, get yer hide outta my tavern!" the bouncer shouted after him, before turning and glaring at the pair.

Ezra stared slack-jawed at the gap-toothed monster.

The bouncer slapped Ezra in the back and bellowed, "You two outta luck. Just girls in there, no goats." He brushed past them and, pleased by his own joke, laughed all the way back into the tavern. "No goats! Ha! Ha!"

Left Hand beamed at Ezra. "See, he thinks we're Aryans. We got it covered."

Ezra quickly realized the stories didn't do reality justice. The dizzying reek of sweat, food, and sex saturating the cavern made Ezra anxious. The tavern's wicked energy swept Ezra up like a wild mountain stream. He didn't know how a place so dark could be so alive. Bodies packed shoulder-to-shoulder lined the edges, raising goblets, laughing and shouting. Long tables and benches filled the middle, each packed with not only soldiers, but a colorful hodgepodge of Hur-ar's well-to-do, including minor royalty and wealthy outlanders. Slave girls danced on the tables to the tune of drums and lyres.

Left Hand rubbed his palms. "I think this will do." He began to push his way to the nearest long table, packed with soldiers, until Ezra snatched him back.

"No. Trust me. We should find a small table along the wall."

Left Hand opened his mouth as if to protest, but relented.

Ezra kept his face low as they pressed into the crush and, by some miracle, found an open table in a small alcove in the cavern's dim recesses. Here, two round tables had been stuffed and forgotten. Slightly elevated, it gave them a good view of the tavern.

A burly Sammujad, furs heaped over broad shoulders and face and bald head grotesquely crisscrossed with scars, hunched over the other table. He shot them a look of indifferent hostility, and then returned to nursing a goblet. Heavy tapestries depicting hunting and battle scenes covered the cavern wall behind the tables, giving the alcove an isolated feel from the rest of the open tavern.

Ezra was grateful for the anonymous corner, but not having a quick avenue of escape made him uneasy.

"What gives? We'll never get a drink crammed all the way back here." Left Hand fidgeted. "It's too far from all the action."

"Believe it or not, I know a thing or two about this place. All those long tables are lined up in the center for a reason. Each belongs to a noble house." He pointed at the closest long table. "The table you almost sat at, that's Prince Sharakar's standard hanging above it, and those are his warriors. No one sits there unless they are in the service of that house, or their guest. If you would have sat down, this night would have ended quickly and badly."

"Hmm." Left Hand considered this.

"Look over there, just to the right of the King's Shield, the one with the Golden Calf painted on it. Do you see the banner with the Kupar Tree on it?"

"What, that scraggly bush?"

"That 'bush' represents my house. I know all those people and they know me. If they see me, I'll be back at the palace whether I want to be or not."

A burst of laughter erupted at Azubuhl's table as a tall warrior stood and raised a mug high in toast.

"Damn." Ezra slunk down and lowered the cap over his face.

"What?" Left Hand perked up.

"That's Zrula, second-in-command of my father's guard."

"What, the goofy looking fellow with the pitted cheeks?"

"That goofy fellow is a deadly swordsman."

"He don't look so tough."

"Let's go. The city is loaded with taverns."

"I don't think so. The more you try to talk me out of it, the more I want to stay." Left Hand craned around. "Tell me, why are there so many noblemen here drinking with their warriors. I don't get it. You know, don't they have nice places to get drunk?"

"Asul told me once 'A good warrior must march with his men, bleed with his men, and drink with his men.' It's said even the King comes here from time to time."

"Why didn't Asul want you here, then?"

Ezra shrugged. "He thought I wasn't ready. He wanted me to lead the division in battle first, to 'wet my sword before I wet my lips'."

Left Hand's eye drifted to a few slave girls gyrating atop a long table to the cheers of drunken warriors. "I could wet my sword a time or two tonight," he muttered, and then turned to Ezra with a grin. "You gotta quit being afraid, brother. Like I said, tonight Ezra dies and Blade is born!"

In one fluid movement, Left Hand leapt onto the table, almost knocking over the heavy oil lamp. He held a gold piece high over his head and shouted above the crowd and music. "What does it take to get some wine and whores over here for me and my friend?"

A small cheer went up from a few nearby tables and, as if by magic, a tavern slave materialized with two full goblets.

Left Hand tossed a few coppers to the bar slave and, still standing on the table, hoisted his goblet high and shouted. "A toast to the King, to the Commander, and the great house Azubelh!"

Another cheer briefly went up, and then quickly died. Ezra slid even lower, and dropped the cap completely over his face.

Left Hand lightly dropped off the table and onto the stool. He stared at Ezra with a self-assured smirk. "See, no one gives a pile of donkey dung who you are."

"You're crazy."

"Me? I'm not the one who ran away from a palace and possibly being master of the world."

Ezra cringed.

Left Hand stared at him in a way that shamed Ezra. "We're the only free men in this place. Me and you." He looked around and shrugged. "These warriors, they're not free. And the noblemen *damn* well aren't free." He considered Ezra. "You've shown me that. Someone holds their leash, just like someone will hold your leash if you go back." He tapped his chest. "No one, not even Slug himself, holds my leash. I am the true king of Hur-ar. If I die tonight, I die a free man. Let go, or go home, remember? So quit your damn whining, or I'm going to walk up to Pit-Face over there and tell him to take you back to your mother's skirts."

Speechless, Ezra stared at his friend with rising fury. He'd never wanted to strike Left Hand before, but now the urge swelled within.

"What's wrong with you?" A female voice broke Ezra's trance. He looked up at a Sammujad slave girl, not much older than himself, dressed in a beaded scarlet loincloth. A beaded top and tumbling rolls of black hair barely concealed her full breasts.

"I said, what's wrong with you?" She glanced over at Left Hand. "Is your friend dumb?"

Left Hand took a big swig. "No, darling. You see, he needs someone to remind him what it is to be a man. You know, teach him the boff-boff."

She nodded thoughtfully. "Oh, I can do that."

Left Hand laughed and slid a silver piece into a small pouch attached to the leather string, which stretched tantalizingly over her full hips. He winked at Ezra. "This one is on me. If you still want to hit me after she's through with you, well…we'll see how it goes."

"Left Hand!" Ezra began to protest, but she straddled him before he could continue.

He felt Left Hand snatch something from his side. "I've got your purse."

She pouted playfully. "I wouldn't steal, promise." She bent down and kissed Ezra hard. He could taste the salt on her skin, the wine on her open lips. Her soft breasts, rubbed against his neck before she pushed them into his face.

"Let go, or go home," Left Hand laughed, and called for another round of drinks.

She jostled her hips against Ezra's groin, seeking, teasing, overpowering. His hands dangled clumsily by his side, unsure where to touch. He'd never been this close to a woman. Even in his adolescent fantasies, he never expected a lowly slave girl would be his first experience. Ezra knew what he wanted to do, he just didn't know how to approach the issue. In all his training to be a warrior and king, he'd never had a single lesson on this particular subject, other than what he could glean from listening to the palace guards.

She straightened and considered him suspiciously. "Well, *he* knows what to do," she glanced down at his lap, "even if you don't." She crossed her arms. "You're no Aryan, that's for certain." She lifted his cap. "You're just a babe, with eyes much too pretty to be an outlander."

Ezra glanced at Left Hand, but he had already found his own slave girl and had begun the process of trying to suck her face off.

She shoved the cap down over his head. "Do you want to watch them, or play with me?"

"Uhm…" he flushed.

She leaned in and whispered in his ear. "It's okay, I won't tell anyone this is your first time."

He flushed even more, if such a thing were possible, and stole a quick look at the Sammujad's table. Two others had now joined him, both with their back to Ezra. Only an arm's reach from Ezra, a small bald man and a shaggy giant leaned in conspiratorially. None of them seemed particularly interested in what transpired beside them, even when Left Hand's woman released a moan.

"Do we go somewhere, like, in private?"

The slave girl giggled and tugged the conical hat even lower, almost covering his eyes. "If you want privacy, why don't you push this silly hat down lower. This is the City Wall, hon." She glanced over at the next table. "Here, men take what they want, when they want, where they want." She leaned over, breasts hanging tantalizingly low before of his eyes, and whispered. "No one cares."

She's right, no one cares, Ezra thought and surrendered.

She guided his hands to her thighs, and then around to the narrow of her waist. "Just follow my lead and it will be so good, I promise. Just let go."

A single word, almost whispered, shook Ezra from his rapture. It should not have reached his ears over the din echoing through the tavern, or the moans of the girl straddling his lap, or the heavy breathing and warm tongue intimately invading his ear.

Yet, it did.

"*…Sarah…*"

Part Three: Midnight

12. The Conspiracy

Ezra froze, unnoticed by the slave girl continuing to writhe on his lap. Her fingers inched toward the leather strap holding the baggy goatskin trousers around his waist. Ezra feigned interest, and listened intently to the nearby conversation above the deafening raucous.

"Her name is unimportant, just as long as I deliver her to the block tomorrow evening," said one of the men at the table beside him.

That voice, he thought. *I know that voice.*

The slave girl's kisses slid down his neck, affording Ezra an opportunity to slowly turn toward the Sammujad's table. He tilted his cap up just enough to see.

"Her name is why I want her," the small, bald man said. "Her name is what's paying for your merchandise. I also need your assurance her name won't prevent me from taking her from the city."

"By this time tomorrow no one inside the city will give a damn about her name, including the King and Prince Hector. She will be yours, free and clear."

Ezra's passion evaporated, all thoughts of pleasure exiled as he recognized Bal-eeb sitting at the table beside them. He turned and drove his face between the slave girl's breasts, hoping his step-brother didn't see him.

"Free and clear," the bald man reiterated. "No other bidders to jack up the price beyond our agreed terms."

"She'll be the next to last item at tomorrow's final slave auction. All the arrangements have been made, deals struck."

"You promise much," the small man said. "How do I know I can trust you?"

"Because it's in your interest to do so."

"I need more than that. I need concrete proof that I won't be running afoul a powerful royal family. I need friends, not enemies. If I can't trade in Hur-ar, my network collapses. If it collapses, I can't bribe the Scythians." The small man leaned back. "You are Sammujad, like me, eh? You know what happens when the Scythians are displeased.

"My client is Scythian, and he wants to bed a Hur noblewoman, a virgin. If I fail to deliver, well, let's say it will go badly for my business interests on the steppe and then I will have no business. Even the marshes would offer me no protection then.

"I am taking a great risk with this deal," the bald headed man said.

Bal-eeb leaned back, crossed his arms and smiled like a wolf. "Rest easy, slaver. Only moments before my arrival here, the Commander himself appointed me Captain of the Wall. By dawn I will be heir to the House Azubehl and second in line for the throne of Hur-ar. If what they say about Hector's health is true, I will soon be first in line. Your client will have more than just a noblewoman, he will bed the Golden Princess herself, the girl selected to become queen." Bal-eeb laughed. "Or at least was selected. Just show up at the auction with your gold, I will do the rest. Fulfill your end of the bargain as we agreed on the steppe and you and your men will pass the gates, *my gates*, with your prize."

"Captain of the Wall, eh?" the small man mused. "So I can count on you letting us pass without fear of inspection or additional tariffs?"

Bal-eeb shrugged. "So be it, no tariff or inspection just as long as you are out of the gates before sunset tomorrow."

The small man lifted a set of chains with shackles on the ends and jingled them. "That will depend on you delivering the goods."

Ezra struggled to remain calm. Sarah and his mother were in danger. He had to get out of this tavern, all the way across the city, and into the palace without Bal-eeb knowing. Not knowing what else to do, he continued to kiss the slave girl to buy time and listen.

The bald one continued. "I know a thing or two about Hur-ar's nobility. Isn't there already a prince of the House Azubehl?"

A flash of anger momentarily darkened Bal-eeb's face. "He will be dealt with, do not worry about that." He knew Bal-eeb well enough to detect the venom in his voice. "Prince Ezra will be dead before dawn."

"I'm not worried," the bald man said. "However, I don't want your complications to become my complications. Any vengeful princes coming after my prize, or my life, will reflect badly on our arrangement."

The slave girl sat up with hands on hips and raised her voice. "Hey! Are we going to do this or not, because you don't seem interested in the least bit."

And then Ezra made eye contact with Bal-eeb. They stared at one another for what seemed an eternity; the usurper in disbelief, the prince in horror.

From his left, Ezra heard Left Hand's slave girl scream. Left Hand stood and shoved his slave girl toward Bal-eeb's table. She fell over the small bald man, sending them sprawling to the floor where they blended into a blur of limbs, furs and profanities.

Left Hand grabbed Ezra by his vest and hurled him out of the alcove just as Bal-eeb's dagger whizzed by. Left Hand snatched the table lamp and hurled it at the tapestry behind the conspirators. It erupted into flames as Left Hand upended the table.

Ezra stumbled back from the blistering heat as smoke quickly filled the cavern.

"Time to find another tavern." Left Hand shouted and shoved Ezra toward the entrance.

A wave of panic swept over the tables and benches as the crowd bolted toward the tunnel. Swept up in the herd, Ezra could no longer see Left Hand. Tendrils of flame licked the highest reaches of the cavern roof and ignited the house banners.

Ezra caught a glance of Left Hand springing to a tabletop. Snagging the bottom of a banner, the thief launched himself over the mob and swung toward the tunnel entrance. Ezra followed suit.

Almost tripping on platters of half-eaten meat and over turning dozens of ceramic mugs, Ezra leapt for another banner before crashing face first on a table.

He spun about, kicking at whomever had grabbed his ankle, only to find himself staring up at Zrula's snarling face.

Sword held high, the warrior prepared to plunge the blade into Ezra's chest. "You're not going anywhere, you sniveling pile of…"

Two feet struck Zrula square in the head, sending him flying backwards onto the floor to be quickly trampled. Left Hand swung back and touched down on the table. "Quit lying around. It's Festival, you know. Places to go, things to see."

Ezra scrambled up, and glanced back to see Bal-eeb fighting his way through the crowd toward them. Ezra grabbed a banner, and swung behind Left Hand over the smoky cavern. They dropped into the throng and blended with the coughing mob spilling into the streets.

.

13. The God of Chaos

As soon as Ezra and Left Hand pushed their way through the coughing crowds, they slipped into an alley and ditched their disguises.

Ezra stuffed the goatskin underneath a trash heap. "How did you know?"

"I caught you staring instead of kissing. Then I heard your name. It didn't take much to figure it out."

Ezra looked at the crowds milling outside the City Wall. Black smoke vomited from the cavern's mouth. "I hope everyone got out."

"Too late to worry about that now. C'mon, we gotta go before someone comes looking for us."

Ezra turned around and saw Left Hand sliding into a sewer drain.

"Where are you going?"

Left Hand looked at Ezra as if he'd asked the dumbest question possible. "Getting the hell out of here."

"My mother and sister are in danger."

"They'll nab you the moment you step out there." Left Hand nodded toward the street. "We'll take the Narrow."

"But that will take all night!"

"The roof tops are no longer safe, and the streets will be crawling with soldiers." He slipped farther down into the drain. "This way or no way."

Ezra exhaled and followed Left Hand down the hole. As he descended into darkness, a thought occurred, like a rope thrown to a drowning man.

Asul, he will know what to do!

***

"I don't know who they were, lord! Mercy!" she screamed again as Bal-eeb continued to twist her arm.

"A little more pressure," he said, "And I'll pull your arm right out of its socket.

"You expect me to believe you took those two as Aryans?" Bal-eeb said. His fine waist wrap and tunic were now scorched and reeking of smoke. The stench served only to remind him of the insult he'd just suffered at Ezra's hands.

"I swear, I swear, I swear!" she gasped, the pain becoming unbearable. "They had money. If I don't please the patrons my master will beat me."

"Your master is roasting inside the cave, thanks to those two."

She cried out in anguish, but Bal-eeb didn't care. He needed to know why Ezra was in the bar eavesdropping on his plans.

Bal-eeb had found the two slave girls he'd seen sitting on Ezra and the other boy's lap shortly after escaping the City Wall. He'd dragged them through the milling crowd to this guard shack a few blocks west. Questions roared through his mind. Had Ezra known all along? What did this mean for the conspiracy? His well laid plans teetered on the edge of failure.

If he wasn't angry enough, Virag stepped into the crowded shack, the singed fox furs on his shoulders still smoldering.

"Captain of the Wall, your complications are becoming my complications."

He ignored the insult and continued his interrogation. "Who was the one sitting beside you?" He increased pressure on her arm. "Speak, bitch, or you'll end up like your friend." He pushed her face toward where the other slave girl lay sprawled unconscious on the dirt floor. "Perhaps your memory will be better than hers. Who threw the lamp?"

"I don't know his name." She winced. "One of them said something about a hand."

He cuffed her and she fell to the floor in a whimpering ball.

"You're wasting your time," Virag said. "The wench doesn't know anything."

Zrula stormed in, streaked with soot, his nose swollen. "We've searched five streets in every direction." He dropped goat-hair garments at Bal-eeb's feet. "We found these in an alley, but no trace of the two who wore them."

Bal-eeb kicked the clothes away. "I saw both their faces. One was young Prince Azubehl, I'm sure. As for the other one, I've never seen him before."

Virag took the clothes and smelled them, before dropping them in disgust. "Why would a prince wear the goat fur of an Aryan trader to sneak into a tavern he could otherwise openly stroll into?"

"I've served several of the noble houses. Their brats go slumming all the time," Zrula said. "His being there tonight was simply coincidence. The prince is likely trying to sneak his way back into the palace now, or maybe he's hiding in his friend's palace."

Bal-eeb shook his head. "That other boy, he was no snot-nosed princeling. I've committed every royal family to memory. He was too damn fast, and too damn lean to be a royal."

Virag sighed. "Do we have a problem?"

"This incident has no bearing on our business."

"Oh, it has a very real bearing on *our* business, but tidying up this mess is your problem."

Virag knelt down and gently patted the whimpering slave girl, speaking like a concerned father. "Did you serve your master well?"

Trembling, she drew away slightly and nodded.

"I'm sure you did. What's your name?"

"Lumina."

"That's a pretty name. Your friend there, what's her name?"

"Natasha."

Virag patted the passed out slave girl's cheek. "Natasha, wake up. Wake up, precious."

She groaned. Her eyes fluttered open. Momentary disorientation gave way to terror. "I don't know, I told you! I don't know who they were."

"Shush." Virag placed a finger on her lips. "I know. No one is going to beat you." He held up her hands and enveloped them in his, softly kissing her knuckles before slipping a set of manacles around her wrists. She frowned in confusion as Virag secured another set on Lumina.

"What are you doing?" Bal-eeb demanded.

"I'm taking these slaves as compensation for the misery I've endured this evening. Their master is dead, therefore they revert to the crown." He pointed to Bal-eeb. "As newly minted Captain of the Wall, you represent the king. I therefore accept your gift."

Zrula stepped forward, hand on hilt. "He made no offer, you ass. I've had enough of your disrespectful tongue."

Bal-eeb held Zrula back with a hand to the chest. "These slaves are of no consequence. Take them if you like, compliments of the crown. Just be at the appointed place tomorrow."

"Wouldn't miss it." Virag gave a slight nod and dragged the slave girls from the shack.

Zrula spat once as Virag strolled out of earshot. "A viper, that one."

"More like a fox. When he's no longer necessary, I'll go fox hunting."

"What do we do?"

"Ezra will try to warn his mother and sister. Double the palace guard and post a sentry at Sarah's door."

His whole life, Bal-eeb had fought to remove the god of chaos from his affairs. Now, at the moment of his victory, she returned to plague him.

A guard with a singed beard and sooty uniform approached the shack door. His green waist wrap signified he belonged to the Sewer Patrol, the lowest echelon of the City Guard.

"Great Captain, I am Gilga. I witnessed the events in the tavern tonight."

"What of it?" Zrula said.

"The two masquerading as Aryans, those who started the mess, I recognized one of them."

"I see," Zrula snorted. "And what do you want for this information?"

"Nothing, except the honor of serving the Great Captain." Gilga bowed to Bal-eeb.

Zrula laughed. "He'd say anything to get out of slum patrol."

"If what you tell me is useful, I might be able to find a posting for you on the wall. If not," Bal-eeb drew his sword. "I will permanently assign less strenuous duties."

"It is most useful, I swear," Gilga spoke quickly. "They stepped over my table as they fled. I got a good look at both. One I did not recognize, but the other I knew well. They call him Left Hand."

"He is lying." Zrula frowned. "No one's gotten a good look at Slug's second-in-command."

Gilga raised his hands and backed away. "I saw Left Hand last year in the Third Tunnel. My patrol had him cornered, but he vanished. The Untouchables do that, like ghosts."

Bal-eeb lowered his sword and turned to Zrula. "Didn't you say they vanished into an alley?"

Zrula nodded. "But it's too farfetched. No way a notorious outlaw and a prince would be running together. It makes no sense."

Bal-eeb pounded his fist against the wall, rattling the shack. "It explains everything, like Ezra's disappearances. He'll use the sewers to sneak into the palace and warn his mother. Send our fastest messenger to the King's palace and tell my mother her presence is required immediately at the House Azubelh. Tell her breakfast will be served early, she'll know what it means."

Zrula bowed. "As you wish."

"Mobilize our forces, send as many into the sewers as we can spare to hunt Ezra and this *Left Hand*. Enlist Gilga in the hunt and any former sewer soldiers you can scrounge up."

Zrula looked doubtful. "Only the five Great Tunnels are capable of being patrolled. The rest are too narrow. The thieves will cut our men down in the dark. Not to mention, telling our warriors to crawl the sewers during Festival could lead to mutiny."

Bal-eeb leaned toward Zrula. "At least twenty soldiers lay roasting in that tavern. The whole Army will want revenge, especially when House Azubehl offers fifty Gold Crowns for the head of the one they call Left Hand." He poked Zrula in the chest. "Find Left Hand, and you'll find Ezra."

Zrula grinned. "Of course."

***

"Does anyone sleep in this city?" Wadim remarked as he walked beside his master.

"Not during Festival," Virag said.

Virag and his armed entourage progressed slowly through the crowded streets, the two slave women shuffling behind, heads down and chains clattering.

Glad to be away from the tavern's burning stench, Virag mused aloud, "Have no doubt Bal-eeb is a powerful warrior, but he should stick to fighting and leave conspiracies to those more adept at subterfuge, like his mother. Now *there* is a woman worthy of the Golden Throne." He had paid a tidy sum to learn all he could about Bal-eeb and his mother. It quickly became apparent their success climbing Hur-ar's hierarchy rested solely with her.

"Bal-eeb is under the illusion he understands the Hur-po, that he can become one of them. He is mistaken. He's just a filthy Sammujad trying to steal a little glory for himself. As for this young Prince..." He trailed off. "Did any of you get a good look at the Azubehl boy in the tavern?"

Wadim shook his head. "No, my lord, none of us did."

"Too bad," Virag said dryly, regretting that he hadn't, either. "My business partner obviously miscalculated his opposition within the House Azubehl."

"Is it wise to meddle in royal feuds?" Wadim asked. "Perhaps we should return to the Steppe until events in Hur-ar settle down?"

Virag frowned, irritated by his underling's question. "The die is cast when the forge is hot. Besides, hunting down the young prince is Bal-eeb's problem, our problem is securing the princess."

"What if Bal-eeb cannot fulfill his end of the bargain?"

"Then I will have to ensure he can."

They stopped before a busy stoop, where a crudely carved sign of a strutting rooster hung over a doorway.

He placed two golden crowns in Wadim's palm. "Go to the Street of Moons in the city's Twilight quarter. It's dangerous, so keep your blade ready. There, ask around for a man they call the Jackal. Follow the sounds of baying hounds and you'll find him. He's an old business acquaintance, and also dangerous. Give him the coins and tell him where he can find me. Waste no time. As for the rest of you, wait in the tavern common room. Don't get drunk." Virag snatched the chains securing the slave women from Spako's hand. "I'm going to my room to assess these women's proper value."

14. The Narrows

"I must get to the palace."

"That might happen quickly, or it might take a while." Left Hand crouched in the intersection of two small tunnels, each barely large enough to stoop. He rubbed his chin thoughtfully. "If we go left, we'll come to the Third Tunnel. It's got some water in it, but not too much. We'll climb the walls until we find the passage to the Narrows leading to the Four Gates. And you know what that means."

"Slug."

"Yep." If they traversed the Four Gates, a major sewer intersection, they would have to deal with Left Hand's gang leader, someone Ezra preferred to avoid.

"That could get complicated, I suppose, but we still have the bag with all the food," Ezra said. "He'll let me pass just as long as I can pay the tax."

"Yeah." Left Hand looked around, uncertainty clouding his face. "I'd just rather not have to answer any questions tonight."

Left Hand pointed to the right, where only a dim light trickled down from drains leading to the street above. "*Or* we could go that way, which might be equally complicated."

"Where does it go?"

"The Fourth Tunnel."

"I thought that tunnel was flooded?"

"It is. Really bad. We'd have to scale the wall practically at the ceiling, and hope our grip, and luck, hold out. It would take us to the Narrows on the other side of your palace."

Ezra thought himself a better than average climber, but didn't relish the idea of scaling a crumbling brick wall in the darkness above a roaring flood.

"You don't have to come with me," Ezra said after a pause.

Left Hand looked back with uncustomary seriousness. "I don't. And you don't have to go. You left that world behind, remember?"

"They're my family," Ezra said. "You can't expect me to abandon them."

"Haven't you already?"

Ezra stared hard at his friend. "I'll go alone if I must."

Left Hand picked up a pebble and turned it over and over, deep in thought. Ezra could not read his expression.

After a few moments, Left Hand spoke. "You won't make it without me."

"You taught me well."

"Not my best tricks." He paused. "I'll help you, but for a price. When I save your sister, she gives me a kiss."

Ezra fought the urge to laugh, knowing Left Hand was completely serious. "Why just a kiss?"

"Because, you idiot, after only one kiss she'll fall madly in love with me. Then I can be a prince, and you can be a sewer thief."

Ezra grinned. "I think it can be arranged."

They turned to the sounds of shouting echoing in the distance behind them.

"Untouchables?" Ezra asked.

"No. Too loud. That's the sound of cussing and complaining."

"Soldiers," Ezra said. "They're coming after us."

"They'll never catch us." Left Hand tossed the pebble down the right tunnel. "Maybe we'll catch old Slug in a good mood. Remember, same as always, when we get there I do all the talking. You still can't talk like a thief."

"Can, too."

"Cannot." Left Hand jumped to his feet and trotted down the tunnel, Ezra close on his heels.

***

"I thought you said there was only a little water in the Third Tunnel?" Ezra shouted over the roaring flood.

"You should be thankful," Left Hand shouted back. "Not enough to force us to crawl the ceiling, but just enough to keep the soldiers out."

Ezra slid along the sloping wall's damp granite, seeking hand and toe holds memorized since the first time Left Hand brought him here. Enveloped in total darkness, he couldn't see the water roaring only a few feet below. Nor could he see or hear Left Hand only an arm's reach ahead.

Before the Narim walled themselves into the Black Fortress in ancient days, the god-men created enormous stone walls stretching the length of the canyon's three sides to route the avalanches away from the city. They also built the Five Great Tunnels.

Carved out of living granite and originating from flood ponds surrounding the city, the tunnels both acted as flood control for the snow melt and water supply. The thieves and city dwellers above both referred to the Great Tunnels simply by their number, starting with One in the north and ending with Five in the south. They ran underneath the wall and overflowed to the grassy flats beyond the city. Well-constructed, warriors often patrolled the cavernous tunnels from mid-summer to early winter. Otherwise, they were impassable the rest of the year, or so the Sewer Patrol thought.

Ezra smelled the gaping hole in the tunnel wall before his fingers found its ragged edge. Built by men years after the Narim sealed themselves in the Black Fortress, the Narrows were constructed to carry the contents of Hur-ar's chamber pots to the Great Tunnels. Built of sun-baked brick, these poorly built secondary tunnels were extensive, but narrow and often crumbling. Many thieves had lost their lives in cave-ins.

For this reason, even the street gangs avoided the Narrows, where size and numbers counted for nothing. These were the kingdom of the Untouchables.

Accustomed to the stench, Ezra half-crouched and caressed the moss covered wall, careful not to slip on the slimy floor.

"You know, it's not Slug I'm worried about," Ezra said. "Lucatta isn't happy with you after the last time you ditched her."

"I told you, relax," Left Hand's voice came from the darkness ahead of him. "She only acts upset. Deep down, Lucatta is crazy about me."

"Obsessed is more like it," Ezra sighed. "I think she's just plain crazy. You keep messing with her, she's likely to knife you."

"She just doesn't know how to take 'no' for an answer, that's all."

"You never tell her no."

"Of course, dummy. No one tells Lucatta no. She's crazier than hell, haven't you heard?"

In a low crouch, he followed Left Hand's voice deeper into the blackness. Soon, the air felt less stifling. The tunnel had widened. Water and light dripped from a wide pipe climbing vertically to the street. They had arrived at The Four Gates, a four-way intersection spacious enough to fully stand and the heart of Slug's territory. Laughter, mixed with drums and flutes, filtered from above. They were near the Grand Market, and the tunnel ahead would lead them to Palace Azubehl.

103

"Wait," Left Hand whispered.

"Do you think anyone is here?"

"Someone is *always* here," Left Hand replied.

"Always!" shouted a voice from above.

With several sharp cracks, heavy wooden gates slammed down over the tunnels in each direction, trapping them in the intersection.

As if the crumbling baked bricks gave birth, ghostly arms and legs slid from cracks all around. Flint and copper blades glinted in the pale light.

Ezra stood shoulder-to-shoulder with Left Hand as a gang of children, from perhaps seven to a few about his age, surrounded them.

"Left Hand finally sees fit to drag his butt home," a voice sneered from behind one of the blades.

"I see fit to do whatever 'da hell I please," Left Hand laughed.

The boy who challenged Left Hand stepped forward, stringy black hair and narrow eyes like a rat. "Papa Slug ain't happy wid you."

"Rat, Papa Slug ain't never happy."

Ezra knew enough about Rat to never turn his back on him. Rat had been itching to become second-in-command. Ezra knew Rat's kind; the court crawled with such whisperers and deceivers. Ezra suddenly thought of Bal-eeb, and suppressed the urge to plant his fist in Rat's face.

"Open 'da gates. Got places to go, ping-ping to be a'takin'." Left Hand reverted to the dialect of the Underworld.

Ezra understood tunnel-speak well enough, but still found it difficult to talk convincingly as one of the Untouchables.

"We know what you'd been a'takin'." Rat let out a squeaky laugh. "Slug does, too, and he ain't none to happy wid you or Blade."

"I said let us pass." Left Hand folded his arms.

Rat puffed out his chest. "You pass when Slug say so."

The other children closed in, knives extended.

104

Since running with Left Hand, Ezra had endured his share of turf battles. If it came to a fight, they would keep their backs to the wall and use the close confines to their advantage. If the gang couldn't swarm them, they couldn't defeat them.

In times like this, Ezra usually kept quiet. This time, however urgency compelled him to intervene. "What does Slug want?"

Rat waved the knife in Ezra's face. "You ain't got no voice here. You not *Untouchable*."

Ezra took the bag from Left Hand and knelt. "Since I'm not Untouchable, I bring the tax." He looked at a girl he'd seen before, perhaps ten, and winked. She smiled back, but didn't lower her knife.

"What'dya bring, Blade?" asked a little one-armed girl. She tucked a sharpened bone splinter into a cord around her waist and inched forward, trying to peer inside the bag.

"Nobody care what's in 'da bag," Rat sneered.

Ezra knew these children cared. They led violent lives cut short by hunger, disease and the streets.

Ezra handed her a chunk of cheese.

"Blade's got d'tax!" she shouted and retreated to the shadows with her treasure.

The rest lowered their weapons and rushed forward.

Rat shot Ezra a nasty look and faded back. "Won't help none. Slug won't care nuttin 'bout no tax."

Ezra looked up at Left Hand, who grinned and nodded. Ezra handed him the bag and stepped back.

"Lemme see! Wadda we got here?" Left Hand poked around in the bag. "Is 'dat meat Ima whiffin?"

"Meat! Meat! Meat!" the children shouted. To Ezra's shock, more children slithered in from unseen cracks and crannies, so filthy some looked like floating eyes in the darkness. As they scurried into the light, Ezra saw some were missing limbs, some horribly deformed, all emaciated.

"Meat, huh?" Left Hand said in mock concern. "I got some nice wormy cabbage. I keep da yummy fo good ol' Left Hand! Who up for wormy cabbage?"

"Left Hand!" they screamed in glee.

He grinned and began tearing the flat loaves into strips for eager, frantic hands.

Ezra struggled to hide his feelings, to play the role of calloused thief. He would never grow used to their suffering, and hoped he never would. In the world above, these children were objects to be rounded up, tortured and killed for the twisted pleasures of the powerful.

"What mischief bring 'da pretty boys down here when pickens so easy up top?" a deep voice rumbled from the unbroken darkness.

The children snatched the last morsels and scurried into shadows, wiggling back into the cracks from which they had emerged.

Something slithered overhead. Ezra looked up to see wide eyes staring back at him from the Underworld's eternal twilight.

What looked like a big, bald infant slid from an upper pipe. Like an owl, his whole body slowly rotated upright, followed lastly by his head. Then, Slug dropped straight down onto his legless torso with a splash.

Ezra shivered, wondering how Slug didn't hurt his balls doing that.

Like a gray maggot, Slug had no legs, not even stumps. Wearing only a loincloth wrapped around his torso like a diaper, a thin leather strip secured a wickedly curved knife to his back.

The Sewer Patrol called him "The Tunnel Monster," a reputation well deserved. With forearms as hard as iron and hammer-like fists, Slug could tear his enemies limb from limb, or pummel them into a bloody smear. Ezra knew well Slug's skill with that blade, especially within the sewer's tight confines. Even more feared than Slug's knife were his fists, which he often shod in thick metal plates he called *The Pounders.*

Some said Slug was immortal, a demon condemned by the Narim to wander the sewers for eternity. His smooth, almost translucent skin and bald head concealed all signs of life's passing. A deeply cleft palate gave him a permanently sinister grin.

Below the streets, the Underworld revered him as the Legless Lord and the Gray One. Unlike rival gang chieftains, Slug sought out the weak and the unwanted. His scouts scoured the streets and garbage heaps for crippled children and babies abandoned to die, with which he built his army of Untouchables, the most powerful gang in Hur-ar.

The one-armed girl reappeared beside Slug, still chewing on the cheese.

Rat glared at them from his chieftain's other side. "Trapped 'em here, just like you said boss."

Slug ignored his underling. "Why Left Hand runnin' down da Narrow so fast, dragging Blade 'wid him?"

Left Hand stepped between Ezra and Slug. "Not runnin, Slug. Look'n fo 'da action, bring back Slug some ping-ping,"

"Lodes a ping-ping down 'da Avenue. No ping-ping here." Slug tilted his head and stared unblinking at Ezra.

Left Hand shook his head, as if the answer were obvious. "Too many sober spears on 'da Avenue. Blade and me, we crawlin under."

"He's lying," Rat said. "'Da smoke don't lie."

"Narrows fo hiding, not runnin." Slug said.

"Don't know why boss treat'n his best thief like dog when he bring 'da tax." Left Hand removed the last of the bag's contents, the choicest chunk of salted goat and presented it to his chieftain.

Slug sniffed it, never taking his gaze off Ezra. He ripped it in two and gave half to the one-armed girl, who attacked in voraciously.

"What's all 'dis 'bout, Slug?" Left Hand asked.

Slug looked up, closed his eyes and sniffed. "The streets a' whispering, telling Slug trouble coming. Trouble smells like smoke a'following you down 'da Narrow."

Ezra's unease began to fester as the children reemerged and encircled them.

"Smoke bring truth," Slug's obsidian eyes bore into Ezra. "Smoke say careless thief a dead thief. Smoke tell Slug lots a' things."

Slug took a bite and began to chew slowly. "It good. Stuff 'dis good gotta come from 'da Avenue, eh Blade?"

Ezra shrugged, but didn't answer.

"Blade don't say much," Slug continued. "Never see Blade 'cept following Left Hand like a dog hunt'n scraps. Slug not sure who 'da dog, Blade or Left Hand."

"Hey, Slug!" Left Hand intervened. "Blade's a friend. He pay 'da tax."

"Blade got my respect," Slug said, "Take longer to get my trust."

Slug returned his gaze to Left Hand. "Dragon snatched Lucatta tonight in 'da Market."

The Untouchables called anything having to do with the priest of Ba'al "the Dragon." Ezra turned to Left Hand. The terrible news penetrated his cool exterior.

"She's too fast for 'da Dragon."

"Got careless, 'suppose. Snagged by a outlander trying to lift his ping-ping. She in 'da Belly of d'Beast, waiting t'die." Ezra heard sadness in the chieftain's voice.

She's being held in the Temple of Ba'al, Ezra thought.

"What we gunna do about it?" Left Hand asked.

"Code say careless thief a dead thief." Slug said with finality. "Tell me, Left Hand, you been careless?"

"What are you talking about?" Left Hand asked.

Now Ezra knew they were in trouble.

"I'm talking about you and Blade at 'da Wall, draggin 'da soldiers down on us."

"We just havin' some fun." Left Hand didn't even try to bluff.

"Don't mind fun, unless it put my family in danger." Slug patted the little girl's head. "Tonight, you and Blade brought 'da city down on us." Slug drew his knife from over his back.

"Slug, I'm 'da best Left Hand you ever had."

"True, but you messed up." He sniffed the air. "Smell da smoke? Torches burning in the Great Tunnels, driving rats dis way. Soldiers dead, Captain of 'da Wall looking fo Left Hand. You started a war. Too many soldiers even for Slug. Should throw you both in da Hole, but I'm gonna ransom your head before deh kill us all."

Slug faded back, and the thieves closed in. Left Hand and Ezra drew daggers and turned back-to-back.

"We can't fight this many and Slug." Ezra's mind raced, trying to think of a way out.

"There's a lever above the right-hand tunnel," Left Hand whispered. "If I can get to it, it will open all four gates."

Ezra struggled for another way out of their predicament. "We can save Lucatta!" He blurted.

"No way back from 'da Belly of 'da Beast," Slug said.

"I know a way. We get her out, or die trying."

'What'ya got to lose, Slug?" Left Hand chimed in. "Lucatta's life fo ours."

Ezra couldn't read Slug's expression, but after a few long moments he spoke. "So be it. Bring back my daughter before she burn, or I burn you." He shoved Rat forward. "Go wid 'em."

Rat turned in astonishment. "Why?"

"If I gotta kill my old Left Hand, you gotta prove worthy as new Left Hand. Any of you come back alive, Lucatta better be wid you, or don't come back."

Slug turned to the other thieves. "Call all my children to 'da Wide. We'll be safe der until soldiers go back topside." He looked down at the little girl. "Open 'da gates."

She scurried up the wall, using her one hand better than most use two. Grabbing the lever with her teeth, she pulled it with her weight and a grinding noise filled the chamber.

The gates lifted, and Slug and the Untouchables melted into the darkness, leaving the three boys alone in the intersection.

"Nice thinking," Left Hand said casually. "How did you know Lucatta was his daughter?

"I didn't. It was a guess. He seemed really upset."

Left Hand frowned. "He looked like he always does."

Ezra just shrugged.

"Good guess," Left Hand said. "I've known Slug and Lucatta since I've been down here, and I never knew."

"Everyone know Lucatta Slug's girl!" Rat scoffed.

"Whatever, Rat." Left Hand turned to Ezra with a queer expression "I wonder how he did it."

"Did what?"

"You know, boff. Without legs."

Ezra doubled over in laughter at the absurd image in his head, and the tension broke like a damn.

He'd brushed against death twice tonight. He'd take the laughter where he could, because Ezra had a feeling they would brush against death a few more times before dawn.

"What you two laughing at?" Rat asked. "We all die tonight. No one gone down 'da Dragon's Belly and live to tell."

Ezra looked at Left Hand. "Any ideas?"

"No," Left Hand smiled. "No one has been brave or stupid enough to try. I am not that brave, and I ain't stupid, but I'm desperate and handsome, and that'll have to be enough."

"We still have to save my mother and sister."

"Mother? What sister?" Rat looked back and forth between them, but they paid him no mind.

Left Hand screwed up his face in thought. "The Gleaning could happen as late as high noon during Festival. We could nab her while she's waiting in line."

"She'll be guarded. Black robes and guards everywhere," Ezra cautioned.

"It's settled, we nab Lucatta before Gleaning, and grab your family now."

Ezra felt relieved, even though Left Hand had just put his life, and Rat's, in further jeopardy by placing Sarah's predicament ahead of Lucatta's.

"Let's go. I'll get my kiss from your sister first!" Left Hand slapped Ezra's shoulder and raced down the tunnel.

"What sister? Where 'da hell you going?" Rat shouted and followed after them.

In a chorus of splashes, the three thieves raced down the tunnel.

15. Sunflowers in the Moonlight

Unable to sleep, Sarah slipped from beneath the covers and draped a bed fur over her shoulders. As she did many sleepless nights, she stood at her balcony window and stared out over the courtyard. Tonight, a crescent moon frowned down upon a city vibrant with celebration.

"Here I am, alone...*again*," she whispered despondently to the night, angry at the invisible chains the world seemed to forge just for women. "Why can't I run away like Ezra?"

Some nights on her balcony, Sarah dreamt of love. She longed for a lover who cared for her heart, not her title. Sometimes when she stood on the balcony in the moonlight, Sarah could not shake the feeling of eyes upon her. She fantasized a handsome man would step out of the shadows and whisk her away from her fate. He would be a good man, a gentle man, a loving man. Sarah swore she would forsake the throne and all the gold in Hur-ar for such a love.

The girl still dwelling in her heart ached for this ideal lover, but the emerging woman whispered no such man existed, at least in Hur-ar. The emerging woman always seemed to speak with her mother's voice; the voice of family, the voice of duty. Her mother's voice issued the proclamation that chained Sarah's fate to Prince Hector's to secure the family's future in Hur-ar's royal hierarchy. Her mother's voice, which had become more distant and cold as Sarah had grown.

Oh, how Sarah resented that voice.

Men's shouts, the creak of pulleys and the groan of the wooden gates signaled a midnight arrival in the courtyard below, stirring Sarah from her thoughts. The courtyard's comings and goings seldom drew her attention, but now a conspiracy of laughter and clattering wagon wheels compelled Sarah to slip into the balconies shadow, out of sight. Sarah stepped to the window in time to see her father's wagon clatter to a halt. Sarah held her arms tightly around her shoulders; not so much against the chilly air, but at the scene playing out below. The night lifted every infuriating whisper to her balcony.

"We didn't expect you back so soon," the watch sergeant said.

Father mumbled something unintelligible as a slave knelt like a human step stool at the bottom of the wagon's steps. Ashtoreth stumbled down first, laughing in that superficial way that made Sarah sink her fingernails into her biceps.

"Don't spill the goblet, darling!" Ashtoreth called back to Prince Azubehl. "Or we'll have to go right back and fetch more of that delightful wine. The King promised he would send several jugs for our party tomorrow night."

Sarah groaned inside as Father stood and belched so loudly several of the courtyard guards actually turned. He swayed for a moment, almost falling over had it not been for Mother supporting him from behind. Even from here, Sarah could see the wine and food stains streaked down the front of his robes.

Probably vomit, too, she thought.

With much assistance from Mother, Father stumbled out of the wagon. He would have fallen face-first if Ashtoreth had not caught him at the last moment. Sarah would not have thought such speed and strength possible for a small, apparently drunk woman.

"Now, now! We wouldn't want the mighty prince to break his neck, would we?" Sarah looked away as Ashtoreth kissed Father like a prostitute.

The giggling pleasure women followed, each dressed in a nearly transparent gossamer wrap. Sarah didn't recognize the raven haired slave, but soon realized the tall woman was none other than Tazrech's mother, Yalani, Second Wife of House Azubehl.

During Festival, differentiating between pleasure slave and patrician could sometimes be difficult.

Ashtoreth supported Father toward the open double doors leading to the Prince's inner chambers. Firelight flickered from beyond the threshold, alluding to secrets and deeds Sarah did not want to imagine. Yalani and the slave girl strode behind, arms intimately encircling each other's waist. They occasionally stole glances over their shoulder at Mother, who still remained in the wagon.

"Come, girls," Ashtoreth called seductively over her shoulder. "Let's take this party inside. The Prince needs some special attention."

Yalani whispered into the slave girl's ear and they both giggled before hurrying after Ashtoreth.

Mother remained still as stone as the rest of the party vanished into the bedroom chamber.

"Rise," Mother softly instructed the prostate slave. Princess Meribeph had long ago banished the whip from within the palace walls. Anyone caught beating a slave would themselves be beaten. Sarah marveled at how her mother could command even the most unruly warrior with only a whisper, as if her voice carried magic.

"It's not magic, it's respect," her mother had once chided Sarah. "Respect bought with fear buys obedience only until the master's back is turned. Respect bought with kindness yields loyalty. Let the courage and conviction of your heart fill your voice, and even mountains will obey."

"Welcome home, Princess." The young slave smiled warmly and held out his hand.

"Thank you, Gregorious." Meribeph took his hand and hopped lightly down. She glanced around the courtyard until her attention rested on the wagons parked along the eastern wall.

"Why are preparations not underway for tomorrow's journey?" she asked the watch sergeant. "And where is Captain Asul?"

"I do not know, Your Highness," he replied. "I can send for him if you wish."

Mother didn't respond and glanced around the courtyard and palace walls. "Who gave the order to double the guard?"

"Prince Bal-eeb. He sends word of trouble near the city wall and thought it prudent."

"I see," she said. "Return to your post."

The guard nodded and strode away, leaving the First Wife alone.

Sarah suffered a pang of guilt spying on her mother from the shadows, but could not turn away. Mother strolled to the courtyard's center. There, she lovingly caressed the lush sunflowers surrounding the lion fountain. Ever since Sarah could remember, Mother had ordered sunflowers planted in pots around the fountain.

"They're pretty, but why just sunflowers?" Sarah had once asked as a little girl.

"Because they're my favorite. And because they always turn their faces to the sun, no matter where it is," Mother had said. "Even when the courtyard is in shadow."

"What about at night, Mama?"

"At night, they turn east and patiently wait for the sun." She remembered Mother leaning over and kissing her nose. "They remind us there will always be a morning, no matter how dark the night."

"Meribeph!" her father's voice roared from the chamber, followed by decadent laughter and velvet moans.

Don't go in there! Sarah screamed inside.

Mother slowly turned toward the chamber and took a few steps. Then, she paused, closed her eyes and dipped her head. Mother took a deep breath and slowly exhaled. She pulled the pins from her hair, letting her luxurious locks spill over her shoulders. Moon and torchlight conspired, painting her hair silver and gold like a goddess come to life.

Meribeph opened her eyes and turned her gaze up at the balcony, and tenderly smiled at Sarah.

Ashamed, Sarah ducked behind the curtain.

Her mother's voice, full of long-absent love and gentleness, floated into Sarah's bedroom. "Go to sleep, beloved daughter. Sunrise will be a time for new beginnings."

An urgent need overwhelmed Sarah, to hold her mother tightly, like she did when she was a little girl.

"Mother!" Sarah pushed aside the curtain, but she was gone, the chamber doors shut.

Except for the babbling fountain amongst the sunflowers, the courtyard fell quiet once again. Sarah slipped into her bedroom, longing for morning, and to hear her mother's voice again.

16. Fireflies

Sarah stood before the tree that held up the sky, and knew she'd returned to the kingdom of dreams. The twilight meadow wore the raiment of eternal spring. Fireflies twinkled all around, melting in and out of the glorious stars stretching above.

Strolling beside the stream, Sarah approached the meadow's center. There, the stream widened, forming a small circular island where the ancient tree boldly stood. Titanic boughs sagged almost to the crystal water. Unlike previous nights, the Golden Woman wasn't waiting for her on the island.

Did she really feel the soft grass and cool dew upon her feet? This dream possessed a sensual clarity lacking in her previous visits, as if the vision's blurry edges had been sewn up tightly to mimic life's jagged reality.

"Do not touch the water," an unseen female voice resonated.

Sarah spun about, searching. "Hello?"

As if in answer, the fireflies swarmed around her feet, then congealed into a graceful, twinkling bridge arching over the stream.

"Come," the voice called.

Excitement coursed through Sarah as she stepped lightly across the sparkling bridge, expecting her heel to fall through, or at least be covered with crawling insects. Instead, it felt like warm stone basking in the afternoon sun. The fireflies scattered, revealing a stone bridge where none had existed moments ago.

"The only way home is forward," the voice called again.

Sarah held her breath, stepped across, and soon found her toes deep in lush grass crisscrossed by gnarled roots. She dashed around the tree searching for the Golden Woman. Caressing the trunk, its smooth bark felt more like flesh than wood.

What she thought was one stream was actually four. All originated from the moat surrounding the tree and flowed away in cardinal directions until they vanished into a distant tree line. Imagining how cool and inviting the water must feel, Sarah desperately wanted to touch it, but heeded the unseen woman's warning.

Sarah remembered the bridge, and ran around searching for the glittering causeway, but it had vanished.

How can I return if I cannot enter the water?

Then, before her eyes, a thin tendril sprouted from beneath a gray bough. Fascinated, she watched as it thickened into a twig and extended to just above her head. Buds emerged and blossomed into tender green leaves along its length. Then, a single bud on the tip burst open into a light pink flower. It opened in an aching way, stamens dancing within the petals' center as if calling for a lover.

She glanced around, looking for other flowers on the tree, but none bloomed. Her heart ached for the lonely flower. She fell sobbing to her knees.

"Why do you weep?" the voice asked.

"Because the flower will soon wither and die."

Then, something buzzed past her ear. She looked up and a fat bee landed upon the delicate petals. Sarah stood and perched upon tippy-toes for a better look. Her sadness turned to elation as she watched the clumsy bee stumble from petal to petal, but happiness was short lived as the blossom turned brown and shriveled. The petals withered and enveloped the bee in a deadly embrace. The bee simply folded its wings and accepted its fate.

"Why?" Sarah gasped.

As if in answer, the dead bud fell away and transformed into two dancing fireflies. They flittered around each other until they joined the twinkling cloud beyond the moat.

The stem's tip began to expand and sag under the weight of the engorging green orb until it rested at eye level. The orb swelled and turned a light shade of yellow and orange. Unable to resist, Sarah held out her hand.

With a gentle pop, the luscious fruit fell from the stem into her palm. Covered in a light fuzz, it felt perfectly ripe, begging to be eaten. She lifted it to her mouth, but stopped.

The Golden Woman stood before her.

The beauty considered Sarah with opal eyes full of blue fire, like captive lightning. Two ivory pins held a bun piled high with midnight hair, with tendrils falling across skin perfect as pearl. As in all of Sarah's dreams, she wore a flowing white silk robe encircled with an embroidered golden dragon, held in place with a wide crimson sash.

Sarah considered the fruit, suddenly realizing with the utmost clarity this morsel wasn't for her. She offered it to the Golden Woman, who took it and bit deeply. She held Sarah's gaze while clear juice dribbled between her fingers. Sarah looked down to see fat crimson drops, like blood, splatter in the grass.

Sarah looked up. No evidence of the mysterious fruit remained except for a pit resting in the Golden Woman's outstretched palm. The pit looked like a ragged corpse, freshly denuded of flesh by some terrible beast. A horrible dread gripped Sarah. A door had just opened, one leading to a place from which she could not return.

The Golden Woman's expression softened. The blue glow faded, revealing soft brown eyes, tear-brimmed with sorrow as ancient as the roots of the earth. "Lead them, Sarah. Take it, and you shall become like a light upon a dark shore."

Sarah's hand recoiled from the pit. "I can't. I am afraid." She wanted to wake up and forget this dream forever.

The woman's hand closed around the pit, and lowered her head as if defeated.

"What shall I do now?" Sarah whispered.

"Run."

Hands ripped Sarah back into the waking world.

17. Awakening

"Run!"

Someone dragged Sarah from a warm bed onto cold stone. She opened sleep-filled eyes to see Rashka ransacking her wardrobe by the dim light of a dying fireplace. Rashka rushed to her bedside and shoved a plain white linen robe into her hands. "Take this; you can put it on later."

She glanced at the balcony, where the stars still hung against pitch black. "But it's not time to go."

The servant dumped over the small chest on her vanity, spilling gold coins onto the floor. She knelt down and frantically stuffed them into a small silk purse, and hastily drew the string closed.

"Must flee! He'll be here any moment," Rashka said breathlessly and pulled her off the floor.

Fear crept into Sarah as surely as the cold soaked through her thin gown. "Rashka, you're scaring me."

"Get dressed, you're in terrible danger." She shot a nervous glance out the window. "Dawn will be here soon, and then there will be no escape."

Rashka helped her don the plain white robe. "Ashtoreth has supplanted your mother as First Wife."

"No, that's impossible. Father loves..."

"I have no time to stand here and explain this!" Rashka snapped. "If we tarry you will die."

"Where is Mother? Where are we going?"

"We will get your mother out soon enough. She will join you in a few days, perhaps outside the city. I don't know." Lies were written all over Rashka's face.

"Your brother...well, no one can find him." She shook her head in disgust.

The old woman hastily tied Sarah's robe and crammed the purse down the inside flap. "Seven pieces of gold. That is all you have. It must be enough to bribe your way to freedom." She grabbed Sarah's face and stared intently into her eyes. "That gold is your life, do you understand?"

Sarah nodded as tears streamed down her cheeks. "I'm afraid."

Rashka slapped her. "Stop crying! The time for tears is over. Harden yourself, or the world will rip you to shreds." A dagger, black and wickedly curved, appeared in Rashka's hands. "Thrust it first into an enemy's throat and then run." She slid the knife inside the robe opposite of the gold.

"I cannot..."

"Don't, and you die all at once. Do, and you only die a little at a time. Defend your gold, not your virginity. If sleeping with a man will gain your ends, do it. Use them every bit as ruthlessly as they would use you."

Sarah finally saw the Scythian in Rashka.

"Hur-ar and the House Azubehl is dead to you. Don't look back, ever. Keep moving, never rest too long in one spot. The way back home is always forward." The old woman pulled Sarah's head down and kissed her forehead. "And always remember, I love you."

Rashka cast a glance toward shouts echoing in the courtyard. She grabbed Sarah's hand, dashed to the door and threw it open.

Sarah only had a few moments to register Bal-eeb's devilish grin before a savage backhand sent Rashka sprawling limp across the floor.

"Hello, sister."

Sarah screamed and knelt beside Rashka's still form.

Zrula stepped around Bal-eeb and seized Sarah by the arms, hefting her off the floor.

She kicked and screamed to no avail. "Take me to my father immediately!"

Bal-eeb ignored her demands. "Where is your brother?"

"I don't know, and if I did I would never tell you."

Sarah's cheek erupted in fire under an open hand slap. "Liar."

Zrula slowly tugged her elbows until it felt as if her sternum would rip apart. Sarah cried out in pain.

"Tell us where Ezra is hiding," Zrula hissed

"Enough. We can't damage her," Bal-eeb said, as two palace guards stepped into the room followed by a flood of young women. The daughters of Prince Azubehl's other eight wives fanned across the room, ransacking Sarah's belongings.

"I am the new First Daughter!" Tazrech squealed with glee. "The room is mine!"

First, they raided Sarah's wardrobe, sending gowns, robes and dresses flying. Nicu and Shalba, the Third Wife's portly daughters, bickered over her golden headscarf, tugging at it like two dogs fighting over a scrap.

"Stop!" Sarah tried to shout, but the ebbing pain only permitted a hoarse whisper. "Get out of my room."

Wearing a mask of frenzied hatred, Tazrech marched across the room toward Bal-eeb, snatching the golden scarf from Nicu on the way. Tazrech kissed Bal-eeb deeply before turning to Sarah and striking her hard across the head with her own silver mirror.

Bal-eeb snatched Tazrech's arm. "Now, now, dear sister. We can't have that. We need to keep Sarah's face pretty for the slaver's block."

Sarah slumped in Zrula's grip as the girls descended upon her, spitting, clawing, kicking and spouting foul obscenities. Zrula dropped her and stepped back. Sarah curled into a ball, shielding her head from the blows.

"I said enough!" Bal-eeb barked, but the assault continued.

Even as she tasted her own blood, disbelief reigned. Sarah rejected the unthinkable.

This cannot be happening. Where was Mother? Father?

Zrula finally dragged her away from the mob.

"I am now First Daughter," Tazrech said haughtily and pointed to where the golden silk nightgown poked from Sarah's plain robe. "I demand all her golden robes; they are mine by right."

Bal-eeb grinned and caressed the material, touching Sarah's skin in the process. Sarah remembered the dagger tucked in the robe just inches from Bal-eeb's hand. For a moment, he acted as if he would yank off her robe, but then took the scarf from Tazrech and tenderly tucked inside the white linen. "Being first daughter is far different from being promised to a crown prince."

Tazrech stomped and pouted. "That's not fair!"

"There is no word on the steppe for *fair*," Bal-eeb said. She thought of the dagger again, but Zrula firmly pinned her arms. "Sarah will be sold on the block wearing golden silk to prove her lineage. It will drive up the price, and I want the bastard buying her to pay until it hurts."

Bal-eeb caressed her chin and ran his hands through her hair. "Of all the daughters of Azubehl, you are the prettiest. If I had my way, I would make you my wife." He held her jaw with a stone-like grip and kissed her. He reeked of acrid smoke, and she tried to turn away.

When he finished, she spit in his face.

Bal-eeb calmly wiped the spittle from his cheek. "Ashtoreth is now First Wife by your father's own decree. You are to be sold before sunset in the Grand Market. By Hur law, your mother will become a kitchen wife.

"As the new High Prince, I will kill Ezra. I can do this in the most agonizing way imaginable, or I can do it quickly. That choice is yours. Tell me where he is hiding."

Sarah met his stare with silence.

"As you wish." He motioned to Zrula. "Take her to the Master of the Block. Make sure she is sold in the golden silks, is that clear?"

He turned to one of the guards. "Drag the handmaiden to the courtyard and behead her with the other prisoners."

Sarah screamed.

"Tell me where your brother is, and I'll only sell the old bitch."

"I don't know," Sarah sobbed.

Bal-eeb shrugged. "You will be sold to a Scythian chieftain. When he's finished with you, his generals will use what's left of you and pass your desecrated shell to the common horse warriors. There will be nothing left of you. If by some miracle, you're still alive, my messenger will find you and deliver your brother's head."

With that, Zrula dragged Sarah from the chamber.

Part Four: Dawn

18. Battle Cry

"I know what is in store for you, *Princess*," Zrula sneered.

He snatched Sarah's hair in his fist and dragged her over the smooth marble floors toward the east courtyard. Despite the agony burning her scalp, she clawed at his fist. The more she struggled, the louder he laughed.

He burst from the palace, dragging her over rough cobblestones that tore at her thighs. Sarah wanted to scream, but somehow held her tongue.

Zrula snatched her up, and slammed Sarah against the wall. One hand gripped her wrist almost to the point of crushing bones, while his other hand roamed her body. He had a horribly swollen nose and the same burnt odor as Bal-eeb.

She squirmed to escape, and conceal the blade and gold tucked beneath her robe.

"How I'd love to have a go at you before some Scythian dog has his way." As Zrula roughly pressed his lips against hers, she freed a hand and went for the knife. The hilt caught in the folds of her robe.

"What's this?" He twisted her wrist, easily took the knife, and tossed it over his shoulder.

He looked about at the empty stable grounds. "Maybe I *will* take a go at you."

Sarah clenched her teeth. "I'll rip out your eyes!"

"I've ravaged more women than I can remember. Some scream, some bite, some claw. In the end, I break 'em. Just like I'll break you."

Having never faced danger, Sarah didn't know where this fire in her belly came from. She welcomed the rage and drove her knee into his groin, but her knee only found armor.

"You must have a little Scythian in you, eh?" Zrula laughed and tightened his grip.

Unexpectedly, Zrula released her. He clenched his throat, stumbled backwards and fell to his knees. To Sarah's shock, his head slid off and bounced dully against the cobblestones.

"She doesn't have any Scythian in her, but I do." The dimming stars silhouetted an avenging spirit astride a black horse. Clasping a bloodied sword, old Leonus dismounted.

"Come, your Highness." He scooped up the dagger and lifted Sarah onto the horse. "The sky behind Black Fortress is brightening. Time is short."

Sarah glanced down at Zrula's headless body and shivered. Blood spread across the cobblestones, reflecting the starlight in its smoothness.

"I have to save Mother."

"We will bring her later."

"I command you to help me get Mother. I'm not leaving without her." Sarah tried to dismount, but Leonus held her firm.

"The High Princess foresaw this. She knew Ashtoreth would try to overthrow her. We weren't just leaving for the mountain retreat, we were escaping. Somehow, the witch learned of your mother's plans and struck first. There are many still loyal to your mother. We will save her, but you must ride for the city gate now."

Her eyes grew wide. "Rashka! They're going to kill her."

"We will save her, too."

Leonus gave her the dagger. He grabbed the Sijeva's reins and led the horse along the wall toward the main courtyard.

"Do you have any gold?"

Sarah patted the pouch still in her robe. "Yes."

Leonus led the horse by the reins. "Once you leave the compound, ride straight for the city gate," he whispered. "Trust no one. Lie and bribe as much as it takes to gain the open steppe. Ride north along the river until you come to the cliffs. Do not go to the villa! Ashtoreth will have spies there. Turn east until the slopes meet the mountains. There, you'll find a narrow footpath going north up a canyon. Dismount and lead your horse. In a few miles, you'll come to a grove of scrub cedars and a cave guarded by loyal warriors. It is well stocked with provisions. Stay put until we come for you."

"Where is Asul?"

"I don't know."

They approached where the wall came closest to the palace, the transition between the east and main courtyards.

"Be quiet," Leonus whispered and peered around the corner toward the palace gate. "Damn. They doubled the guard and I don't recognize any of them."

"Halt!" she heard someone shout.

Leonus leapt onto the horse behind her and seized the reins. Wheeling Sijeva about, he galloped back into the east courtyard and, with a clatter of hooves, halted beside the stable. "Jump onto the roof. You'll have to climb the wall and make your way on foot."

Guards appeared from around the corner, swords drawn.

She fumbled to pull the knife. "I'm not leaving you."

He grabbed Sarah by the back of the robe and hurled her toward the stable. She grabbed the eaves and scrambled onto the roof.

Leonus drew his sword and faced his attackers.

"Leap to the wall," he said, not looking back. "Make for the city gate. You won't have much time before they come looking for you"

"Leonus…"

"Your brother jumped it easy!"

"Thank you!" she sobbed.

"Go," he whispered.

Leonus patted the horse's flank and sweetly whispered something unintelligible.

The warriors parted around Zrula's body, spread out and cautiously advanced.

Leonus raised his sword and shouted. "Come get a belly full of Scythian steel, you Hur bastards!"

Sarah took a deep breath, and leapt. She cleared the gap, landing in a crouch on the wall. Sarah peered over the side into the empty alley before lowering herself until she hung by her fingertips.

From the courtyard, hooves thundered and Leonus shouted a war cry. "In the face of death, I fight! Father Sky, take my spirit. Mother Earth, drink my blood. *In the face of death, I fight!*"

She dropped to the ground and fled, the sounds of battle and a screaming horse chasing her into the city

19. The Courtyard, Part 1

"Is the pipe still sealed?"

"Yeah." Ezra pushed up on the cage bolted over the drain pipe. "Won't budge. Anyway, we're too late."

"Ain't no other way in," Left Hand said.

"I know. *I know*." Ezra struggled against an encroaching feeling of helplessness.

Lodged in the pipe using their backs and knees, the boys were stacked on top of one another.

With a strained look, Rat shouted up the pipe. "'Dis Royal Row! Somebody tell me what 'da hell we doing here?"

"Someone is gonna see me unless you shut up!" Ezra whisper-shouted from the top of the stack.

Immediately below Ezra, Left Hand hissed down at Rat and stomped his head. "Yeah. Shut up!"

"Whatever." Rat relaxed his legs just enough to slide slowly down. "Be waitin at d'bottom. Hurry up." His voice echoed as he vanished in the darkness.

Ezra planned on telling Rat as little as possible.

Left Hand looked up at Ezra. "What do you see?"

Ezra poked his head slightly above the pipe. The raised iron grill surrounded his head like a cage.

Ezra had no words to communicate the true scope of the disaster unfolding in the courtyard. He finally summoned the will to speak. "There's a pile of dead men in the center of the courtyard, and a bunch in shackles, too."

Ezra recognized many of the dead as warriors and slaves who held unwavering loyalty to Asul and his mother. "They've got most of Mother's servants and a few soldiers tied up."

"Where is your sister?" Left Hand asked. Ezra thought he heard trepidation in thief's voice.

"I don't know."

With the palace's exterior behind him, the stairs leading to the great double doors blocked his view left. However, he had an unobstructed view of the palace's right wing and most of the main courtyard.

Only the fountain's gurgle broke the morning silence. His mother's most trusted slaves were hunched on their knees, heads down and hands tied behind their back. Then he saw Rashka a few paces away, the side of her face swollen and bruised. He wanted to call to her, but a guard stood nearby.

"I don't know what to do," Ezra whispered and slowly shook his head.

"We can try the cellar pipe again," Left Hand said.

"We're too big, and you know it."

Ezra heard a creak and then several slow footfalls as the main palace doors opened to his left. He took a sharp breath when he saw his mother's back. Two guards held her elbows and marched her before the line of kneeling slaves.

"They've got Mother."

"Is she okay?"

"As far as I can tell."

Ezra winced and tightened his fist when the guards forced Mother to her knees. Head held high, Meribeph faced the west colonnade and the double doors to Father's chambers. A few moments later, laughter and talking floated into the courtyard from beyond his sight.

"People are gathering along the eastern colonnade. They're going to make a show of it." Ezra rubbed his eyes, fighting back the tears.

The chamber doors flung open and his father stumbled out with Ashtoreth on his arm. Ezra recognized Yalani following close behind. The two women were all but naked, only thin gauzy robes covered their bodies.

Ezra knew all was lost when he saw the Golden Scepter around Ashtoreth's neck.

The Prince lumbered forward, almost tripping over one of the kneeling slaves. "Ashtoreth is my new First Wife," Prince Azubehl mumbled, barely coherent. "I'm going back to bed."

With that, he turned around and unceremoniously shuffled into the chamber.

Light applause rippled from the unseen crowd.

"I'm going to kill him, I swear to all the gods," Ezra hissed between clenched teeth.

Ashtoreth's pleasing smile faded the moment the chamber doors shut. "Bring me wine," she commanded a nearby guard. "Bring wine for all. This party is just getting started."

The unseen crowd cheered.

With a fresh goblet in hand, Ashtoreth strolled around the line of kneeling slaves until she stopped before his mother.

"On the steppe, when a woman wants to take another's man, she simply kills her. You Hur-po make things too civilized, too complicated."

Yalani giggled.

Ashtoreth squatted in front of Meribeph, who stared straight ahead. "I actually feared you once. I kept expecting you to have me killed. With every new dawn, I still lived and so did my son. Then I thought you were perhaps a fool. Soon, I realized he actually loved you, and you foolishly thought that love protected you." She licked her lips seductively and caressed Meribeph's face. "It only takes time, and the right skills, to make any man forget about love. I can make a man forget *anything*, especially a haughty wife."

She stood and addressed all in the courtyard. "As you all have heard, I am now First Wife. The first thing a new wife should do is clean house." She considered the pile of slaughtered warriors. "Those died as an example." Ashtoreth pointed her goblet at the handful of shackled warriors. "And these will burn in the Dragon's belly. Take them away."

Bal-eeb's men dutifully prodded the prisoners out of sight.

Ashtoreth turned her attention to the line of kneeling slaves. She pointed to the guard standing behind Rashka. "Bring me your sword."

The guard left his post and presented his weapon.

She traded her goblet for his sword. "Don't spill it."

Ashtoreth returned her attention to Meribeph. "I admired the way you ran the household. I have my own way of doing things, but I still value your opinion. I'd like to ask you about your slaves. They are so very loyal to you, and loyalty is difficult to earn."

"Slave," she nudged Potbelly with her toe. "How long have you served Princess Meribeph?"

"Twelve years," he croaked.

She looked back at Ezra's mother. "Meribeph, was he a good servant?"

His mother nodded once. "There is no finer steward in all of Hur-ar."

"Yes, I heard that about him." Ashtoreth turned to Potbelly. "You should be proud of such high praise. As your new mistress, I shall reward you with your freedom."

Hope lit Potbelly's face. "Thank you, mistress!"

Ashtoreth swung the sword with surprising speed and skill, severing Potbelly's head with one clean stroke. His head rolled down the line of slaves until it stopped near Ezra, a hopeful smile still on his face.

Gasps and cries rose from the crowd, along with a smattering of laughter.

"He's free." Ashtoreth strode through the spurting blood, letting it drench her feet and soak into her gauze robe, until she stood before the next kneeling slave.

"And this slave?" She casually gestured to Gregorius, a young Sammujad that Meribeph had saved from the Black Dragon several years ago.

"No," Ezra's mother raised her hands in supplication. "If you want me to beg, I will beg. Spare them."

"Answer me, was he a good servant, one worthy of freedom?"

"No," Meribeph clasped her hands together. "Just let him go."

Gregorius considered Meribeph with loving adoration. "Let the last words on my lips speak the blessed name Meri…"

The sword flashed and Gregorius's head went flying.

"Thank you for the advice. I can't have unworthy servants in my house." Ashtoreth wiped the back of her hand against her cheek, leaving a bloody smear.

"Cleaning makes me thirsty," Ashtoreth laughed and took the goblet, drinking deeply. Wine trickled down Ashtoreth's chin and over her crimson-spattered body. Her blood soaked clothing clung tightly, leaving no secrets. She handed the goblet to the guard and looked about, as if confused. "Where was I? Oh yes."

The sword flashed again and again in a blood-fueled frenzy. With each stroke, the crowd cheered and Ezra flinched.

Ezra could not look away. Each stroke tore away a comforting hand, a beloved caretaker, a friend, a piece of his childhood.

"Come away, Blade," Left Hand whispered. "There is nothing you can do."

"No," Ezra said. "Where is Asul? Why did he let this happen?"

"*Ezra,*" a voice whispered. Rashka smiled directly at him from where she knelt only a few paces away. He didn't understand how she could have spotted him in the dark recess beneath the grate.

"Do not be afraid." Peace and patience filled Rashka's voice. A soft blue glow, barely visible, filled her eyes. "Sarah will lead them to a new land. She will be like a light on a dark shore."

Ezra rubbed his eyes, wondering if they played tricks on him. "Lead who?"

"Look beyond your heart's own desires, Ezra. Only then will you rule in a land washed clean by the tears of the dead."

Ashtoreth approached, swinging the drenched sword side-to-side. "I will not have Scythian dogs in my house."

Ezra slid lower in the pipe until he could only see the top of Ashtoreth's head, and praying she couldn't see him.

A commotion rose across the courtyard.

"Prince Bal-eeb," someone announced.

Ashtoreth lowered her sword and turned as Bal-eeb appeared by her side. "We must talk. There has been trouble."

Her voice turned sharp. "Why is it whenever I give you a simple task, there is always trouble?"

He took her arm and pulled her out of earshot of the guards. They stood almost on top of the grate. Looking almost straight up at the mother and son, Ezra slid even lower.

"The princess has escaped."

"What?" Ashtoreth shouted.

"The stable master killed Zrula. She climbed over the wall and ran into the city."

"How did that old man kill Zrula?"

"I don't know, but the stable master is now dead. I've summoned the Wall Guard to search the city. She can't get far. Rest assured, I'll find Sarah and have her on the slave block by sunset."

"We made a blood contract with the Master of the Block." Cold rage dripped from Ashtoreth's full lips. Anger flushed her cheeks, almost as bright as the blood soaking her body. To Ezra, she looked like a demon. "He expects us to deliver a princess of the House Azubehl for tonight's auction. Do you know the price for breaking a blood contract? It will not be my head that is served up in payment."

"I will deliver her."

"You better, or I'll take care of this myself. Too many arrangements have been made, too many deals. My informants in the King's palace, as well as the House Vadaz have assured me they will not stand against us. Hector has even made arrangements to wed Azubehl's third daughter."

Bal-eeb grunted. "The fat one, eh? Why not Tazrech?"

Ashtoreth stifled a cold laugh and whispered in even a lower voice. "She's too promiscuous to be useful. The fat one is stupid, easier to control. Not that it matters, Hector will be dead before the leaves fall in the mountains.' She grabbed her son's bicep, leaving a bloody smear. "And you will be the Crown Prince.

"Listen, my son." She slid closer to Bal-eeb, her expression as sharp as a lance. "The Five Families think they can control this Sammujad wench, that I have done their bidding to eliminate their rival. They are wrong, but my plans will only work if they think I've effectively dealt with the spawn of Meribeph. Tell me, son, have we? What of Meribeph's other brat?"

Bal-eeb looked down. For a moment, Ezra was afraid he would glance into the grate.

"That is the other problem."

Bal-eeb quickly gave her the details from the previous evening.

Ashtoreth slapped Bal-eeb hard across the face, leaving a bloody mark like a cat's scratch. "*Thieves?* He's running with thieves?" She shook her head. "Right under your nose, and you couldn't catch him. He will try to save his sister, and perhaps even his mother."

Bal-eeb's jaw clenched and unclenched, but Ezra could tell he would not dare challenge his mother. "I have laid traps for him. He will be dead by sunset, I promise."

"Bah! You like to make promises, just like your worthless father." She returned her attention to Rashka. "I never make promises. I make deals."

She raised the sword under Rashka's chin. "You're Meribeph's favorite pet aren't you, Scythian?" She turned to the guards. "Make sure the former First Wife watches this."

A guard snatched Meribeph's hair and yanked back her head.

Rashka looked up at Ashtoreth defiantly. "Soon, witch, the cold abyss will be your bedchamber and demons your lovers." She spat at Ashtoreth and looked about. "And this place will be forgotten by even the gods."

The blade fell. The crowd cheered. The sword clattered to the ground and Ashtoreth snatched the goblet from the guard. "Put all these heads on poles along the wall. The city must know there is a new First Wife in the House Azubehl."

Goblet swinging lazily, Ashtoreth strolled to where Meribeph sobbed. "Get her to her feet," she commanded. "Strip her."

Bal-eeb obeyed, and Ezra averted his eyes from his mother's naked figure.

Ashtoreth folded her arms and looked Meribeph up and down. "You know, if you would have used that body the right way, things may have turned out differently. Too bad." She *tsked.* "You are still a royal wife. Hur law says I cannot kill you, but I can make you wish for death. You will be a kitchen wife, lower than a slave, lower than a dog. Your body will service the depravity of any who desire to take it. If you beg nicely, perhaps I will permit you to take your own life."

"I will suffer a thousand living hells before I beg at your feet again," Meribeph replied. Even in the clutches of her enemies, she remained defiant, a Princess of Hur-ar to the end.

Ezra struggled for control, not to shout out, "I am here!" to give his mother hope.

Ashtoreth motioned to the guards. "Take her to the kitchens. Tell the slaves they may do to her what they wish."

The guards dragged Ezra's mother out of sight.

138

Ezra's grip tightened around his knife hilt as he let the tears flow freely. Hate course through his blood as he imagined plunging the blade into Ashtoreth's heart.

"Draw me a bath, and have all this cleaned up," Ashtoreth commanded a slave waiting by the chamber doors, and then turned her attention to the crowd. "Get rested, we have more to celebrate tonight!"

Wild cheers met her statement.

Ashtoreth snapped her fingers. "Ah, I almost forgot Yalani, come here darling."

Yalani stumbled forward, and wrapped her arm around Ashtoreth's waist.

"Where is Tazrech?"

Yalani looked about for her daughter and then smiled. "She's right there."

"Bal-eeb, take Princess Tazrech to the block in Sarah's stead."

Yalani turned pale.

"Mother?" Tazrech's voice echoed weakly from beyond Ezra's sight.

"Don't worry, if my son finds Sarah, Tazrech can come home." Ashtoreth casually kissed Yalani's cheek. "He promised he would."

A moment later Bal-eeb dragged Tazrech toward the gate.

"Momma, don't let her do this. Don't let them take me away!" Tazrech screamed over her shoulder.

Yalani trembled, but offered no protest as her daughter vanished beyond the gates.

As the sun crested the mountains golden rays reflected off crimson pools. Blood oozed through cobblestone cracks until it dripped into the drain. Red streams trickled over Ezra's feet and back. Below him, he heard Left Hand shift position to avoid the blood.

They slid down the pipe.

"Where's Rat?" Left Hand looked about.

Ezra leaned against the tunnel wall, as if he would pass out any moment. He slowly sank to his knees and splashed the filthy water over his body, trying to scrub away the blood.

"Blade?" Left Hand spoke softly. *"Blade?"*

Fighting for self-control, he looked up at Left Hand. "This is war. That's what Asul would tell me. He used to tell me stories about how the Scythians would taunt their foes by torturing captives in front of their enemies before battle. The Sammujad would see their people suffering and charge blindly." He shook his head. "I can't do that. Must not charge blindly. Gotta keep my head. Vengeance will have to wait."

Left Hand blew a long breath. "That's better than I could do. I'd want blood now."

"I'll have blood. But my sister is still free. She'll be figuring things out, finding out where to hide." He paused. "My mother is still alive, but beyond my help, at least for now." Ezra slid his knife back into his drawstring. "We must save Lucatta first. Otherwise, her death is certain."

"Rat's gone."

"Screw Rat."

"Works for me. Enough of this standing around, then." Left Hand grinned. "Let's go get her!"

The thieves splashed down the pipe at a full run. Ezra led them on, but his thoughts lingered on the courtyard, and his mother's fate. In his distraction he failed to notice the dim flicker dancing on the tunnel walls.

They rounded a corner and came face to face with a band of warriors.

20. The Place of Mazes

The stench.

Sarah never imagined the city would smell this way. Mostly, it reeked of human excrement, often to the point of suffocation. As the city came to life, women stepped out onto their stoops and dumped chamber pots into the gutters. More than once she hurried past people directly relieving themselves on the streets.

Sarah struggled to contain the panic welling up inside. Thoughts of her mother's whereabouts, the image of Rashka lying unconscious on the floor, and the memory of Leonus's screaming horse threatened to overwhelm her. Yet, somehow, she managed to keep her mind on what needed to be done - find the gate and escape.

Escape, however, became a dimming prospect. A few moments after fleeing into the alley outside the palace, it occurred to Sarah she had no idea how to get to the city gate, and she quickly lost her way.

She kept her head down, and her robe pulled tight, making sure all signs of golden thread where hidden. She felt naked without a headscarf. The weight of the gold on one side, and the dagger on the other provided little comfort.

She had thought Rashka's choice of plain robe wise, but could not help but notice how much this simple gown, though torn and soiled, stood in stark contrast to the deject poverty surrounding her.

Emaciated children, filthy and covered in sores, played in the streets. Sleeping drunks lay on trash in almost every corner. Sometimes, people stared at her as she passed. Sarah dared not make eye contact and hurried on. Thankfully, the stares became less frequent as the city came to life, and the streets more crowded.

She wandered from street to street, crossroads to crossroads trying to find a way to the city gate, or at least a major avenue. She never knew how dark the city truly was. Her palace occupied an entire block, with lots of open space. These narrow streets were mazes, winding here and there with no sense of order. Unable to see the surrounding mountains, Sarah couldn't get her bearings.

She knew the city had been built on a slope, so she tried walking downhill. Soon, the street would curve back uphill, and interact with others in an almost random pattern. A few times, she thought about following one of the narrow alleys downhill, but could not work up the courage to step into their darkness.

Fear crept over her. She wanted to ask for help, but dared not. More and more soldiers began to circulate in the crowds, forcing Sarah to slip from one street to the next just to avoid the patrols.

Soon, she came to a wide street filled with potters and food mongers. Vases and pots of all sizes lined its edges. A slight breeze blew, diffusing the stink. Hope kindled anew, as she knew this must be the Pottery District. One of these streets would lead directly to the Grand Market and, from there the City Gate.

Food vendors began to set up their carts and shout to the crowds. Her tummy growled at the scent of roasting meat and fresh bread. She would need food and drink for her journey.

She patted the pouch tucked beneath her robe and it jingled in response. Perhaps if I buy a loaf of bread, I can make small talk with the vendor and ask directions to the Avenue of Kings, she thought. She'd never been to market before, and had no idea how such things worked. How hard could it be?

Ahead lay another crossroad, where this street split into two, forming a triangle intersection. Just before the crossroads, a frumpy old woman hawked fresh loaves of flat bread from a cart. Her filthy dress appeared stitched from old linen bags, but she looked better fed and clothed than most.

Sarah made up her mind, and stepped behind several large pots. There, she turned her back to the crowd, extracted one gold coin and resealed the pouch. She stepped across the now bustling street and approached the vendor.

"Bread fresh as the morning sunshine, m'lady. Made'em myself, I did." The old woman's smile revealed a mouth full of black gaps.

Sarah flashed a brief smile in return and examined all the stacks of thin, oven-baked loaves.

The old woman swished away the flies with a horsetail swatter and looked Sarah up and down. "Long night of Festival, hmm? Gunna make a early go of the parades, eh?"

Sarah nodded quickly and pretended to examine the goods intently. Making a quick guess as to how many loaves she'd need, Sarah picked up three and handed the woman a gold coin.

The old woman's eyes grew wide, and Sarah knew immediately she'd made a mistake. The old woman bit it with a few of her remaining teeth, and her eyes grew even wider.

"Is that too much?" Sarah blurted, and regretted is instantly.

"Oh no, dearie!" The old woman's voice transformed to a smooth, fawning tone. "It's just enough.

"Wake up, Bathlar" the old woman kicked a man sleeping behind the cart Sarah hadn't noticed before. "Wake up and meet the nice lady."

A tall, spindly man with a beak nose and sallow cheeks slowly rose from behind the cart. He grunted, broke wind and rubbed his eyes. "Someone given' you a rash, Mum?"

She slapped him in the chest. "Mind your manners, boy. We got us a lady here."

He grinned at Sarah with a stupid leer. "Uh, a lady."

"Look what the nice lady paid with," she held up the coin, and the oaf displayed the same look of amazement the old woman had.

"Anything else you like?" the old woman said cooly and gestured to the bread and assortment of strange herbs that hung from the cart.

Sarah opened her mouth to ask how to get to the Avenue of Kings, but thought better of it.

"No, no…not at all. Thank you, goodbye." Sarah held the bread tightly to her chest as if it were a shield and backed away.

"No need to run off so soon, dearie," the old woman called.

It took all her willpower not to bolt. She strode into the the thickest part of the crowd, not caring where she went, only that it was away from the bread vendor. To her horror, she looked over her shoulder and saw the bread man, this time with two smaller men, trailing on the far side of the street.

They carried clubs.

Her breath and pace quickened. She frantically looked about for an escape, and spotted an alleyway to her right. Sarah feared the dark alley as much as the men tailing her.

She glanced back. They had closed to only a dozen yards. The oaf's egg-like head bobbed above the crowd, leering down as if about to eat her.

Shouts and cries rose from ahead. The throng began to part for horsemen plowing through the street.

"Make way for the city guard!" someone shouted.

Sarah froze when she saw Bal-eeb, now bedecked in the bronze armor of the Wall Guard, leading the horsemen. He lashed out at those blocking his way with a cropped whip. Flanked by several other horsemen, he waded through the crowd, eyes searching.

She ducked behind the line of people retreating to the street's edges, and slipped into the alley. Not even bothering to see if the thugs followed, she ran with all her might. Lungs burning, she hid behind a stack of firewood and looked back. The thugs were nowhere to be seen. Sarah almost stood to run again, when she saw a horseman pass in front of the alley. Peeking over the split wood, she saw him peer down the alley before riding out of sight.

Sarah knew she could not return to the street. She gazed down the deserted alley, which curved left and vanished into blue shadow.

Sarah ran into the unknown.

The alley existed in perpetual twilight, though the bright blue line above spoke of a day nearing mid-morning. The rancid smell here far exceeded anything she encountered in the main streets. A few times, she heard a crying baby and a dog barking, but didn't see anyone.

Soon, she came to an intersection of another, slightly wider alley and realized these were the backs of the buildings which faced the main streets. A few people sat on stoops, or lounged in upper windows. A child, not much older than a toddler and dressed only in filth, stood a few paces away. Staring at Sarah, the child held a dead rat by the tail. Except for an oddly protruding belly, the child was nothing more than a collection of bones.

Sarah knelt down before the little girl. "What's your name?"

The child said nothing.

"Can you talk?"

The little girl nodded. "Are you 'da angel?"

Sarah smiled despite herself. "No."

"You so pretty. I thought you was 'da angel. 'Dat means I'm not dead yet. Momma say when I see 'da angel, dat's how I know I'm dead. She says Narim send 'da angel to take good people away."

"Where's your mother?"

"With 'da angel."

The child pointed to the bread and held out the rat. "Wanna trade?"

Suddenly self-conscious, Sarah held out all three loaves. "Take them. Keep the rat."

The little girl hesitated, and then snatched the bread away with surprising quickness.

"Little girl!" Sarah called to her.

The child stopped and turned around.

"Do you know how I can get to the City Wall?"

"Find 'da angel, she take you." The child turned a corner and vanished.

Sarah stood up and sighed. Now she had one less gold piece and no bread. As far as she could see left and right, intersecting alleys spilled into this one.

"Where do I go now?"

That's when a scream poured out of the nearest alley. A woman begged some unseen attacker to spare her life, and for someone to help her.

Sarah turned to flee, but her feet wouldn't budge.

"Don't be stupid," she said to herself. "You're in no position to help anyone." Yet, she could not turn her back on the woman's plea.

If she turned and ran, that voice would haunt her to the end of her days. Sarah took another deep breath, steeled her courage, and entered the alley.

21. Alley of Blue Shadows

Sarah peaked around the corner. A raven haired beauty squirmed on the ground under a whip, her cotton robes reduced to bloody strips. Lash marks covering her trembling arms bore testimony to futile resistance against the squat anvil of a man beating her.

"Tell me where the money is, and I might let you live!" the woman's attacker bellowed.

Sarah's heart told her to run. The vengeful voice echoing throughout the alley chained her feet in place.

Beneath his whip, the woman thrashed on the ground like a wounded animal. Sarah never beheld a slave, let alone a woman, being beaten, and her heart broke at the sight of a soul suffering under the cruelty of another.

This doesn't concern you, she scolded herself. Yet, Sarah knew she could do nothing of the sort. The screams had already seared her.

The woman looked up and their eyes met, witness and victim now entwined for all eternity.

"A whore does not invoke *my name*," he poked a thumb in his own chest, "while her thieving friends rob my own men."

The lash fell with each word. The woman abandoned the struggle, yet the warrior beat her with increased ferocity. Sarah knew he meant to kill her.

She recognized the bent spear emblazoned across his bronze armor, signifying him a warrior of the House Sagar, a minor princeling and loyal client of House Azubehl. Like many of the city's warriors, he had been likely loaned to the crown for a duration of service.

Her decision came without conscious awareness. Sarah slipped behind the corner, removed her white robe exposing the thin silk gown below, and covered her face with the golden scarf. She took a deep breath and stepped into the alley. Trembling inside, she strode boldly toward the warrior armed only with the golden silk and her mother's voice.

"Stop!" she said in a clear, stern tone.

His arm froze in mid-strike, mouth agape.

Not giving him time to collect his thoughts, Sarah pressed her advantage. "Is this how men of Hur behave during Festival?"

He blinked. "She...she stole from..." he stammered and gazed upon her golden gown, and then around at the filthy alley. "Your Highness, what are you are doing here?"

"That is my business!" He flinched as if her voice were itself a lash. "Give me your name and your whip," she demanded, hand extended palm up.

He hesitated, as if trying to summon courage to question why the Golden Princess lurked in the most unlikely of places. The suggestion that she really wasn't the Golden Princess probably never crossed his mind. To falsely don the Golden Robes carried a sentence of living immolation.

Emboldened, Sarah kept pushing. "Obey, or your only remaining decisions will be either to have your head on a pike on the city wall or disembowelment."

She didn't know if disemboweling was a real punishment, but she needed to say something.

"Magus, Watch Officer," he blurted and handed over the whip. Astonished at how quickly this man turned from monster to mouse, a memory stirred of something her mother once told her.

Most men with just a little power are often cowards, Mother had said, *and will easily bend to those with more.*

Sarah tried not to recoil at the feel of the sweaty, bloody whip in her hand. "The men of the House Sagar should know better. Festival is a time of forgiving debts. My father will hear of this."

"I beg your Highness!" The man seemed to physically shrink. She half expected the big man to grovel at her feet.

"Beware, for when I am queen, you can expect my eyes and ears to be everywhere. Now go, and if I hear of you hurting this woman, or anyone else, you can expect an unpleasant reassignment shortly thereafter."

He stepped back, but then she caught the hint of doubt swirling behind his thick brow.

"Begone, before I forget Festival is a time of mercy."

The battle of wills won, Magus the Watch Officer turned and fled from sight. Sarah's knees suddenly went weak and she fought the urge to vomit.

Something touched her foot. The raven haired woman had crawled to Sarah's feet and kissed her sandals. "Thank you," she whispered over and over.

Sarah knelt and lifted the woman, not paying attention to the blood now staining the golden robes. "What is your name?"

"Ezmoria, beloved lady. May the Narim revere you soul, may the Psatina and Oetesy shower blessings on you and your children."

Sarah didn't know who shook more, her or the woman. "Please, there is no time. Hide me, I beg you."

For a moment, confusion swept over the woman's face and then understanding. "Help me up. I know a place."

***

After a few turns, Ezmoria pulled Sarah behind a stack of crates. "Hide your robes, or people will remember our passing."

Sarah quickly concealed the golden robes beneath the plain white garments.

"The cloth is still too fine." Ezmoria grimaced and smeared dust over the white linen and then took Sarah by the hand and led her deeper into the city. The raven-haired woman led her through more winding alleys, each nearly indistinguishable from the next, until they came to a barren wall that had likely never seen sunlight's kiss. Ezmoria pushed open a rickety, worm-eaten door and led Sarah into a cramped and musty cellar.

Ezmoria shut the door behind her and slid a thick wooden dowel into a slot to secure the door. She hobbled to a corner where a coal bed smoldered in a crude fireplace. Ezmoria winced as she picked up a stick from the dirt floor and stirred the ashes. It flamed to life before she tossed in the stick.

Ezmoria slumped on a hay-stuffed mattress in a dark corner and stared at Sarah for what seemed an eternity. Sarah wandered the claustrophobic space, the only light coming from cracks in the door and the blood red embers.

"Thank you for saving my life," Sarah said to break the uncomfortable silence.

"I would say the same thing."

"This place, is it safe?"

"There are no safe places in Hur-ar," Ezmoria laughed before breaking into a coughing fit. "I often hide here after a customer gets too rough."

Sarah wrung her hands and looked about. This place stank of desperation. Appropriate, I suppose, Sarah thought. She glanced back at Ezmoria. Her blood encrusted robe had begun to stick to her shoulders.

"Is there any clean water in here?"

Ezmoria nodded to a tall clay jar standing in the corner.

Sarah placed her finger in the tall jar and tasted it. She looked about for something to make bandages, but only found the filthy blanket on the mattress. That wouldn't do. Sarah removed her white robe and began tearing the hem of her golden robe into strips.

"What are you doing?" Ezmoria said astonished.

"I'm going to clean your wounds."

What was once a long silk nightgown had been reduced to a ragged scrap, barely reaching mid-thigh.

Sarah found a chipped pottery bowl and wiped out as much dust as she could before pouring water in it. She then knelt beside Ezmoria, placing the bowl and strips beside her on the mattress. "Be still. It'll probably hurt."

She'd never dressed wounds before, but had seen Rashka do it enough. Ezmoria remained quiet as Sarah peeled the tattered, bloody cloth from her back. Sarah held her hand over her mouth, trying not to let nausea overwhelm her. The lash had sliced into the skin as cleanly as a knife.

"Why was he beating you?"

"Because he could." Sarah could almost taste the bitterness in Ezmoria's voice.

Sarah shook her head and dipped a strip into the water. She gently brushed Ezmoria's hair aside and began to clean the wounds.

Only the sounds of the street and of dripping water interrupted the silence. When she finished, Sarah wrapped a few strips around Ezmoria's torso as a crude bandage.

Ezmoria picked up a golden strip and caressed it between her fingers. "This is real silk." she whispered, eyes wide in astonishment.

"Yes," Sarah said casually.

Ezmoria pulled away and slid to the other side of the mattress. "I thought you were just a foolish girl, pretending to be the Golden Princess for Festival." She fell prostrate before Sarah. "Forgive me, your highness! I didn't... I couldn't believe it was really you."

Sarah lifted her chin. "I am Sarah, First Daughter to the First Wife of High Prince Azubehl." She took a deep breath and sighed. "Or at least I was. Now I am being hunted and need your help."

Sarah briefly explained all that had happened that morning up to their meeting in the alley. Ezmoria listened, arms wrapped around her knees. After Sarah had concluded her tale, Ezmoria finally spoke.

"It's likely Magus knows all this now. His men are probably scouring the district looking for both of us. He'll kill me and turn you over to those that hunt you."

"I must escape the city. Can you help me?"

"There is no escape from Hur-ar."

Sarah fought back the tears. "I have nowhere to go. They mean to sell me to Scythians."

"I thank you for saving me, but you've only delayed our deaths." Ezmoria's shoulders sagged. "You should have left me to die under Magus's whip." She considered Sarah with both pity and contempt. "You won't last past nightfall. Anyway, I'm just a whore. I cannot help one such as you."

"Maybe you know someone who can?" Sarah removed a gold piece from inside her robe. "I can pay."

Ezmoria's eyes flashed at the sight of the coin, and then grew stern. "Put that away! That will feed a family for a winter. If anyone sees that, they will kill you and leave your body for the dogs."

Ashamed at her own stupidity, Sarah returned the coin to the purse and stared at the floor. "He was going to kill you. I couldn't just stand there and watch it happen."

"He might as well have killed me. They will hunt me as surely as they are hunting you." A tear rolled down Ezmoria's cheek. With some effort, she stood and examined the makeshift bandage around her torso. Blood had begun to seep through. She gave a short laugh behind the tears. "The Golden Princess! The girls in the alley will never believe this." Then her face darkened. "I can't go back to my brothel. Magus, or even the one you call Bal-eeb, are probably ransacking it now and beating my girls."

Ezmoria's voice possessed a strange, almost melodic, accent. Sarah couldn't place it, but suspected this woman wasn't Hur-po.

Ezmoria hobbled over to a nook hacked from the unbaked brick wall, withdrew a tattered wool shaw and wrapped it over the gold cloth. She slumped back down against the wall and sighed. "Like it or not, we are both in this together now, your highness. Is there anyone you can trust?"

She shook her head. "I don't know who is alive or dead. I have a brother but," Sarah stifled a sob, "I don't know where he is."

Ezmoria sighed impatiently. "Alright, alright! Don't start crying. That will do us no good. I need to think."

They sat facing one another for what felt like an eternity. Sarah felt useless, like everything up to this point had been her fault. She prayed Asul was looking for her right now. Of all the men in her Mother's service, he would have been the last to betray her. "How much gold do you have?" Ezmoria finally spoke.

"Five pieces." She withdrew the dagger. "I have this, too."

"Give me three gold pieces and the dagger," Ezmoria held out her hand impatiently.

"I don't think I want to."

"Iron and gold are only as useful as the hand that wields them. From what you've told me, it's obvious you don't know how to use either."

"Tell me why you want them."

"I know someone who might help, but it will take gold."

"I'll give you one gold piece, but no more."

"Fine, give it here." Ezmoria shook her palm impatiently. "And the dagger. Hurry, we haven't much time."

Ezmoria slowly stood, obviously fighting back the pain. She placed the coin in a small pouch attached to a thin waist strap, where she also slid the dagger. She pulled the shawl tightly around her shoulders. "Can you see any of the gold cloth?"

Sarah shook her head.

"I'm going to leave you here, but only for a little while. I need to get a message to my friend. He might be able to smuggle us to the gate unnoticed."

"Are you coming back?" Sarah leaned forward like a child begging her mother to return home soon, but caught herself. She leaned back and folded her hands, trying to regain her composure.

"I shouldn't," Ezmoria turned her back and made for the door "I stand a better chance without you." She stopped and turned around. Something in the prostitute's face lifted like a dark curtain, momentarily betraying an underlying tenderness. Hope swirled inside Sarah at Ezmoria's pity.

"If I have not returned by sunset, that means I am captured or dead. Make your way to the City Gate under the cover of darkness the best you can." She pulled the dowel and tossed it to Sarah. "Lock it behind me."

Ezmoria vanished with a slam of the door.

Sarah quickly replaced the dowel before collapsing on the mattress in a fetal position. Every noise, every shout, echoing in the alley beyond fed her worst fears and sent her heart pounding. All the day's horrors bubbled up in the darkness. She never imagined she could feel so alone, so powerless. She wanted to cry out for her mother or for Asul, but the words would not form in her mouth. Instead, Sarah buried her face into the fetid blanket, spoke her brother's name, and quietly cried.

22. Gabereph

The kitchens, which could prepare food for over a hundred guests at a time, should have been bustling with activity preparing for Festival. Now the comforting smell of warm bread and roasting meats only served to taunt Meribeph, a perverted setting for what horrors soon lay in store.

The Princess stood naked before slaves and guards. Only Meribeph's hatred burned brighter than her shame, hatred for Ashtoreth, hatred for her husband. She had known of other royal wives cast to the kitchens by princes grown bored of them, but never imagined this fate awaited her. What had she done to earn such an end? She dutifully followed the old ways, the righteous path taught to mortals long ago by the Narim. Yet, deep in her heart, she sensed this might be punishment for her secret sins.

She closed her eyes and prayed. *Are my sins so heinous they deserve such judgment?* She beseeched the Nameless God, the forgotten deity to which legend said even the Narim bent their knees. Only silence and bitterness echoed in her heart. Meribeph opened her eyes and hope drained away.

The big guard, who looked like a mountain bear and stank like a pig, paced haughtily between her and the slaves. Meaty hands behind his back, he smirked at their downcast faces.

She recognized every slave, knew every name. She'd bought many of them in market, often after being passed over by other households as being too weak or too old. The slavers knew that when the Matron of Azubehl visited the block, chances were good they could sell their low-end stock at a good price. She didn't care. If it saved one soul from the belly of the Black Dragon, it was worth it.

A dozen kitchen slaves, mostly women, children and old men lined up against the far wall next to the blazing pit ovens. On the opposite wall, standing beside a long table, stood seven burly men; common slaves used for heavy labor. All stood meekly, heads down either not to make eye contact with the warriors, or perhaps not to look upon their shamed former mistress. Only the children looked on with brimming eyes. One child knelt, holding the kitchen dog, a good tempered yellow mongrel responsible for cleaning the scraps off the floor.

She recognized neither of these guards, likely Bal-eeb's loyal men. She knew any men suspected of harboring even an ounce of loyalty to her were dead and piled in the courtyard. She fought back the tears at the thought that Asul's body likely lay under that pile.

A young henchman with stringy hair and barely old enough to wield a sword approached. With one arm he pinned her elbow painfully behind her back while pressing her face-down against the butcher table. He gnawed loudly on a drumstick, all the while rubbing his crotch against her.

She'd set her mind on scratching his eyes out if given the chance.

"As a gift from her Highness, Princess Ashtoreth, the new First Wife of the House Azubehl," the burly warrior began, "you are presented with this wench as a kitchen wife." He laughed and held out a meaty hand magnanimously. "Her flesh is now at the disposal of all the household slaves, as a token of your mistress's love and affection."

The guard holding Meribeph stopped his smacking and wiped the chicken grease down her back. "They don't look very excited," he said with mock sincerity.

"You're right." The bearlike man stroked his beard as if contemplating, and then snapped his fingers. "Perhaps they don't know what to do with her."

The greasy guard giggled with almost girlish glee. "I think that's it. I mean, obviously too rich for their taste. Yeah, she's too good for the likes of them," Greasy pressed Meribeph's face against the roughhewn boards. "Think we should get first go at her, eh?"

She heard burly guard close the kitchen door.

"Shouldn't we run 'em out while we take our go?"

"Naw," the burly guard laughed. "Someone needs to show them how to use her, as an example."

Greasy began to giggle again.

Out of the corner of her eye, Meribeph saw one of the slave girls press a little boy's face into her skirt and say, "Don't look."

That's when she saw a knife, partially covered with a rag, only a few inches away from her head. She slowly inched her free hand toward the blade.

"Hold her," Burly commanded. "I go first." She heard the clink of buckles, and then the sound of bronze falling to the floor.

She fought to contain her horror as, glancing back, Burly approached. She could only hope Greasy remained preoccupied with her back end that he failed to notice her fingers crawling toward the blade.

She froze as Burly's forearm pressed into the small of her back, squeezing the wind out of her. Meribeph lunged for the knife, but seized only the damp rag.

She spun her head to the left and saw the wizened old slave Janus standing beside the table, impassively staring up at Burly. Barely taller than a child and quiet as a mouse, the tiny old woman had been a fixture in the kitchens since Meribeph arrived in the palace as a young bride. With close cropped silver hair and dark eyes, she was sometimes mistaken for an old man, as Burley did now.

"Bugger off, old fellow. If you have anything left worth using between your legs, you can take a go later." Burly kicked Meribeph's feet wider. She closed her eyes and prepared to endure the unendurable.

Burly screamed, and the weight lifted from her back. Meribeph scrambled on the table and turned in time to see Burly doubled up on the floor. Hands over his crotch, blood oozed around his fingers.

Bloody knife in hand, Janus stood emotionless as stone.

"You crazy son of a bitch!" Greasy pulled his dagger. Before he could lunge, a labor slave's muscled forearm encircled his neck from behind, snapping it with a wet pop. Janus stepped over Greasy's body and plunged the knife into Burley's neck.

Janus tossed the blade onto the table with a clatter, and barked something in crude Scratch. The men sprung into action. They picked up the dead bodies and vanished out the back archway. Janus turned to Meribeph and nodded once. Then, without a word, she ambled to the ovens and began to slide in unbaked dough as if nothing had happened.

Slave women quickly surrounded Meribeph. From somewhere, a blanket appeared and tender hands wrapped it around her trembling shoulders. They gently helped her off the table.

"Gabereph," they whispered and tugged her toward the back of the kitchens.

Gratitude and utter sadness washed over Meribeph. By saving her, they had doomed themselves. Someone would answer for the deaths of Bal-eeb's henchmen and she knew Ashtoreth wouldn't hesitate to slay every slave present that morning as a warning to others.

"Thank you," she said, fighting the tears. Her quaking legs finally gave out. Yet, hands and arms lifted the fallen princess toward the back archway all the while whispering, *"Gabereph. Gabereph."*

The word burned itself through her pain. At first, she merely thought it perhaps a Scratch bastardization of her name. Then, it came to her. She'd only been a young girl in her father's palace the last time she'd heard this antiquated term of endearment, a name the palace slaves called her mother.

Gabereph, *beloved.*

Meribeph sobbed in gratitude at an answered prayer, and at the terrible weight at all that had been lost.

The slaves pulled away the curtain separating the kitchen from the pantry and gently drew Meribeph over the threshold.

She looked up and caught her breath.

23. Allies

The thieves of Hur-ar say that in the sewers many things are lost, but few are found. They say that the gods of water and darkness always demand tribute from all who tread their domain.

At this moment, Ezra was losing time, and hope, of saving Luccatta. The Market and the Gleaning Ceremony lay out of reach at the end of this long tunnel. Every moment he clung to the ceiling like a spider was a moment she drew closer to the belly of the Black Dragon.

If they didn't go now, they may never save her.

The strain he had endured last night, when suspending Left Hand above the guards, paled in comparison to the agony his muscles now endured. He screamed inside for his arms to cease their complaining and obey. He needed to concentrate, to focus his hatred toward the men meandering only a few feet below him in the dark tunnel.

The warriors had surprised them, and the boys fell back around a corner and resorted to one of the oldest, and most successful, thieves' tricks. Instead of running, they climbed the tunnel walls all the way to the ceiling. The ancient bricks, jagged and irregular, provided ample hand and footholds. A strong thief could cling like a bat and wait for their enemies to depart the murky domain.

Yet, these intruders stubbornly refused to leave. They clanked and sloshed back and forth, torches and swords held out, not once suspecting their prey lurked in the shadows just over their heads.

The warriors of the House Azubehl splashed through the ankle-deep water, the smoke from their torches curling around Ezra and Left Hand like snakes. He struggled not to cough, fighting to listen.

"I saw them, I swear! They couldn't have disappeared so quickly." Ezra recognized Helzba's voice, one of the sergeants in his father's garrison.

"How do you know it was him?" one of the other warriors asked.

"I saw the gray-eyed shit well enough," Helzba laughed. "Always clinging onto Asul's skirts, acting like he was king already."

"Nobody will be hanging onto Asul's skirts anymore." A warrior with a high pitched nasal voice laughed as he randomly prodded the walls with his sword.

The warriors' laughter echoed, a hammer pounding anger deeper into Ezra's heart like a spike.

The memory of Asul's voice spoke, *Cold rage is the best rage.*

Five of them, Ezra calculated.

"They're gone, Helzba. Let's get our asses outa this stinkhole," said another Ezra did not recognize.

Judging by their unfamiliar voices, several of these men must be Bal-eeb's. But Helzba once pledge himself to Ezra, with praises on his tongue for Princess Meribeph. Asul trusted him, too.

I've sparred Helzba many times, he thought, remembering the crushing strength the battle-hardened veteran delivered with a wooden sword. If the sword had been real, Ezra would have died many times. Squat, but solid, Helzba would maneuver to lure his opponents into the sparring field's wide center. There, he would pummel and slash his enemy relentlessly while hunkered down behind a tall shield.

Ezra looked down. None of them had shields, but all carried long swords. A slashing attack would be difficult in the tunnel's close confines.

"You lost them, Helzba," said the one with the irritating nasal whine.

"They're here. I can smell 'em. Look low. Thieves are like ticks, love to wiggle into filthy cracks. You could pass 'em a dozen times and never know the better."

"Let's go, its smells awful down here."

"I know how it smells. Stop your belly-aching and keep looking."

"Bal-eeb said Ezra would try to reach the palace through the sewers, and that means he'd have to go through here."

"But we saw them coming *from* House Azubehl," Nasal said.

"The better," Helzba dismissed. "That means they're trapped."

"How come you know so much about these tunnels?" Nasal said with a hint of insult.

"Let's just say I know this tunnel, so shut up."

The bastard was a Sewer Soldier, Ezra thought.

Soldiers caught stealing from another soldier were given a choice, lose their right hand or spend one year chasing thieves in the sewers. Assigned to the lowest ranks of the City Garrison, most Sewer Soldiers became sick and died in only a few months. Many were killed. Being a Sewer Soldier marked one as being untrustworthy. Those that survived their sentences often hid their past.

I bet Asul never knew, he thought. Like many commanders, Asul had banned Sewer Soldiers from serving in House Azubehl. Welcoming Sewer Soldiers in your ranks was a mark of a desperate, or despicable, commander.

Craning backward, Ezra spied Left Hand's face, wet and ruddy in the dim torchlight. Left Hand clung easily with nary a tremble.

Left Hand fought well, but could not stand toe-to-toe with these battle-hardened men.

In any battle you will have silent allies, hidden from you and your enemy. Memories of Asul's instruction drifted around Ezra in the smoke. *Find these allies while your enemy boasts. As he savors his imminent victory, lay your plans and prepare your traps.*

The men stood directly below in a semicircle. "Maybe we should double back to the compound?" Nasal offered. "Let's get back and get our share of the spoils. I hear tell they threw the old First Wife to the kitchens. If we go now, there may be a little for us."

As the men laughed, Ezra began to quickly formulate a plan. He glanced around and, in a moment of clarity, his hidden allies revealed themselves.

Be bold, they whispered to him, *for Fate offers only a single path forward.*

Ezra's decision came quickly. *The Fate Tile is on the field of battle. Fight them on my terms, commit everything and leave the tunnels victorious, or not at all.*

He looked back at Left Hand and whispered. "Get Lucatta and meet me at the Wide."

Left Hand frowned and opened his mouth as if to disagree, and then nodded once as if sensing Ezra's plan. He turned around as nimble as a spider and began to slowly crawl away into the darkness.

Ezra slowly crept along the ceiling away from Left Hand.

"Do you hear that? They're here!" Helzba barked. "It's just like the other times. Chase a bunch of runts down a hole, just to have them disappear. Well, it ain't happening again. This rabbit ain't getting away."

The men began to look about. "Yeah, I heard it, too. Maybe it's rats," one of them said.

"That ain't no damn rats." Shadows danced on the curved walls as Helzba thrust this torch about.

163

Nasal glanced up in time to see Ezra drop onto his shoulders.

Riding piggyback, Ezra plunged his knife repeatedly into the warrior's eyes like a pecking bird. Screaming frantically, Nasal dropped his torch and sword and swatted at Ezra.

One torch down.

The remaining warriors lunged toward Ezra, but not before he slid off Nasal and bolted down the tunnel, drawing the warriors away from Left Hand. The men pursued, charging through the water with torches held high.

Ezra rounded a corner. Momentarily out of his pursuer's sight, he held his breath and slipped into the embrace of his first ally, the shallow water.

The first warrior burst around the corner, looking ahead for his fleeing quarry. Lying flat in the water, Ezra snatched his ankle. With a crash, the warrior fell face-first, and the water claimed his torch with a sizzle.

Two torches down.

Ezra snatched the sword and rolled out of the way just as the next warrior bungled forth. Ezra sliced this one's hamstring, sending him plunging beside his companion. The water claimed another torch. Darkness, Ezra's second ally, further asserted herself.

In the darkness never look directly at something, Left Hand had once taught him. *Use the corner of your eye to see movement. Listen to the sounds echoing off the tunnel walls and splashes.*

Ezra had the initiative, and sensed his advantage growing. Hatred replaced doubt. Icy fury guided his sword to the necks of the fumbling warriors thrashing in the water.

His heart as cold as the water sloshing about his feet, Ezra faced his remaining foes. Helzba and the other warrior stood below their torches, jaws agape. Ezra wasted no time pressing his attack.

Ezra threw his knife at Helzba's companion. It found his neck. Another warrior, and another torch, fell into the water.

"Welcome back to the sewers, Helzba. I'm not hiding behind any skirts. Come and get me."

Helzba hefted his weapon, craggy face set in grim purpose. "I've been looking forward to this for a long time, runt."

"You have no shield, *Sewer Soldier*." Ezra stepped forward, hugging the curved wall. The tunnel, his third ally, would serve to protect his left flank, while his sword protected his right.

In his peripheral vision, Ezra spotted the bodies beginning to bob and turn the water a new shade of black. With breastplates scraping tunnel bottom in starts and stops, the corpses inched toward Helzba.

Ezra took another step and spread his arms. "Come, Helzba. Isn't this what you do best, kill thieves?"

Helzba shifted right to avoid the deepest water and the bodies, placing him even closer to the curved tunnel wall.

With a battle cry, Helzba lunged and swung with a high overhead arc, just as Ezra had seen him do a hundred times. This time, his sword scraped the ceiling in a shower of sparks. Ezra dropped beneath Helzba's sword arm, spun and slashed.

Cut in two, Helzba's torch fell into the water and died.

"No!" Helzba exhaled.

Cloaked in darkness, with the dead at his feet, Ezra commanded the field of battle. Wrapped in the tunnel's embrace, he quietly set down the sword and once again scaled the walls. He followed the racket of Helzba floundering down the tunnel.

"My eyes! My eyes!," Nasal whimpered in the distance. "Please, someone help me."

"Are you going to help him?" Ezra whispered.

Helzba's slashed blindly at the darkness.

"You missed," Ezra laughed. "Try again. I'm sure you heard the stories, about soldiers lost in the tunnels with no light." Ezra's voice echoed. "How many friends did you lose down here?"

"I can pay. Just let me live. What do you want?"

"*Vengeance.*"

Ezra fell upon him.

***

Ezra found Nasal crawling on all fours, begging for help. He momentarily thought about killing him out of mercy, but instead kept running.

To his surprise, he came upon Rat resting against the wall a dozen yards down the tunnel.

Rat stood. "Left Hand told me to wait for you. He went for Lucatta. He said meet him back at the Wide."

"Where were you?"

"I went back up da Narrow while you two crawling 'round da pipe, den I hear da soldiers coming and hid."

"Why didn't you warn us?"

"No time."

It made sense. Rat shared most thieves' strong instinct for self-preservation and lack of honor.

Rat craned around Ezra where Nasal's pleading voice echoed louder. "You kill all 'dem?" he asked, almost reverently.

"Yes."

"Damn."

"Let's catch up to Left Hand; he'll need our help."

"What 'bout him?" Rat nodded at Nasal's shadowy form crawling out of the darkness. "Want me slit his throat?"

Ezra looked back into the shadows, and could just make out the blind soldier crawling their direction. Then he heard the scraping of bronze on brick as the bodies slowly floated by.

He began to shake. The tunnel, the darkness, the bodies…allies transformed to curses.

Shaking, Ezra crumpled to the tunnel floor.

"Blade, you okay?"

Ezra shook his head, trying not to vomit.

"You never kill before, eh?" Rat put his hands on his hips. "Well, dat's 'bout da best start a'killing I've ever see."

Ezra blurted out a laugh, "I guess."

"Help!" Nasal pleaded at the sound of their voices.

166

"It's alright. Help me up." With Rat's help, Ezra stood.

Rat removed his knife and turned to Nasal. "I'll finish him."

"No," Ezra commanded. "He's not a threat."

Rat shook his head. "You killed all 'dose soldiers. And now you showin mercy?"

Ezra shrugged and looked down the tunnel. "I hope Left Hand got there in time."

"Me too."

"C'mon, we have to hurry."

"I know a shortcut," Rat said.

Ezra frowned. He didn't know the Underworld like thieves who'd been brought up below the streets. A good thief always kept secrets, ways that gave him an edge against enemies and hunger. Rat had a reputation as a good thief. If he could shave precious minutes it might mean the difference between life and death.

"Left Hand brought us here the shortest way he knew. I doubt there is a faster way except through the streets."

"My way shorter." He pointed up the tunnel.

Ezra turned, and something hard slammed into the back of his head. The world went black.

24. Behind the Curtain

"My Princess," a weak voice greeted Meribeph as they entered the back pantry.

Asul lay against bags of grain, ashen with blood stained linen strips wrapped around his bare chest. His sword lay by the side. The sight proved almost too much to bear, the reality far more brutal than the mere thought of his dead body lying in the courtyard.

The laborer who snapped the guard's neck, a dusky skinned mountain of a man named Samuel, spoke, "We found him before dawn, left for dead in the cellars. Janus removed the arrow and bandaged him up the best she could."

Meribeph turned to the slaves peering into the pantry from the kitchen. Summoning all the dignity she could muster, Meribeph addressed them once more in the manner of a princess. "Blessings upon you all. I can never repay you for what you've done. You are all in great danger and must flee the city."

They looked at one another quizzically, and then at the princess. "Where shall we go?" Samuel asked.

"The wagons are likely still loaded. If so, take them and go."

Samuel lowered his head and shook it sadly. "Slaves cannot pass the city wall without a master. They say the Bastard Prince is now Captain of the Wall. His men will be keen to anyone from House Azubehl trying to slip the gates."

She considered them, irritated at how calm and docile they acted in the face of certain death.

"Then flee to the streets! There must be many places to hide in Hur-ar. What about the sewers? Everyone knows the thief guilds hide there."

Samuel glanced at the others, who seemed to be looking to him as a spokesman. He extended his arm, displaying the house brand seared into his flesh, and spoke patiently as if to a well-intentioned, but ignorant child. "Thieves catch runaways and resell them to the priests for a bounty." He lowered his arm. "The Snake won't kill us all. Many of us will end up where you found us, destined for the belly of the Dragon."

"Thieves and dogs have more rights under Hur law than a slave," another spat.

"You must try." Meribeph raised her voice, searching their faces for any glimmer they would try to save themselves.

"You gave us hope, Gabereph," Samuel said. "We could not allow the guards to take that precious gift from you. If it means our lives..." He shrugged and said nothing else.

Janus pushed her way through the door, followed by the little boy. She distributed kitchen knives and cleavers while the child handed each slave half a loaf of fresh flatbread, hot and baked to perfection.

"You mean to fight?"

No one answered her.

"They'll cut you all down." There had been too much death today at her expense, too many had perished because they served her.

"A better way to die than the jaws of the Black Dragon," Samuel said.

Resolution, firm and unswayable, stared back at her. She knew no power under the sun could change their minds. Here, they would make their last stand. Here, they mattered. Here, they would die.

Only one course of action lay before Meribeph.

"No matter what happens, you will meet your fate with unconquered spirits." She touched Samuel's chest over his heart. "Here, you are already free."

Samuel turned the cleaver over in his hand and smiled. "Your name will be on our lips as we fight."

She shuddered. "My name bears too much blood this day."

Without a word, they bowed and slipped into the kitchen, pulling the curtain behind them, leaving Meribeph alone with Asul. She pulled the blanket tightly around her shoulders and knelt beside him.

Wheezing breath battled its way in and out of his broken body. She extended a hand and touched his clammy cheek.

He took her hand in his and pressed it against his lips. "Thank the Narim that I may look upon your blessed face once more," he whispered.

Meribeph struggled to fight back the tears, to remain as brave as he expected her to be. "How?"

"No time," he whispered. "You must do something, before it's too late."

"What?"

"Rip off the bandages." He tapped his chest.

"You'll bleed out."

"Do it."

Hands shaking, she parted the drenched linen. Blood welled up, dark and rich, and began to run down his side. The gurgling sound in his chest proclaimed Asul would soon die, drowned in his own blood.

"Take my sword," he gestured feebly to the weapon propped against a grain sack. "Place the tip in the fire until it is red. No time to waste."

Meribeph stood and snatched the heavy weapon. She rushed into the kitchens and plunged the blade into one of the blazing oven pits. The slaves watched as the princess turned the sword over and over. Under her breath, she impatiently urged the fire to quickly work its magic upon the steel.

At the first hint of a red glow, she ran back to the pantry and knelt by his side.

Asul lay still, head cocked to the side and eyes closed.

"Wake up!" she slapped his cheek. "Tell me what to do."

The captain's eyelids fluttered, and he looked about confused before focusing on Meribeph and regaining lucidity. "Put the linens in my mouth."

She obeyed and, with surprising quickness, Asul grabbed the red-hot tip and pressed it flat against the pouring wound.

The warrior arched backward, eyes clenched in agony. Instead of jerking the sword away, he pressed his other hand against the flat of the blade, pushing the metal harder against his skin. His flesh sizzled. Meribeph tried not to breathe in the sickening smell of burning human flesh. She tried to pull away the sword, but he fought her until the blade turned a dull gray and the sound of searing flesh faded.

The sword clattered to the floor, and Asul slumped unconscious against the grain sacks.

Wrapping the blanket tightly around her, Meribeph returned to the kitchen and fetched more linen strips and a bowl of clean water. In the quiet, she cleaned the wound, as well as a less serious sword gash near his hip.

As he slept, the gurgling sound vanished.

Any moment, she expected guards to burst into the kitchens, to shout of their comrades and ask the whereabouts of the fallen princess.

Mercifully, all remained quiet. She didn't know what Samuel and the rest of the slaves had in mind, but sounds of baking and the clanging of pots resumed their normal cadence beyond the curtain.

Asul stirred in a fit of deep, racking coughs. Meribeph held him as bloody flecks flew from his lips. After a few moments, he settled back down and she wiped down his mouth. She said a silent prayer of thanks as color returned to his complexion.

"Ambush…cellars," Asul rasped "The witch knew we were planning to escape. We were betrayed. The children?"

"On the run. No one knows where."

Asul stared ahead, as if peering through the pantry shelves beyond the wall to the city. "Ashtoreth needs the children out of the way. As long as they live, we are not defeated. Ezra, he can take care of himself. Sarah can, too," he paused. "If her heart does not betray her, like…" his voice trailed off.

"Like me?"

"Like us." He kissed her palm.

"I should have acted sooner. Ashtoreth spun her webs faster than I could tear them down," Meribeph said. "Her spies seemed to spring up everywhere at once, from court to the temple. She must have learned our secret and told the Prince."

He shook his head. "The Prince is too far gone into madness to even care. Now that she has swept you aside, Azubelh will soon follow."

Her teardrops mingled with his blood. "Why didn't she just let us go? By now, we would be far to the south, to a new life. Nothing could have stopped her from claiming First Wife after we were gone."

"She would still have claimed First Wife, and she have hunted us down. Nowhere in the mountains or steppe, not even Havilah would have been safe." He turned away and shook his head. "I could have killed Bal-eeb a hundred times. I should have killed her, too."

"And then you would have been like the rest of them. That is why I love you. That is why I have always loved you."

Meribeph leaned over and kissed him. She opened her blanket and slipped beneath it next to him. Pressed against Asul, she used the heat of her naked body to warm his.

Finally, she found the courage to tell him what had transpired since last night. Despair rushed over her again with renewed fury as she told him the tale. Meribeph's heart wanted Asul to rise like a vengeful savior, to shake off the bloody rags and storm from the kitchen with sword raised. Her heart told her to embrace him as the last vestige of a once beautiful life now in ruins. More than anything, her heart wanted him to save her children.

Their children.

"We cannot hide here much longer," she said as she finished the account. "The noon meal will soon be upon us. Bal-eeb's men will be looking for the missing guards, and for me."

He said nothing, and only stared up at the ceiling as if it would deliver them. His silence frightened her as much as the silence coming from the kitchen.

Meribeph fell quiet, and ran her fingertips over his chest. The touch of his skin seemed to calm her, and perhaps calm him, too. His breathing seemed to strengthen with each passing moment. These moments were unexpected gifts, and curses, bestowed upon the condemned on both sides of the curtain.

Fate had stripped Meribeph of her wealth, her dignity, and her family, and even the clothes from her back. She faced the realization that all she had right now was all she would ever have. Fate had taken much, but given her three precious gifts to carry beyond the grave - the hope her children may yet escape, the loyalty of those waiting beyond the curtain, and the love of the man in her arms.

Meribeph breathed in Asul's scent and tried to make it a part of her. She stared at his face, willing his eyes to burn into her soul. She needed to know she'd carry the essence of the only man she ever loved into the next world.

Strong, gruff voices barked beyond the curtain.

"We could have been happy." She buried her head into his chest.

He gathered her hair into his hand and bestowed a long, deep kiss. His lips radiated heat and life.

"Enough talk of death. Hand me my sword." He gently pushed her away. With considerable effort, Asul rolled over and, leaning heavily on the pile of grain sacks, stood.

She handed him the blade. "You're in no condition to fight."

Asul laughed. "I'm in no condition to die."

Beyond the curtains, the gruff voices became angry.

He gripped the blade and set his grimace on the curtain. "Stand behind me, Meribeph."

She glanced around, and then remembered the door leading out of the pantry to a narrow walkway between the palace and the compound wall.

The angry voices turned to shouts.

A single thought sparked a glint of hope, and she began to push Asul backwards.

"What are you doing?"

"Do what I say! We only have one chance."

Shattering pottery. Clanging pots. War cries.

She continued to shove Asul toward the door. "Find a way to the dungeons, there are loyal men imprisoned there."

"I'm not leaving you."

"Ashtoreth will not kill me, not yet. She's not done humiliating me. She thinks you are dead." She kissed him hard. "Save our children!"

Asul slipped out the back door as screams announced the slaughter beyond the curtain.

25. The Gleaning

"Mother!" Sarah screamed and scrambled into the corner, arms outstretched as if warding off a blow.

Another soft tap at the door yanked her fully awake, reminding Sarah where she was and banishing a dark dream unremembered. "It's me," Ezmoria hissed on the other side of the door. "I am alone."

Sarah leapt up and pulled the dowel. Ezmoria entered and secured the door behind her. She carried a burlap bag and began to rummage through it. She pulled out a loaf of flatbread and handed it to Sarah.

"Eat. Hurry, we have to leave. There are soldiers two streets over searching every house."

Ezmoria pulled out another loaf, and began to eat as well.

"Did you talk to your friend?"

"No." Ezmoria said with a full mouth. "We will have to look for him."

"Who is he?"

"A thief, and a good one."

"Can you trust him?"

"No, but he desperately wants to sleep with me. He's high up in one of the city's most powerful gangs. If anyone can get us out, it's him."

Ezmoria removed a plain, homespun wool dress similar to one Sarah often saw the palace slave women wear. "Put this on."

Sarah obeyed. "Did you pay for all of this with my gold?"

"I wouldn't dare show that coin to anyone," Ezmoria scolded. "I went to a secret place where I had food and money hidden. We will need both for our journey."

Sarah took off the white robe, but kept the remnants of her silk slip on beneath the wool dress.

Ezmoria raised an eyebrow.

"This thing itches. The silk keeps it from chafing. No one will see it."

Much too big, the wool dress sagged and rubbed in the wrong places and stank like horses. Thankfully, it had a pouch sewn on the inside waist she could safely tuck her coin purse.

She decided not to ask Ezmoria to return the dagger. She hated the way it felt in her hand.

After Sarah had changed, Ezmoria took her white dress and stuffed it into the bag. "We can trade this for food."

She knew it was irrational, but Sarah resented Ezmoria. The white dress was one of the last traces of her old life, and now Ezmoria snatched it away without so much as asking.

Sarah spied her golden scarf lying on the mattress. She picked it up and stuffed it down her dress. Ezmoria opened her mouth to say something, but refrained. Then she looked at Sarah's feet.

"Give me the sandals."

"Why?"

"Look at them, the stitching has golden threads! You might as well shout who you are wearing shoes such as those."

"What will I wear?"

"Nothing."

"Won't my feet hurt?"

Ezmoria stared at her incredulously. Sarah looked down at Ezmoria's dirty, calloused feet and shame washed over her again.

The sandals quickly ended up in the bag.

Ezmoria scooped up dirt from the floor and smeared it into Sarah's hair and over her face. "Keep your mouth shut. Stay close. Act casual. Look no one in the eyes. We make for the Grand Market. There are always people in my friend's gang there, they will be able to find him."

Ezmoria listened at the door before pulling the dowel and peaking out. "It's clear. Come."

Once again, the sights, sounds and smells of the streets overpowered Sarah. The sun had just crested the lip of the eastern mountains as morning drew to a close. Maybe it was the sun beating on her skin and face, or perhaps the way Ezmoria casually strolled beside her, but a welcome calmness settled on Sarah.

Sometimes Ezmoria stopped and examined a vendor's piece of cloth or trinket. As if reading her mind, Ezmoria said, "Running won't get us to the market any faster, and might draw the wrong attention."

Ezmoria haggled for a few minutes with a man selling succulent strips of meat on sticks. The spicy aroma made Sarah's mouth water. After what sounded to Sarah as a heated argument, they settled on a price of a quarter copper dragon. Ezmoria handed the vendor a small coin, and he handed her two sticks.

Sarah remembered the morning fiasco trying to buy bread and felt utterly stupid.

"Here." She gave one to Sarah and resumed their stroll to the Grand Market.

Sarah closed her eyes and savored the spicy meat, so tender it almost fell off the stick. "Thank you, this is delicious!"

Ezmoria nodded. "He's the best dog meat vendor in the Market Quarter. I wasn't leaving the city without one more."

Sarah stopped chewing and stared at the small remaining morsel clinging to the stick. "I guess I like dog," she said and devoured the rest. "How can you be so calm?"

"We're either going to make it or not. Anyway, I doubt they'll be looking for either of us in the most crowded place in all the city."

Sarah so wanted to share Ezmoria's confidence, or perhaps fatalism. She kept looking over her shoulder expecting to see Bal-eeb galloping through the streets.

"How much farther?"

"See where the buildings end?" Ezmoria pointed to a place about a hundred yards ahead where the rooftops gave way to open sky. "That is the Grand Market."

Sarah let her stick fall to the ground and wiped her hand on her dress. "If we make it out, where will we go?"

"The Great Sea."

"I've heard of it. Is that where you come from?"

"Yes." Ezmoria stared straight ahead, as if gazing beyond the city walls to a place Sarah could only imagine.

"What is it like?"

"It cannot be described to one who has never seen it. There are no words."

"Try."

Ezmoria sighed. "A place with no fear, where people are taught love makes you strong. There, no one is a slave, and even orphans have a family. When you see the sunset over the sea, you know the gods truly love us."

"How did you end up here?"

"A foolish girl wanted to see what lay beyond the reeds and fell under a slaver's noose." She looked at Sarah. "It only takes a step, you know, to become hopelessly lost. It takes a lifetime to find your way back home."

They walked in silence for a few moments before Ezmoria spoke again. "If we make it out of the city, we will still have to travel several days over the steppe. It's been years since I made the journey in a slaver's caravan. The way is perilous. If we fall into the hands of the Scythians, we will wish we were dead."

"If we make it, will your people accept me?"

For the first time, Sarah saw Ezmoria genuinely smile. "Among the Lo, salvation is given just for the asking. It is our way."

Sarah wanted to believe her, but couldn't. No people could be that good.

The merry sounds of music rose above the crowd's din. Sarah looked behind them to see men and women about her age dressed in rainbow colored robes dancing gayly down the avenue, throwing flower petals over the watching crowds. A band of old men strolled behind them, playing flutes, cymbals and drums.

"The day's Parades have begun," Ezmoria said. "They will make it easier to go about unnoticed."

"I've always wanted to see a Festival parade." Sarah found herself smiling and swaying with the music. Revelers joined the dancers in the street. "Who are they?"

"I don't know, maybe a krewe from the local slum, maybe a fertility cult. Many parades just happen." Ezmoria smiled again. "Those are always the best ones."

The music penetrated the air, energizing it with a kind of magic infecting old and young, rich and poor alike. It infected Sarah, too.

A beautiful young man with long, curly hair and a smooth face threw rose petals over Sarah and Ezmoria. He grabbed Sarah by the hand and pulled her into the dancing throng.

"Get back here!" Ezmoria scolded, but it was too late. Sarah found herself surrounded by a crush of young bodies, firm flesh and inviting smiles. Sarah twirled from hand to hand, embrace to embrace and, to her shock, heard herself laughing. The old men changed the tune, and an excited cry went up from the crowd. One of the old men sang out in a high tone and the dancing renewed, this time with everyone holding hands and spinning in circles. Sarah had never heard this song, but everyone else seemed familiar and sang along.

The singer began with a bawdy tone, "The wind is blowing, *blowing fast*, So swift it rushes down apace, *Woosh-woosh* it sounds in avenue's race!"

"Who's going to take me home to-night?" The crowded raised their hands and shouted in chorus. Then they rejoined hands and resumed the dancing circle in the opposite direction.

Sarah couldn't quite make out all the words, but the song told the story of a love-lorn warrior, a beautiful maiden and a stormy night. The dancers whirled by in a blur. Growing up in the palace she'd never danced like this, with such reckless joy.

Sarah let go of her fear and danced and laughed as if she might never laugh and dance again.

Then a shrill, blood curdling horn blasted high and clear above all other sounds. The old men lowered their instruments and the music died. The dancers grew still, the crowd hushed, and all turned and faced the Grand Market.

Sarah didn't know why, but the horn banished the joy from her heart.

A hand shot from amongst the crowd and snatched Sarah. "That was stupid!" Ezmoria scolded and dragged Sarah to the edge of the street.

"I'm sorry. I didn't mean to," Sarah stammered.

The distant horn trumpeted again, summing a wild roar from the market ahead of them.

Ezmoria turned pale. She pulled Sarah to the edge of the street until they stood with their backs against a wall.

Around them, the parade quickly dispersed. Many of the revelers eagerly hurried toward the Market, but many others shrank away from the horn's call and rushed the other way.

The hair on Sarah's neck stood up at the rolling thunder of a hundred drums and the dry screech of countless rams horns.

"Blood Drums." Ezmoria flattened herself against the wall, closed her eyes, and covered her ears. "I thought it would be over by now. We cannot go into the Market. I cannot bear it."

"What is it, Ezmoria?" She craned around Ezmoria and peered over the crowd. The statue of the Black Dragon could be seen above the rooftops, jaws smoking.

"The Gleaning."

Sarah's blood turned icy.

She had overheard the palace slaves whisper of the horrible rite. Not even Rashka would speak of it, only to say Mother had saved many from the Gleaning.

"You can hear their screams," Ezmoria said, voice shaking. *"They make them watch!"*

26. March of the Damned.

On that cold winter's day long ago, a grain merchant returned home drunk again after a night of gambling. This time, he'd lost the last of the merchandise. The storehouses were bare, the once prosperous family destitute.

Alone by the light of a dying candle stump, his dour wife had also been drinking. She'd stared silently at the candle all night, ignoring her little boy's pleas for a morsel to eat.

She calmly put her husband to bed, snatched a length of rope, and took her only a child by the hand and into the streets.

"Where are we going, Momma?" he asked as they made their way to the Market Square. They stood in a long line, at the head of which loomed the scary statue, the one that terrified him every time he accompanied Papa to his market stall.

The cold wind bit through his thin linen over shirt. The icy stone pavers turned his bare feet numb. Yet, even from here, he could see the flames licking the sky in front of the Black Dragon. Colder still were the moans and cries floating up from those in the line around him.

"Why are we here?"

Mother remained silent, staring ahead, lips tightly pursed and face as blank as the gray sky.

Priest rushed up and down the line, keeping the pressing crowds away from those waiting. The boy thought they might be black ghosts, or maybe the demons. Father told him that long ago, demons once reigned in the Hur Valley, and would inhabit the bodies of men and make them do horrible things. When the Narim came, they drove the demons away.

Maybe the demons had returned, the boy thought.

He wasn't sure what terrified him more, the priests or the howling mob pressed all around. Underneath the all-seeing eyes of the Black Dragon, the mob ebbed and flowed like sloshing water, threatening at any moment to surge forward and drown him. The boy didn't understand why they were shouting, or why they appeared both happy and angry at the same time. They guzzled wine, their lips and robes stained purple. Mixed in the mob, he saw men and women doing things to one another, things he didn't understand, things he'd seen dogs do in the streets.

Not wanting to see anymore, he pressed his face against his mother's bosom, but she pushed him away.

Tears formed at the corners of his eyes. "Momma, I want to go home."

"Shut up!" She knelt down and tied his wrists.

Bewildered, he repeated "Momma" as snot and tears ran down his face.

"Shut up, I said! It's all your fault. He was a good man until you came along. We were happy. I can have another child, but I can't find another husband."

Then the drums thundered, followed by the ram's horns blaring in shrill, demonic harmony. The crowds packing the market roared.

Descending into hysterical tears, he pulled at his mother's robe, begging her to pick him up.

The voice of instinct stirred deep inside. Run!

Screams rose from the Black Dragon's feet. Screams that didn't abate, screams that sounded like someone being turned inside out.

The fire between the Dragon's legs flared higher.

Black smoke billowed from the statue's nostrils.

The line began a slow march forward.

"A child," a frantic voice called out. "The Dragon desires a child!"

"Here is a child!" the mob shouted gleefully and pointed at him.

Priest surrounded them like a black wall, leaning down at him with big yellow teeth while their bony fingers tugged, prodded, and poked. His mother shielded him, and hope flared in the boy's heart. *She will protect me, she'll take me home,* he thought.

"How much?" she demanded.

"Six pieces of temple silver," a voice purred.

"I need ten!" she countered. "Ten or nothing."

Run! The voice in his heart pleaded louder. *Run before it's too late.*

"Seven, woman. No more." The priest's voice took on a sharper, more impatient edge.

Hidden behind his mother, the boy tried to wriggle his wrists. The hastily tied knots gave way slightly.

Run or burn, the voice inside cried.

"Eight, then. But you must watch. To cry out or show any remorse dishonors the Dragon, and you will be paid nothing."

"Agreed." Those were the last words he ever heard his mother speak.

Other than the sensation of his wrists slipping between the ropes, of dashing between a hundred legs and a thousand hands grabbing for him, the boy remembered little of actually fleeing into the Avenue of Warriors. Elation at clearing the mob evaporated when he glanced back to see black robes in pursuit.

Hide! His inner voice shouted.

He found himself curled into a ball at the bottom of a sewer drain, slunk away from the shaft of light penetrating from the upper world. Shadows passed back and forth through the iron bars as the priests searched the street above. With each pass, their voices grew nearer.

Then came a deep rumbling from the deep. "What is your name?"

He didn't know what to tell the disembodied voice floating up from the darkness, so he spoke truth. "K'a."

"Ah 'your father's right hand,'" the voice said. 'And now your father has severed his hand, and sold it for Dragon's gold."

Tears slid down K'a's cheeks. Spotlighted in a cold shaft of light, the boy offered no rationalization, no apologies. "Yes."

"Do not cry, K'a. You gunna be strong and free. Maybe one day, you be my Left Hand, eh?" The Gray One emerged from the pit. He should have thought a demon. Yet, he perceived him a savior. Slug reached up for the boy. "Join me, and never fear again."

K'a didn't resist as Slug's arm enveloped him and lifted him like a leaf in the wind. Together, they sank down into the fetid warmth.

***

On that day long ago, Left Hand vowed never to return to the Market during a Gleaning. Today, he broke that vow.

The closer he came to the Grand Market, the stronger his fear grew…

…Fear he was too late, and would arrive only in time to see Lucatta tossed into the fire pit.

…Fear he would hear the screams, and smell the sickly reek of the burning innocent.

…Fear terror would seize him, and he would become K'a again.

He wanted to be back in the sewers, fighting along Blade's side, but Left Hand knew his best friend would be alright. He had no doubt of Blade's skill with a sword.

The fight will be good for him. Builds character, that sorta of thing, he thought.

In reality, he didn't want Ezra here. Not yet, at least. He had to face his past alone, to discover if he could hear the Blood Drums again and keep his courage.

He leapt over the last alley remaining before the Market. The closer he drew to the parapet, the more Left Hand melted away, and memories resurrected K'a. Chest heaving, he approached the parapet and peeked over.

To his relief, the Gleaning hadn't begun. Left Hand settled cross-legged on the rooftop's edge and sighed with cleansing relief. He had a great vantage point above and behind the slaver's block and the Black Dragon statue. Here, he could observe most of the Grand Market. He also had a full view of the enormous pit now blazing in preparation to receive its victims.

He'd never seen so many people packed into the Market. The crowds spilled out of the sunken square, up the stone stairs in each corner and down the four Great Avenues.

The temple made sure there were plenty of victims to feed the Beast this Festival. In the shadow of the Black Dragon, the March of the Damned waited. The line of Hur-ar's unwanted and unlucky stretched all the way to the market's opposite side. Condemned thieves shuffled beside debtors. Soldiers prodded infirm, old and unwanted slaves forward to their deaths. Some were the sick and lame, whose families were unable, or didn't care to feed them. Some were Temple enemies, condemned for blasphemy. Then there were the children.

Surrounded by soldiers and priest, orphans, bastards and captured street children were placed at the head of the line. More horrifying still where the destitute mothers holding unwanted babies. When the drums sounded, these would be the first victims tossed into the pit.

K'a wanted to run, but Left Hand kept his feet firmly planted. He could not abandon Lucatta to such a fate.

He scanned the long line looking for her. It didn't take long to spot Slug's daughter slumped between two priests. Covered in tattered rags, her hair hung low over her face. She stood among the condemned thieves, a lucky break as it placed her farther down the line, giving Left Hand time to figure something out. He didn't see any chains or ropes, which told him they'd likely given her a potion to make her docile, an unfortunate complication.

Soldiers lined either side of the procession, keeping the bloodthirsty mobs in check. He'd have to sneak in amongst the bazaar's vendors to get close. But how to snatch her and get out unnoticed?

He glanced toward the Market's northwest corner, which lay closest to the Black Dragon. Here, the Avenue of Warriors spilled into the Market. Even though Blade wanted to rendezvous at the Wide, he half-expected to see him, and maybe even Rat, weaving their way up the Avenue any moment.

A roar went up from the mob as the High Priest, Shellbaz himself, ascended the platform.

"Let the power of the Dragon, master of this world, master of the earthly princes and mortal thrones, sanctify these proceedings!" Shellbaz turned, lifted his arms to the great black idol and shouted for all to hear. "We give thanks for his dark mercies and beg him to bestow power, wealth, and virility upon his obedient children!"

The priest turned and pointed an accusing finger at the condemned. "In return, we offer up these huddled masses, this wretched miserable refuse. Send this tempest-tossed to him, that he may drag them down into the pit where they belong, and in so doing, purify our Golden City.

"Sound the drums! Blow the horns! Let the Gleaning begin!"

Such a deafening thunder arose from the Market, Left Hand wondered if it would shake the mountains to dust. He covered his ears and looked up at the Black Fortress.

"Why do you let this happen?" he shouted to the Narim, but could not even hear his own words. He had long abandoned praying for justice, or for anything. If truly benevolent gods existed, they would have sent the Black Dragon crashing to the ground and destroyed this wicked city long ago.

As the crowd thundered their loudest, Lucatta broke free from her captors and bolted between the vendor stalls. From Left Hand's vantage point, it looked as if she would try to make the Avenue of Warriors, where a sewer entrance lay in close proximity. At least six priests, young and quick, were in close pursuit. Two warriors observed the unfolding events and joined the chase.

"Good girl!" he whispered.

Left Hand looked about for a quick way to get to the street. Festival banners bearing the symbols of the great houses fluttered in the breeze over the avenue. They hung from ropes secured by iron spikes driven into the brick parapet.

He smiled to himself and, with a quick flash of his knife, cut one of the ropes free. "Blade is going to regret he missed this."

The fear melted away under purpose's onslaught, and K'a evaporated. Left Hand grasped the rope and swung out over the crowd.

27. The Avenue of Warriors.

As the crowd roared again, Sarah guided Ezmoria behind a large stack of heavy pots. "We'll wait until it's over, then we'll make for the gate." Sarah tried to quell Ezmoria's fear, but the events unfolding in the Market terrified her to the point of near paralysis.

"Evil," Ezmoria gasped. "They've taken so many of my friends. I will kill myself before they take me. I would have never come here if I thought it was still happening. We must go back and take our chances in hiding. If they catch us here, they will not hesitate to turn us over to the Black Dragon." Ezmoria slid to the ground and covered her head with her arms.

Her fear began to infect Sarah. That's when she heard shouting coming from the Market. Sarah peaked around the pots and saw a young girl, filthy and in rags, dodging through the crowds with several priest and soldiers in pursuit.

And then a boy fell out of the sky.

He didn't so much fall as he glided to the ground on a rope and stepped lightly beside her. Wearing only a loincloth, he had a mop of unruly hair, twinkling eyes, and big ears.

"Excuse me, ladies, if you're not going to buy the merchandise I need to borrow these pots for just a moment." Then he stopped and did a double-take. "Ez?"

"Left Hand!" She jumped up and hugged him. "We've been looking for you."

The boy turned to Sarah and his eyes lit up with recognition. "You!"

Sarah frowned, sure she'd never seen him before.

"She's getting away!" someone shouted.

The boy peaked around the pots. "Do me a favor. Help me push these pots over. No time to explain; it's kinda important."

Maybe it was something about the boy's voice, or the sparkle in his eye, but without a word, Sarah put her hands against the column of stacked pottery.

"Wait." Peaking around the corner, he held up a hand as the priests rapidly approached. "Wwwait.." He drew out the last syllable. "Ez?"

"Yes?"

"*Run!*"

Ezmoria didn't ask why, she just dashed up the street and away from the Market just as the ragged girl raced by.

The boy shouted "Now!"

Sarah shoved her shoulder against the pottery, and the heavy yellow and black grain jars tumbled.

The nearby pottery vendor didn't have time to shout at them before the column struck several other pottery stacks, sending them tumbling in the streets and right on top of the pursuing priests. With perfect timing, the heavy ceramics toppled upon them, knocking the priests to the ground and shattering all about.

He took her by the hand, winked, and smiled perhaps the broadest, happiest smile Sarah could ever remember seeing on another human being. Together, fled up they Avenue of Warriors behind Ezmoria and the girl in rags.

***

Virag turned at the sound of the crashing pottery in time to see the pots smash down upon the Priests of Ba'al. He caught a glimpse of the two thieves, a teenage boy and girl, dodging through the crowd down the avenue.

He's a sewer rat if I've ever seen one, Virag thought. But the girl with him…

His thoughts trailed off, his eyes narrowing on the fleeing couple running hand-in-hand. "She's well fed for a thief," he said to himself.

"You could be well fed, too," the dog meat vendor waved the haunch at Virag. "Two coppers. I will go no lower."

As the thieves turned to slip into a narrow side-street, Virag saw shiny cloth fall from the folds of the girl's dress and flitter into the gutter amidst a pile of filth. He looked about to see if anyone had seen it, but the crowds milled about without notice.

The priests slowly crawled to their feet and staggered off after the thieves.

They won't catch them, Virag thought.

The frustrated vendor turned his attention to Spako standing beside Virag. "You are very big! I bet you would appreciate a dripping haunch of dog."

"Master, can I buy some dog?" Spako asked.

"Stay here, idiot." Virag walked swiftly across the avenue, one eye on the priests as they doubled back and forth in a fruitless search for their prey.

It only took a moment for Virag to spot what he was looking for, snatch it from the gutter and return to his body guards. A few moments later, the two priests slipped down the side street where he had seen the thieves vanish.

Virag grimly studied the golden silk headscarf. "Prince Bal-eeb has lost control of this situation. The fool has put my business interests in jeopardy."

"Return to the Jackal." He handed Wadim the scarf. "Give him this and tell him to begin his hunt. Make it clear I want her unscathed."

"Yes, Lord." Wadim nodded and hurried off.

"When will we return to the Market for the auction, Lord?" Bolian asked.

Virag leaned up against a wall, crossed his arms and observed the side street. "The auction will begin after the Gleaning has concluded. Judging by what I saw in the market, that could take a while."

As Virag watched, one of the priests emerged from the side street and rushed off toward the market. A few minutes later, a small army of priests led by none other than Shellbaz himself, plowed their way through the busy avenue. The crowds parted before them. They turned and vanished down the same side street.

"Complicated," Virag sighed.

***

The priests gathered in a semicircle along the gutter's edge. Shellbaz considered the narrow drainage hole at their feet, barely wide enough to accommodate a small adult.

The priests shifted their gaze nervously from the drain to each other. "Should we send acolytes down in pursuit, Glorious Excellency?" one of them asked.

The High Priest studied the coins, rubbing his finger over the kupar tree relief on its face. They found the coin purse snagged on the drain's crumbling brick edges.

"All that falls from on high, All that which slips below the mired surface, Belongs to the Beast." Shellbaz handed the coin to an underling. "Brothers, my spies tell me it has been a busy morning in House Azubehl. Fate dangles a most precious prize before us."

Shellbaz, the highest mortal servant of the Black Dragon, turned and glared at the Acolytes of Ba'al. "The Dragon has revealed his will to me. The daughter of Meribeph must die on his altar. Bring her to me, and do not fail."

"Do we pursue them into the sewers?" the same young priest asked again.

"No. Let Bal-eeb flush them out. Send word, and gold, across the city. Watch the guards of the City Wall, as well those of Azubehl. If they find her before we do, I want to know."

"What about the acolytes who let the thief slip away?"

"They will take the thief's place at the Gleaning."

28. The Beauty of the House Azubehl

Sarah would have slipped and fallen a dozen times since they entered the sewers had it not been for the boy Ezmoria called Left Hand.

"Don't worry, we're safe," Left Hand said as he helped Sarah down the nearly vertical tunnel until almost all light had vanished. "They won't follow us down here."

"I can't see," Ezmoria said nervously. "And I keep bumping my head."

"There is light, but it is very faint," Left Hand said. "Your eyes will adjust. Don't worry, the ceiling will rise as we make our way deeper."

Sarah was afraid she'd slip on the steep, slippery tunnel floor and go sliding into the darkness. The raggedy girl and Left Hand, however, navigated the confined darkness with ease.

Sarah heard the panic simmering just below the surface in Ezmoria's voice. "It's hard to breathe. What if we get trapped and can't get out?"

Sarah tried to not breathe the musty stink through her nose, but she dared not complain. Whomever this boy was, he seemed to be an ally. Ezmoria knew him, and seemed to trust him. That alone put Sarah at ease.

The boy slipped from her side and she heard his voice somewhere close to where she heard Ezmoria's. "It's okay, Ez. You're safe. I've been trying to get you alone in the dark for a long time."

"Stop it!" Sarah heard a gentle slap and nervous laughter and some of the tension abate from Ezmoria's tone.

Soon, just as Left Hand had promised, the tunnel expanded and the floor's grade shallowed to a more manageable angle. As her eyes grew used to the darkness, Sarah noticed dim shafts of light shining down from holes about every twenty paces. The feeble illumination gave her just enough light to keep her footing.

The boy took her hand again. "Now, both of you just hold on to good ol' Left Hand and he'll take care of you."

What an odd name, Sarah thought.

He leaned close, whispering where only she could hear, "Don't be afraid."

He gave her hand a little squeeze. Sarah flushed, but didn't stop him. She liked the way his calloused palm felt.

"'Don't be afraid'," the raggedy girl mocked.

"Lefty, who's your friend?" Ezmoria asked.

"My name's Lucatta," the raggedy girl said. Even in the dark, Sarah could feel the venom in the girl's voice. "You gunna be telling me 'bout your friends, *Lefty?*"

Even through the thick street accent, Sarah had no problem detecting the searing jealousy.

"These are my friends, and they helped pull your ass outta d'fire!" Left Hand slipped into the same dialect as the girl.

"Ain't no one help me. I help me!"

"I thought 'dey slipped you 'da sleepin drink."

"'Dey did!" she shouted incredulously. "Just a little go down, rest I spit."

"Don't yell at me. I ain't da one going off and gettin caught."

Sarah knew right away that Left Hand's comment landed a blow. Lucatta crossed her arms and stomped off ahead.

That's when Sarah spied the line of rats scurrying down the tunnel's edge. She tucked close to Left Hand, which made him smile even broader.

Ezmoria cleared her throat. "Where are we going?"

"The Wide. Introduce you two to Slug. We're going to wait on Blade."

"Where is Blade?" Ezmoria asked.

"Goofing off most likely. You never know with that guy. I brought the women, so he better bring some wine when he shows back up."

Sarah thought to ask who these people were but refrained, thankful no one was currently trying rape or kill her.

Left Hand grinned at Sarah. "Ez, who is your friend?"

"I ran afoul a watchman and she saved me. We're being hunted and need to get out of the city. Believe it or not, we were looking for you."

Left Hand slowly turned and considered Sarah with what looked like amazement, though she couldn't quite tell.

"Saved Ez, huh?" He patted her hand. "I guess it runs in the family."

"I don't understand," Sarah said. She'd never met anyone quite like him, funny, confident and not at all worried about touching a princess. She liked the way his ears poked out from beneath his unruly hair.

"Never mind," he laughed, "It means now I get to save you."

Sarah had no reason to, but she believed him.

"Let's go, ladies. Ol' Left Hand thinks he died and gone to paradise!" He wrapped a strong arm around Sarah's and Ezmoria's waists and pulled them both close. Ezmoria actually laughed, and Sarah couldn't help but smile.

Left Hand waltzed them merrily down the tunnel as if they were promenading down the Avenue of Kings into the heart of Festival. His infectious mirth buoyed her spirits and seemed to drive back the darkness and the day's fear, at least for the moment.

***

It was said in the Underworld, that the difference between life and death was as simple as taking a wrong turn down the right tunnel, or a right turn down the wrong tunnel. That fateful day, Left Hand's fateful turn made him the richest thief in all of Hur-ar.

Hunger scratching at his insides like an alley cat, he was driven up the vertical drainage pipe into certain danger. The risk was worth it, as food could always be found in the trash heaps of the rich.

He felt as if his shoulders would dislocate as he inched up the pipe barely large enough for a fat rat. Yet, he made it, and at the top discovered more food than he'd ever dreamt could exist. The thief had unwittingly discovered a secret way into the larder of one of Hur-ar's most heavily guarded palaces.

The first night Left Hand stole only a few balls of goat cheese, some bread and dried meat, and beat a hasty retreat.

A few nights later, he chanced another visit, convinced he'd find the pipe covered, or guards waiting at the top. He found neither and, emboldened, revisited the palace night after night. With each successful foray, he ventured farther into the sprawling complex and began to learn his way about.

At first, he crawled and scurried cautiously in the shadows. Once he learned the guards' rhythms and habits he began to push the boundaries of what was possible until, from the hot spring baths to the kitchens to even the barracks, the Palace Azubehl became Left Hand's secret domain. Over the course of weeks, confidence blossomed into cockiness.

He grew bold enough to walk the roofs under the new moon, confident no one would catch him. Realizing if he kept his stealing to a minimum, Left Hand could get by skimming off the royalty's crumbs undiscovered. Along the way, he picked up a coin here and there from dozing guards and careless princesses.

He dared not share his private paradise with any in his gang, not even Slug. It could have continued forever if Left Hand's success had not become his bane.

The rich food transformed a scrappy sewer rat into a well-fed young man. Each foray up and down the cellar pipe became more difficult. Left Hand knew he would soon outgrow the only passage into the House Azubelh. Other than the narrow drainage pipe leading to the cellar, a gutter pipe into the central courtyard provided the only other way into the palace, and that had a heavy iron grate bolted securely over it.

Resigned to fate, Left Hand determined to enjoy the remaining time afforded him by prowling the halls with reckless abandon.

On a winter night, after a satisfying meal of pickled goose eggs and wine, Left Hand went dancing atop the tiled gables at midnight. Like a rogue spirit, he balanced high above the central courtyard along a roof spine. His misty breath floated up to crystalline stars as he jumped and spun about, landing like a cat one foot in front of the other.

"I wager the master of this house has never done this!" he said with no lack of self-satisfaction. "What a waste. If I owned a roof as fine as this, I'd dance upon it every night."

He relished the winter air's cleansing crispness. He wanted to stay here until the Underworld's filth clinging to his skin froze and shattered, leaving him reborn as a creature of the upper world.

As his heart frolicked, his ear dutifully listened for the tell-tale creak of the guard shack's door below. Left Hand knew the guards would be warming themselves inside the barracks at shift change. Those coming off the ramparts would be taking their first swigs of evening wine. Those coming on shift would be warming their hands and making small talk, delaying taking their post for as long as possible.

He spun about to dash down the roof and begin his dance again, when he caught a silver flash on a nearby balcony. Left Hand instinctively dropped to the cold tile roof and peeked over the edge.

That's when he first saw her. Perched on her balcony railing, the crescent moon transformed her hair to radiant silver. Entranced, Left Hand forgot all thoughts of frolicking, nor did he hear the guard door open and the midnight watch take their posts.

He thought he'd seen all the princesses roaming the palace, but he'd never seen her. Only wearing an ivory slip, she seemed unaffected by the chill. She gazed out into the night with a mixture of wonder and sadness, and he wondered if perhaps this beautiful vision only a ghost. How could a mortal so beautiful carry such longing, such melancholy, in her eyes? Then he saw her living breath transform to mist and float into the night. Oh, he thought, to catch it, and taste the fragrance of those lips!

All mundane concerns of cold discomfort, of roving guards and perilous danger melted away. She lingered there for only a few more breaths before slipping into the darkness beyond the balcony, but Left Hand remained. He didn't budge until frost coated the roof, and the sky lightened beyond the Black Fortress. His limbs shivered violently as the guard shack's door below creaked once again, and the morning shift prepared for their duties.

Left Hand returned to the Underworld, but this time with a new mission. He would visit the palace again, but this time to pilfer neither food nor wine. Now he lived only to feast his eyes upon the Beauty of the House Azubehl.

As winter gave way to spring, he spent his days in the Underworld only counting the hours until sunset, and the opportunity to catch a fleeting glimpse of her again. He even learned her name, Sarah. Sometimes he'd catch himself whispering it to make the time pass more quickly.

Soon, he learned her habits and where he stood the best chance of observing Sarah. She loved to roam the gardens under the full moon, and spend the early evenings near the great fountain with the radiant woman he knew could only be her mother.

In all these times, he never saw his young princess smile, never saw her laugh. He thought of her as his, because one day she would be. One day, he vowed, I will make her smile and make her forget whatever sadness robbed her perfect face of joy. On that day, Left Hand knew his life would be complete.

The nights grew warmer and the little pipe grew increasingly unyielding. Left Hand began to starve himself. A small price to see my princess, he thought. He tried to rub olive oil over himself once, but found climbing the gabled roof almost impossible. He should have abandoned the pipe long ago, but could not bear the thought of not seeing her one more time.

The fateful evening came when the pipe not only refused to grant passage, it trapped him agonizingly close to freedom, his head and one arm free in the cellar, but his shoulder still lodged.

He struggled for what felt like hours to no avail. He knew a slave or, perhaps worse, a guard would venture into the cellar for supplies and his life might soon end.

In the darkness, he briefly fantasized his princess would wander into the cellar and, in an act of mercy, free him.

"Quit fooling yourself, ol' Left Hand," he said. "You're gunna die here because you've been fooling yourself for too long."

That's when he heard the cellar door creak open and lamp light spilled down the stairs, and heard her name.

"Sarah!" a boy's voice called. "If you're hiding down there I will be sorely disappointed. You know it's one of the first places I'll look."

Footfalls, light and quick, descended the stairs and Left Hand grinned. It wasn't his princess, but it was a lucky break.

But he'd always been lucky.

29. The Courtyard, Part 2

An icy splash slapped Ezra across the face, bringing him back to consciousness.

"I don't think we have enough water to wash that stench off him," said a gruff voice, followed by a sinister chorus of laughter.

Coppery blood filled Ezra's mouth and warm stone pressed against his cheek. He cracked one eye to a bright, blurry world.

"Throw more water on him," said a familiar voice.

Another blast of cold water doused Ezra. He tried to move his arms, but they were tightly bound behind him.

"Pull him up."

Someone grabbed him, and Ezra found himself sitting up in the familiar surroundings of the palace courtyard, facing Bal-eeb and at least a dozen fully armed warriors.

His step-brother knelt just out of arms' reach and looked Ezra up and down with an expression of bewildered disgust. "The water is good, yes?"

Ezra remained silent, tugging at the ropes binding his hands behind his back, wondering how he got here.

"When I first came here, I remember seeing that fountain." Bal-eeb pointed to the gurgling lion fountain in the courtyard center. "I thought it was the most amazing thing. Water so cold and clean bubbling up. My people always made their camps next to streams, because water is so rare on the steppe, so precious. The Hur-po waste it, like they waste everything."

Ezra looked about at the courtyard. The bodies were gone, but blood from this morning's massacre still caked the cobblestone. Now dry and covered in buzzing flies, it had begun to stink. He frantically tried to form a plan to get him out of this mess, but his situation appeared hopeless.

"Have you ever seen it rain?" Bal-eeb asked with mock deference as he strolled around Ezra. He didn't wait for an answer before he continued. "It's rare this side of the mountains." He waved his hand toward the canyon walls. "The Sammujad say it's because the peaks curse the wind, and keep the rain in the east." He shrugged. "I don't know and don't care. I've seen it rain once, just once. Water falling from the sky is an amazing thing to behold. Even more amazing is what happens afterwards. Worms rise to the surface by the hundreds. The ground writhes with them. If you spill enough water on the ground they'll do it, too. They all come up at once, thirsty and looking for a drop." Bal-eeb wiggled his finger like a worm and laughed.

"When I found out you'd slipped into the Underworld, I decided to make it rain. Lo and behold, the worms slithered out of the sewers, looking for a sip."

Rat's grinning face emerged from behind Bal-eeb.

Bal-eeb caught Ezra's eye and grinned. With a heavy clink, he dropped a fat purse into Rat's palm. "Tell Slug he is in the Captain of the Wall's good graces, at least for now."

"No hard feelings, *Blade*." Rat turned and wormed his way between the guards and vanished.

Before Ezra could swear an oath of vengeance under his breath, his thoughts turned to Left Hand. Was he safe, or had Slug's treachery already extended to his friend?

Bal-eeb knelt close, so close Ezra could smell the stink of wine on his breath. "I don't understand you. My mother and I came here seeking refuge from all of poverty's hellish misery. You could have ruled the world. Instead, you threw it all away to crawl through the filth." Bal-eeb struck Ezra hard with the back of his hand as one would cuff a slave. "You're weak and stupid, just like the rest of Hur-ar's royalty."

Ezra spit fresh blood upon the cobblestones and glared. "All you know is death and killing."

Bal-eeb raised his arms to the sky, considering Ezra as if he were mad. "Of course that's all I know, because that's all there is. And I will kill, and kill again before hunger burns in my belly, or the icy numbness of a steppe winter robs my limbs of all feeling." He pointed to the palace. "You people don't deserve any of this! I will kill as many of you stupid, spoiled royal brats as necessary to claim the throne. Now, where is your sister?"

"Go to hell."

"Bring the rest of the guards from the dungeon." Bal-eeb commanded one of the warriors, and turned to Ezra, eyes filled with cold dispassion. "I'm going to kill those still loyal to you, one at a time, until you tell me where Sarah is."

"I've already brought them up for you." A strong, menacing voice rose in challenge from behind Bal-eeb's men. One of his warriors crumpled, throat gushing blood. Asul, crimson sword dripping, stepped over the body. "I've come to kill you, Bal-eeb. And then I'm going to kill the bitch that bore you."

Bal-eeb growled and leapt at Asul. Metal clashed as the two warriors locked blades.

Somehow, Asul had freed the warriors still loyal to his mother. They streamed around Asul and fell upon Bal-eeb's shocked henchmen.

Wasting no time, Ezra fell onto his side and rolled to the dead man's sword. As the battle raged all around him, Ezra frantically rubbed the wrist bindings against the blade.

Armed, but lacking armor, he knew Asul's men wouldn't last long against Bal-eeb's soldiers. Ezra glanced at the closed gates, where two guards on the wall fired arrows down upon Asul's men. He'd have to make it to the top of the wall, kill the archers and open the gate before the rest of the palace garrison arrived.

Bal-eeb hacked savagely at Asul, who parried and sidestepped while looking for an opening to strike. Ezra noticed fresh blood dripping down Asul's leg, and pale agony painting his expression. Asul wouldn't last long, either.

The bonds gave way. Ezra grabbed the sword and joined Asul.

"Run before the reinforcements arrive!" Asul shouted.

Ezra didn't listen. The need for vengeance coursed through his blood like a fever. He positioned himself between Asul and Bal-eeb and took the full brunt of the Sammujad's onslaught. He'd never sparred the Sammujad before, and Bal-eeb was an exceptionally powerful swordsman. Without armor, Ezra could afford no mistakes.

"Keep moving. Do not let him pin you!" Asul shouted.

Wild eyed, Bal-eeb bore down on him with all his might, reducing Ezra to defensive blocks. Each blow shook Ezra's sword arm to the bone. Unable to launch a single attack, he could only sidestep to keep the Sammujad's sword arm cutting laterally, and not straight down with full strength.

He's too strong, Ezra thought, his limbs aching with the effort to stay a hair's breadth away from Bal-eeb's blade.

Asul and his remaining men had retreated to a tight defensive circle. Despair fell across Ezra like a shadow when he saw Asul on one knee in the center, coughing blood.

More archers fanned out across the walls overlooking the courtyard. In moments, Asul's men would be cut off and caught in a deathtrap.

Circling one another, Bal-eeb held every advantage and gave Ezra no rest. Bal-eeb fought like the barbarian he truly was, hacking at Ezra again and again without grace or finesse, only with brutal efficiency. Ezra's arm began to numb, his reflexes slowing. Only moments remained before his foe's sword would find him.

"Dammit, *run!* Save Sarah!" he heard Asul shout.

Ezra realized Asul and his men attacked with no hope of victory, but only to give him a chance to escape. If he died under Bal-eeb's sword, all hope of saving Mother and Sarah would die with him.

Only Bal-eeb stood between Ezra and the wall.

Ezra the warrior can't defeat Bal-eeb, he thought, but maybe Blade could.

Bal-eeb swung again, but this time Ezra sidestepped the blow and lunged straight at the Sammujad. Ezra rolled between Bal-eeb's legs as the sword smashed the cobblestones behind him. Ezra felt bits of stone pepper his back. He rolled upright and spun about, slashing deeply into the back of Bal-eeb's thigh.

With a muffled cry, his enemy fell. Ezra raised his sword to deliver the death blow when an arrow shattered on the cobblestones by his right foot, and then another to his left. Ezra hopped from foot to foot to avoid the missiles, affording Bal-eeb critical moments to roll over and raise his sword.

The opportunity to slay Bal-eeb had passed, and Ezra beat a hasty retreat to the wall's shadow where the archers could not get a good shot. He turned and saw Asul for the last time, arrows raining down on him and two remaining warriors by his side.

"*Asul!*" Foolishly, Ezra tried to step out again, but arrows showered from above, forcing him into a retreat.

Asul shielded his head beneath his arms, shafts protruding from his bloody back.

Ezra dashed up the stone stairs along the inside of the wall. He dispatched two archers in quick order, and then leapt onto a hay cart parked outside the wall.

Pursued by rattling arrows, the thief fled the House Azubehl, this time forever.

***

With each arrow plunging into his flesh, Asul's vision dimmed. As the last of his loyal men fell beside him, he watched his son vanish over the wall.

The old warrior smiled and whispered his last breath, "He'll save her."

30. Throne of the Underworld.

The Gray One's penetrating gaze passed through Sarah's flesh, as if seeing all inside and what lay beyond. A knotted mass of muscles and will, Slug perched atop a throne of moss-covered bricks stacked helter-skelter. Sarah tried not to stare where his legs should have been, nor the gaping canyon where his upper lip should have joined. Once, Sarah stood before the King himself in the Imperial Palace's Grand Chamber. That moment hadn't carried nearly the awe and fear as this.

What Slug lacked in missing flesh, he made up for with an aura of uncanny power.

"You save my daughter," Slug's voice reverberated in the small cavern. "For 'dat, Left Hand, I always grateful."

Left Hand crossed his arms smugly. "Well, you know good ol' Left Hand. All in a day's work."

Slug rubbed his chin thoughtfully. "And what should we do wid her, my Left Hand?"

"I thought she'd join us. She smart and quick." Left Hand stood so close she could feel the heat radiating off his skin. His presence seemed to push back the Underworld's clammy darkness.

Slug slightly nodded his head to Lucatta standing to the right of his throne. "I'm feelin like my Right Hand don't agree wid my Left."

Lucatta's eyes flashed between Sarah and Left Hand. "Send her back up wid da whore. Neither got no place here." Lucatta sneered. "Ain't likin da snooty way she talk, no how."

Left Hand shot Lucatta a dirty look. "Dey outlaws now like us! Can't go up. Either we help 'em outta da city, or let'em join da Untouchables."

Sarah greatly appreciated Left Hand's help, but the thought of dwelling in the dismal sewers frightened her almost as much as dying. She also felt certain that if she remained, Lucatta's dagger would find its way into her back.

Only the mountains offered any hope. Unfortunately, she'd also lost almost all her gold when she tried squeezing into the sewer grate. Thankfully, one piece had caught in the folds of her robe, and she kept it clasped tightly in her fist.

"Ezmoria," Slug said warmly. "I heard Left Hand often speak 'bout da Beauty of Pottery Street."

Ezmoria bowed and smiled graciously, perhaps even seductively.

Ezmoria is a survivor, Sarah thought. She's adapting. If I'm going to save my mother, I'm going to have to learn from her.

"What is your name, girl?" Slug commanded Sarah's attention. She almost said her real name, but then remembered the name Ezmoria told her to use.

"Feya."

Left Hand stifled a giggle.

Slug raised an eyebrow. "Feya?" He let the word pass slowly from his lips, as if studying it. "How you came here ain't important. Tell me, Feya, what do you hear?"

"Hear?" Unsure, she looked to Left Hand as if he might understand what his lord was asking, but he only shrugged.

She lifted her ear for a moment. "Well, um, I hear water dripping, ah…and the sound of voices echoing in the nearby chambers."

He leaned his head back and closed his eyes. "Yes, but listen wid your heart, child. What do it tell you?" He opened his eyes and returned his unrelenting gaze on her. She met it, and the fear melted away. Sarah took a deep breath and, struggled for understanding. She lifted her face, closed her eyes, and truly listened.

"The upper world…it thrums above like a heartbeat. People rush to and fro, but their lives trickle down here like the water. The ceiling, it's like the walls of a fortress, like those that guard the city or those that protect the Narim." Sarah suddenly inhaled, as if she had an epiphany. She lowered her gaze and considered the throne room. The dingy cavern was really nothing more than an unusually wide intersection of several tunnels, torch lit with a single ray of daylight shining down a pipe onto Slug. "I hear people all around us, just beyond the walls. There is laughter. Crying. They aren't afraid." She smiled. "There is no fear down here, anywhere. It is a fortress, and you are its lord."

Slug grinned. The cleft parted slightly, giving his smile a demonic element. "Come." He motioned Sarah forward.

She approached the throne and he gently took her hand, caressing the back of it the way a parent might that of a beloved child. "It's been said dat love and fear are da same. You understand dat, child?"

"We fear for what we love most," Sarah whispered, surprised how warm and tender Slug's touch felt. Visions flashed through her mind; of her mother standing in the moonlight, and sunlight shining on Ezra's face as they played Tiles on the rooftop. Grief threatened to overwhelm her. "We fear losing those we love, of the hole it would leave in our heart."

"What would you do to protect 'dose you love?"

"Anything," she replied in hushed tone, feeling as if under Slug's spell.

"Would you kill?"

She hesitated, thinking of the black dagger Rashka had given her. "I would die."

Slug released her hand, breaking the spell. He leaned back. "Bring food and wine."

Several thieves immediately ran off to do their master's bidding.

Slug looked at Ezmoria. "Honor me." He gestured to a pile of bricks forming a stool at his feet. He turned to Sarah and Left Hand. "Take Feya to 'da Wide. Feed her and give her rest until I make up my mind."

"Thanks, Slug." Left Hand took Sarah's hand and led her away.

"What of Blade?" Slug called before they slipped out of the chamber.

Left Hand turned around and shrugged. "I'm sure he'll be along. Rat, too."

Slug's eyes never left Sarah as Left Hand turned and led her away.

They left the throne room behind them and entered a passage that looked more like a natural cave than man-made tunnel.

"I can't wait to meet this Blade," Sarah said. "You all talk so highly of him."

"Are you hungry?" Left Hand quickly changed the subject with what Sarah thought might be a smirk.

"Yes! Famished."

Left Hand took her hand, and led her toward the distant light.

"What is the Wide?"

"You'll see!" Left Hand smiled in a way that made Sarah feel warm and safe.

Maybe staying here wouldn't be so bad, she thought.

Left Hand led her to a cave opening where strong light diffused through a curtain of pouring water. She stuck her hand into the water and yanked it back. "It's freezing!"

"It's clean and tastes sweet as sunshine. It comes right from the mountains by way of the Sixth Aqueduct."

"I don't mean to correct you, but there are only five aqueducts."

"Only five you people above know about. There's actually a seventh, but it collapsed a long time ago."

Sarah wanted to mention she had the best tutors in all of Hur-ar, and was fully versed in the city's history.

"There's lots I bet you don't know about the city, like what's beyond the waterfall. The water is really cold, so best to just step under all at once, you know, get it over with." He stepped into the waterfall and gasped before scrubbing his body all over. She tried not to stare, but watched him out of the corner of her eye. Between his hands scraping the grime from his sculpted body and the force of the water, his loincloth gave up some of its secrets.

Left Hand didn't seem to notice her attentions. "Come on!" he sputtered around a mouthful of water. He reached out and pulled her under. The waterfall robbed her of her breath, but then became welcoming. She opened her mouth and drank deeply water as sweet as any she'd tasted in the mountains. She stood underneath the flow for a few minutes, letting the baptism wash away the days' filth and fear.

"Get as clean as you can. What lies beyond is sacred."

Sacred?

He took her hand and together they stepped across to the other side.

31. The Wide

Once, as a little girl, Sarah asked her mother to tell her
about Heaven. Princess Meribeph told her daughter the
Palace of Heaven had many rooms, each specially prepared
by the God of the Narim for a deserving soul. One moment
we live in suffering, the next we step across a boundary into
perfect happiness.

"Why do we have to wait to die before we know perfect
happiness?" Sarah had asked.

"God gives us little glimpses, every now and then."

"How do you know when you've had such a glimpse?"
Sarah had asked.

"Those are the moments that take your breath away and
leave you in awe." She hugged Sarah and kissed her
forehead. "Those moments are bathed in love, and leave you
eternally grateful to have lived."

Echoing children's laughter, and the roaring of water
greeted Sarah as she stepped through the waterfall and
caught her breath, both from the icy water and the
magnificence that greeted her on the other side.

"Watch your step, it's a little slippery." Left Hand held her arm, and she gladly let him. She didn't want to look down, afraid the grandeur surrounding her would vanish if she looked away.

The breathtaking space shimmered with a turquoise glow, from the pool below to the massive dome perhaps a hundred feet above their heads. Sarah craned her head back to see seven perfectly circular holes in the ceiling high above. Spaced equally around the dome's edges, the holes beamed golden light into the pool filling the massive chamber bottom. The light filled the water, and, as if by magic, diffused a dancing blueish-green glow throughout the chamber. Three well-constructed wooden platforms, wide enough for several to stand side-by-side and connected by ladders, lined the circular chamber. They had entered at the highest platform, about halfway to the dome. The lowest platform rested slightly above the pool, perhaps twenty feet below.

"It's beautiful," she whispered.

"We call it *The Wide*."

Left Hand spoke as he led her along the platform. "We might spend days stealing in the streets or crawling through The Narrow, but this is our home. We draw strength from this place. This is what Slug protects from both the world above, and rival gangs." In the soft light, she saw dozens of people going about their lives along the platforms, from children to those about her age.

They stopped next to one of the massive supports that arched up the chamber's edges and tapered to the dome's center. Here, three children in rags reclined against the wall. The two boys might have been ten, the girl slightly younger. They eyed Sarah suspiciously.

"Hey'ya Lefty," one of the boys said. "Who's 'da girl?'"

Left Hand opened his mouth, and then hesitated. He considered Sarah and said, "Feya. Slug gave her Sanctuary. She's hungry."

The children withdrew bits of what looked like bread and unidentified morsels from stained cloth bags lying beside them. They offered up the food without hesitation.

They look so hungry, she thought. How can I take their food?

"Take it," Left Hand whispered into her ear.

Sarah smiled and thanked them. She popped several bits that might have been dried meat into her mouth and swallowed without tasting.

"So, Feya," the girl said. "You stickin 'round?"

"Sure she's stickin 'round!" Left Hand cheerfully answered for her.

Sarah caught Left Hand staring at her again and her stomach tingled. "I would be honored."

"She talks pretty," one of the boys remarked with an adoring smile.

Left Hand gently pulled her away by the arm. "If ya see Blade, send 'em our way."

As they strolled along the platform's edge, they met more children. Every time Left Hand introduced her, food was freely offered.

"They have so little, yet they give so generously."

"It's our way," Left hand said. "But don't be fooled. There is a cruel code down here. The hand that gives one day, may kill the next. Take me for example, I'm an old man down here. And Slug, he's practically ancient."

Sarah thought about what he said, about how little she knew of this savage place. And how little she knew about the boy holding her hand.

Sarah touched one of the massive support beams running the wall. Beautiful carvings, suitable for the palaces of the Great Houses, adorned its surface. She ran her fingers over an exquisite relief of a sunflower, and thought of her mother. She studied the platform's workmanship, as well as that of the sturdy ladder. "I know this wood. It's called kupar. It never rots. Expensive and rare. It hasn't been used since..."

214

She covered her mouth in astonishment as the hair on the back of her neck prickled. "This place, I know what it is now!"

"The Dominion of the Narim," Left Hand said. "Where the god men dwelt long ago, before they retreated to the Black Fortress."

Sarah recalled the tales of her childhood. "Legend says they buried it so mortal men could never learn their secrets." She craned her head back again and considered the seven skylights far above. "And yet, here it is. It's real."

Then she saw something emerge from one of the skylights. At first, she couldn't tell what it was, but soon realized a bucket tied to a rope slowly descended from the dome. Sarah burst into laughter and slapped her thigh.

Left Hand chuckled lightly. "Makes sense now, huh?"

"We're below the King's Palace. The Garden of the Seven Laughing Wells!"

"Yep," Left Hand said. "The King doesn't realize the Lord of the Underworld is living right below him."

She almost opened her mouth to tell Left Hand how she played in that garden when her mother visited court. She and Ezra would run from well to well, tossing in stones and hoping to hear the laughing ghosts rumored to haunt the wells.

"The royals sometimes throw coins. There must be a fortune at the bottom of the pool." He pointed into the water, where she could just discern geometric shapes wavering deep below. "No one has been able to reach the bottom. It's a lot deeper than it looks. It opens into a larger chamber. There's a village down there, all intact. Blade thinks it once might have been a natural canyon. He called it a "grotto". He thinks the Narim lived at the end of it, and built all of this around it. When they abandoned this place, they flooded the canyon and then sealed the top with this dome. He says the first King built his palace right on top of the Dominion and never knew it.""

"Blade sounds rather intelligent."

"Smart in some ways, kinda dumb in others. He'd be dead by now if it wasn't for me. I taught him everything he knows about thieving."

"I take it you two are good friends?"

Left Hand shrugged. "I only let him hang around me because he has a pretty sister."

Sarah's heart sank.

He winked. "Not as pretty as you, though."

"You're toying with me."

"Only because you make it so easy." He shrugged. "And because I like you."

Sarah flushed and looked down, fiddling with the frayed drawstring on her dress, not really knowing what to say, not understanding why her heart beat so fast.

She finally summoned the courage to look up at him, and found Left Hand grinning ear-to-ear. It infected her, and she couldn't help but smile back. He stepped to a ladder and began to climb down. "C'mon."

She followed him down to the first platform. There, they resumed their stroll, this time in the opposite direction.

Sarah had never been so close, or so casual with a boy. Her formal courtship with Prince Hector had been highly ritualized and chaperoned at every moment. Cold and distant, he cared nothing for small talk. He hadn't even bothered to hold her hand. To the contrary, Left Hand was like a wildfire ready to consumer her.

And she ached for it.

Sarah summoned the courage to look about, searching the platforms but unable to meet Left Hand's gaze. "Blade's sister, is she here?"

"Oh, she's probably wandering around somewhere."

"What's her name?"

Left Hand appeared in deep thought for a moment. "She doesn't have one yet. Everyone down here loses their old name, and gets a new one. Sometimes it takes a while before Slug gets around to it. Sometimes he asks me to help, 'cause I'm good at it and all."

"My, you are talented. Have you picked a name for her yet?"

"No way!" Left Hand exclaimed. "Can't rush these things. It took me weeks to figure out one for Blade."

"Why 'Blade'?"

"'Cause he's good with a knife."

Sarah snorted a laugh. "I can see why that took so long to come up with."

"Are you toying with me?"

"Only because you make it so easy," she giggled, and then her voice dropped to a whisper. "And because maybe I like you, too."

This time, he got quiet for a few moments before resuming the conversation. "She's nice enough, I guess. She's got guts, but she doesn't know a lot. I gotta keep her out of trouble, teach her stuff. Kinda like I gotta do with you. She'd be dead without me."

"How fortunate Blade and his sister are to have a friend like you."

He beamed. "Aren't they?"

Laughter drew her attention. Small children, tended by older girls, swam in the glimmering pool. Some of the children were missing limbs, but seemed to compensate without any problem.

"How did these children come to live here?" Sarah asked.

He pointed to the dome and the upper world beyond. "Abandoned. Slug saved most and brought us here. He teaches us to survive, to steal, and to fight."

Sarah caught herself staring at him, admiring the way his roguish smile and big ears complimented each other. She shuddered trying to imagine what horrors Left Hand might have endured in his life.

He caught her looking at him, and turned away.

He's blushing, she thought, feeling surprisingly in control. This time, she took his hand in hers and they continued to stroll until they found themselves behind the waterfall pouring from the entrance platform above. Sarah realized

217

they were below where they came in. She also realized they were hidden from sight behind the waterfall.

"I suppose you're a good thief," she said.

"In the Narrow and the Wide, there are only good thieves or dead ones." He spread his arms with that same roguish smile, and spun about on his heel. "And here I am!"

Sarah looked about, imagining what life might be like here in the Underworld. She wondered if Left Hand could help her free her mother, and how much it would cost. She rubbed the coin and wondered if Ezra had made it out of the city yet. Maybe Left Hand could help get word to him.

As she considered Left Hand, Sarah thought of all that had happened since dawn. Mother's firm and confident voice rang in her head. *Before you can command the destiny of others you must command your own. Before you can command your own destiny, you must know who your enemies and friends truly are.*

What would Mother do? she thought. She would find allies, and use the Underworld as a safe place to plan the rescue of those she loved.

Sarah voiced the thought as soon as it formed. "You're someone who takes what they want, when they want. Tell me, Left Hand, should I be afraid of you? Will this 'code' you speak of force you to kill me one day?"

The boldness of the question seemed to take him aback. Sarah instantly regretted her words and looked away, afraid she'd stepped too far and offended him - afraid she'd get answer she didn't want to hear. Sarah put her hands behind her back, searching for something to say to break the uncomfortable silence.

He gently lifted her chin. All signs of mirth and wile melted away as Left Hand slid closer, his voice dropping to an intimate tone. "Blade once told me a story about this place. Maybe you can tell me if it's true. He said a powerful god appeared to the Narim here, and made them immortal if they would worship him. Blade said he thought the magic of that god still lingered in the Wide."

"I...," she stuttered. "I have heard that story."

"Do you think it's true?" he pressed. "About the magic?"

She stammered, unable to form the words. He met Sarah's gaze with eyes as deep and clear as the pool at their feet. Sarah slid deeper under his spell, drowning in him as surely as if she had fallen into the pool herself.

It's too much, too fast, she thought, fighting for control, but feeling it rapidly slipping away. This morning I was a *princess*. My family is in danger. I have no time for this.

He slid closer still, as close as he could without touching, so close she could feel the warmth from is skin through her dress. "I think it's true, anyway. Otherwise, you wouldn't be here. You have answered my question, so I will answer yours. I promise I will never let anyone hurt you. Ever."

Sarah didn't know what lay in the depths of Left Hand's heart, but she knew he told the truth. She summoned her remaining strength to inch away, to pour some cool air on the gathering heat building between their bodies.

Sarah summoned her royal voice, her mother's voice, but this time it sounded weak and powerless. Her tongue could simply not betray her heart. "I can never truly repay you for everything you've done." She held up the gold coin. "This is all I have."

He cupped his hands around Sarah's palm, and closed her fingers over the gold. "You might need it later. Perhaps I could beg for a kiss, instead?"

Sarah couldn't stop trembling, until she realized he trembled, too. "I find it hard to believe you've ever begged for anything."

"All thieves are born beggars, my lady." He slid his arms behind the small of her back. They touched and, like lighting in the mountains, their building heat ignited a blaze.

His gray eyes, so much like hers, reflected the water's dancing turquoise. Into those eyes Sarah finally surrendered, and let herself drown.

Sarah drew closer and wrapped her arms around Left Hand's neck. Concealed by the waterfall, beneath the feet of a king and above the graveyard of gods, the Golden Princess and the Prince of the Underworld shared a kiss.

For a moment, Sarah caught a glimpse of Heaven.

32. The Hole

It was only a kiss, yet it seemed like much more; maybe like a new beginning, a second chance.

Left Hand danced about with a little spin, and gave a shout that sounded like half war cry, half puppy yelp.

"You're mad," she giggled.

"If I am, it's your fault." With that, he did a backflip straight into the waterfall and vanished.

Sarah began to shed her clothes, eager to follow Left Hand into the water, but remembered the tattered golden silk beneath her dress. Sarah wasn't ready to chance revealing the expensive silk and the questions it would surely raise. Nor was she ready to leave her dress, with its precious coin, unguarded.

She waited, but after a while Left Hand did not return through the waterfall. Kneeling down on the platform's edge, she tried to peer through the waterfall into the pool.

He erupted to the surface, simultaneously drenching and kissing her.

"That kiss, I stole!" he said and began to slide back into the water.

Sarah grabbed his shoulders and hauled him back up, bestowing her own deep, lingering kiss.

221

Left Hand closed his eyes and leaned back with that silly, self-satisfied grin. "Come swimming with me."

"Not now."

"Oh, you and Blade are so much alike. I have my work cut out for me with you two." He gave her a little splash and pushed off with his feet in a backstroke, disappearing behind the waterfall once again.

She waited for him to reemerge.

And waited.

Sarah stood and walked to the right until she could see around the waterfall. She saw no sign of Left Hand in the shimmering pool, nor on the surrounding platform.

"Left Hand," she shouted, but only heard a vacant echo. That's when she noticed all the platforms were empty. The children no longer played in the water. Unease settled over Sarah as she shouted his name again.

She turned back to the waterfall only to face the two boys who had given her food. They stood side by side, arms folded, expressionless, and unwelcoming. Behind them stood a third boy, about Left Hand's age. He smirked at Sarah, fanning the flames of her unease.

"Have you seen Left Hand?" her voice cracked, betraying her growing fear. They remained silent.

"Do you like it here?" A deep voice sounded from behind. Sarah turned and faced Slug.

He stood a few feet away on his fists, stump of a torso hanging a few inches above the platform. He gave the impression of a gray wall, an immovable force.

Sarah summoned her courage and drew herself up, as her mother had once taught her when addressing royalty. "Where is Left Hand?"

Slug ignored her question, and stepped toward her with thick metal plates over his fists. They thudded with heavy finality against the platform.

He craned his head back to the dome, as if sniffing the air. "*There!* Hear 'dat?" Slug didn't wait for her response. "Its 'da sound of fighting men marching da Avenue. I hear grates being wrenched off gutters, of warriors shuffling down da great tunnels wid torches and swords."

He leveled his stone gaze directly on Sarah. It weighed down on her with the power of truth and doom. "What de lookin' fo?"

"Where is Left Hand?" she asked weakly, fear robbing the strength from her voice.

"Bring her," Slug commanded. Two thieves stepped forward with Ezmoria between them, her hands bound. Head hung low, Ezmoria's black hair covered her face, but Sarah could sense the woman softly sobbing.

"The streets whisper da sad news of Princess Meribeph, and da' fall of House Azubehl. You've got courage Princess Sarah, but cannot stay wid us."

"Where is Left Hand, *please?*" the tears silently streamed down Sarah's cheeks.

"Left Hand loves you, dat make him useless. And dangerous."

Sarah's knees gave way, and the world began to spin. The thieves rushed forward to support her, and quickly tied her hands.

"Prince Bal-eeb knows you here. You placing my kingdom in jeopardy." He turned away. "Take her away."

Deft fingers probed her robe's folds before snatching the remaining coin.

"She has 'dis," the smirking one said as he held up the coin.

"Give it to me, Rat" Slug commanded. He settled his torso to the platform and took the coin, turning it over between his fingers. Even through her own despair, Sarah recognized sadness in Slug's expression.

"Many in 'dis world cursed to pay for 'da salvation of others." He held up the coin for his followers to see. "'Dis coin cursed." He tossed it into the pool and watched it drop out of sight.

He pointed to Ezmoria. "Rat, take her, too."

They began to drag her away when Slug called to her one last time.

"Princess Sarah, your brother is dead."

***

Someone put their foot between Left Hand's shoulder blades and yanked the bag off his head. Warm blood trickled into his left eye and his arms ached behind his back.

Slug looked down upon him in the flickering torchlight. "You been a good Left Hand. I wanted you to know 'dat before I kill you."

"Where is she?" Left Hand demanded, trying to work his hands loose.

"Being traded fo gold, and peace."

"Let me go, Slug, and I'll take her far away."

Two thieves, both strong older boys, flanked Left Hand. He rested on his knees in one of the many narrow tunnel intersections through the city. For a few moments, he didn't know which one until he saw The Hole only a few paces away.

Crumbling bricks lined the ragged edges of the place Slug deposited his enemies. Long before anyone could remember, the earth had given way beneath this tunnel and the Hole was born. So deep that even a tossed pebble would not reveal its bottom, the pit reeked of death and hopelessness.

"I would have never betrayed you." Left Hand tried to stand but the thieves shoved him down.

"If I let you go, you'll try to kill me and save her." Slug scraped his fist plate against the brick floor, producing a terrible grating sound and bright sparks. "It ain't personal. It's just da Code."

"Blade will hunt you down."

"Blade's dead!" Slug slammed a fist into the floor. Bricks exploded into fragments. "Or should I say *Prince Ezra of Azubehl?*"

Slug nodded to the two thieves. "Lower his head. It'll be quick." He raised his shod fist in preparation to smash Left Hand's skull.

One of them pushed their foot into Left Hand's back, forcing his head almost to the tunnel floor. He tried to wriggle his hands from their bonds using every thief's trick he knew, but the Untouchables knew them, too. They had wet the knots, and the rope only tightened.

Left Hand struggled to clear his mind, trying to think of a way out of this. He tried not to dwell on Slug's betrayal, or Blade's death. He stared down the Hole, but didn't see its emptiness, or his impending doom. He only pictured Sarah in his mind's eye, and remembered the taste of her lips and that single moment of perfect happiness.

Left Hand heard a grunt, and the pressure lifted. He looked up in time to see one of the thieves tumbling headfirst into the Hole. Then the second thief dropped his torch and crumpled to the floor, blood pouring from his throat.

"You!" Slug bounded over the Hole, his fist crashing into the tunnel wall where Ezra had crouched, shattering the entire section.

"You're late!" Left Hand shouted at Ezra and rolled to avoid the tumbling avalanche of bricks. Left Hand crouched beside the dead thief and liberated his knife. He manipulated the blade behind his back and, careful not to drop it, began to slice the cords binding his wrists. All the while, Ezra and Slug battled one another.

Ezra dodged around the cramped chamber, narrowly avoiding Slug's relentlessly whirling fists. Like a beast, Slug wheeled and spun, smashing everything in his path, and denying Ezra any opportunity to counterstrike.

"A little help!" Ezra called out just as Left Hand's wrists broke free.

Slug turned on Left Hand too quickly to fully dodge. The glancing blow caught his chest, hurtling him across the

225

chamber. Left Hand slammed into the wall in an explosion of pain.

The wind knocked out of him, Left Hand opened his eyes in time to see Blade thrust his sword at Slug's neck. Slug dropped flat to the floor and, sword extended, Ezra overshot. Left Hand couldn't help but marvel at Slug's speed and grace. In what appeared as one fluid motion, Slug sprung up, pivoted on one hand and struck Ezra fully in the back with the other fist.

For a moment, Left Hand feared Ezra would drop into the Hole, but momentum carried him to the other side, where he writhed in agony, back arched at Left Hand's feet.

"This ain't no time to be laying around," Left Hand chided.

Ezra shot him a look, eyes squinted in agony.

Left Hand caught motion out of the corner of his eye. "Move!"

Ezra rolled just in time as both of Slug's fists came down as one, like a terrible sledgehammer. The floor beneath Slug's fist erupted in a blast of shards and chips. Cracks radiated from beneath the metal fist plates and spider-webbed in every direction.

Ezra shuffled backwards, sword extended, until his back rested against the wall beside Left Hand.

Slug grated his fists against the floor in a shower of sparks. Left Hand looked upon the face of the man who once saved him, the closest thing he had to a father. He saw no vestiges of humanity in the Gray One, only a black-eyed monster bent on crushing both of them.

Then came a loud pop, and the floor rumbled beneath them. The bricks beneath Slug collapsed into a massive crack expanding like a jagged lightning bolt toward The Hole.

The floor gave way and Slug dropped.

Ezra grabbed Left Hand and yanked him backwards out of the chamber as the chasm rapidly widened. The crumbling rim stopped just before completely filling the intersection. Except for a narrow lip, the floor had vanished.

Left Hand and Ezra chanced a peek over the edge into the abyss. No Slug. No bottom.

"Think he's gone?" Left Hand mused.

"If not, he has a long way to climb."

"Took you long enough to get here." Left Hand rubbed his wrists

"I was on my way to the Wide when I saw them dragging you."

Left Hand began to jog back up the tunnel. "We have to hurry, Rat has your sister. He's going to hand her over to Bal-eeb. They've got Ezmoria, too."

Even in the dark, he could see the shock on Ezra's face. "Where?"

Left Hand picked up the pace. "Gotta be the Fourth Tunnel. That's where Slug always holds his hostage swaps. It has a shallow grade and it's big enough to walk in and out."

"That's at the base of the Cliff Road, isn't it? Doesn't it open to face the drainage pool?"

"Yeah, Slug liked it because he can't get ambushed there."

"Smart. Bloodshed at the base of the Black Fortress is taboo," Ezra said. "It's an old tradition no one wants to break."

"Rat betrayed me," Ezra said. "If I see him, I'll kill him."

"Not if I kill him first."

"How do you suppose we can save them?"

Left Hand shook his head. "Don't know. It'll be hard to sneak up on them. They'll be guarding the tunnel. Can't do it from the street, either. There's at least a hundred paces of open ground from where the city ends and the tunnel begins, all open gravel. Either way, they'll see us coming, and we'll be outnumbered."

As they ran, Ezra briefly told Left Hand about all that had transpired since the battle in the tunnel. "Bal-eeb will be expecting me. He'll show up with half the City Wall and most of the palace guard. It's hopeless. We need an army."

Left Hand halted. "We have an army."

Ezra turned and considered his friend as if he were mad.

"Slug is dead. *We* killed him, well, sorta." Left Hand grinned broadly. "That makes me the new Lord of the Underworld."

"Rat would think otherwise."

"Rat doesn't know yet."

"I know what you're thinking, but we don't have time. Anyway, they're just thieves, beggars and bandits. We need a real army."

Left Hand grinned at his own brilliance. "No, we need rats. Follow me, I'll explain as we run. If we do this quickly, we might make it in time."

"Oh, about your sister…" Left Hand said.

"What about my sister?" Ezra said suspiciously.

Left Hand paused. He hadn't told Sarah who Blade truly was for a reason. The moment she knew, the spell would be broken. Sarah would be a princess again, and Left Hand would only be a thief. And then they could never be together.

Then again, he thought, *we might find a way.*

"Your sister's crazy about me."

"I thought they were all crazy about you?"

"They are, but that's not the point."

"What is the point?"

"I'm going to marry her."

Ezra shook his head and held up his hand. "Enough, I don't want to know anymore. I have enough people to kill today without adding you to the list."

Left Hand laughed as the two thieves bolted into the darkness.

33. Battle at the Fourth Tunnel

They stood in the open, several paces from the tunnel entrance. The sunlight stung Sarah's eyes. The cool, dry wind peeled the sewer's moist warmth from her skin. Festival music drifted from the city to the west, and echoed off the mighty white cliff to their east. It surrounded them with an eerie, taunting melody.

"Where are they?" the one they called Rat asked impatiently. He turned to Lucatta. "Word was sent to Prince Bal-eeb, right?"

"Yeah. Slug took care of it," she hissed and looked venomously over her shoulder at Sarah.

"If 'da prince wants to sell her, he better hurry," Rat said as he looked at the sun beginning to dip behind them. "Auction start'n soon."

Sarah looked up, perhaps to catch a glimpse of the Black Fortress high above them, but from this close she could not see it. The entrance to the Cliff Road lay only a short run across the gravel plain. She wondered if could outrun her pursuers up the steep road, from switchback to switchback, until she came to the Black Gate. She imagined pounding on the gate and ringing the bell which summoned the immortal Narim. Maybe the god men would hear her pleas and emerge from their solitude. Maybe they would show mercy.

Sarah looked at the band of thieves. Pale and covered in filth, they looked so out of place in the sunlight. "There is no such thing as mercy in this world," she said absently.

"I have been in worse places, seen worse times," Ezmoria said.

"I've lost everything." Sarah shook her head, fighting tears of despair. "My mother. My brother. Dead. And now…" she closed her eyes and remembered the way Left Hand's lips tasted. "Left Hand had such beautiful smile."

Ezmoria smiled sweet and sad. "That he did, and he'd be the first person to tell you what a great smile it was. And he would be enjoying every bit of you…" she paused and gave a little laugh, "of *us* swooning over him."

From behind her tears, Sarah gave a little laugh, too.

To their right, Sarah heard the crunch of hundreds of feet marching on gravel.

Bal-eeb had arrived.

High upon a midnight mare, he led a cohort of over a hundred warriors onto the plain from the city. Sarah noticed bloody bandages wrapped around Bal-eeb's calves, and felt gratitude to whomever delivered the cut.

Rat took a nervous step backwards. "Slug didn't say 'dare be so many.'"

Lucatta shoved him forward and scoffed. "You da Left Hand now, so act like it."

The soldiers snaked in a double-column onto the barren plain between the cliff and the ragged band of thieves. They halted and, to the crunch of sandals on gravel, turned in unison to form a battle line about fifty yards away. Only a bent, rusted gate lying on its side separated the army from the bandits. Long ago it had blocked the tunnel, but now lay uselessly half-buried in dirt.

Bal-eeb rode to the front of his troops and held up a hefty coin bag. "Send her forward and I'll send over the gold," he called out.

Rat glanced over his shoulder at Sarah and Ezmoria, and then motioned his hand forward. Sarah felt a knife poke the small of her back, and she began to walk.

"Wait!" Bal-eeb called, pointing at Ezmoria. "Who is she?"

"A gift from Slug," Rat shouted. The explanation seemed to mollify Bal-eeb, and he beckoned them forward.

The knife poked her again, and Sarah and Ezmoria began the long walk to their fate. They had taken only a few steps when a hushed roar, almost imperceptible at first, slowly rose behind them.

Sarah saw Rat and Lucatta look nervously around as the noise grew louder. A gust of wind blew from the tunnel and washed over the plain.

"What...?" Lucatta spun around, looking for the source of the commotion.

Bal-eeb's horse neighed and pranced nervously. The warriors across the field looked about in bewilderment and raised their swords.

Two small boys, Rat's lookouts, bolted from the tunnel and fled toward the city. "Run!" one of them shouted over his shoulder.

Then the tunnel vomited a brown, squeaking river. Thousands of rats scurried through the mob of thieves. Sarah jumped and yelped as they scurried around her ankles. The rats scattered across the plain toward the assembled host. A few of the warriors took swats with spears and swords.

"I smell treachery!" Bal-eeb shouted as he struggled to control his steed. "Take the girl!"

Shields raised and swords extended, the warriors advanced.

"What'ya going to do now?" Lucatta taunted Rat.

"Shut up!"

The roar of hundreds of screaming children holding torches erupted from the tunnel behind the vermin. The denizens of the Underworld, children of all ages, poured onto the plain at full speed and overwhelmed Rat's small band.

"Slug is dead! Long live Left Hand!" They shouted, adding to the confusion. They jostled Sarah and Ezmoria, and she felt the knife vanish from her back. Then someone grabbed her from behind and pulled Sarah away from Rat and Lucatta.

The ragged flow of children penetrated the plain halfway to the warriors and then scattered like leaves before a gale. Some ebbed toward the tunnel, while others turned and fled to the city.

Sarah felt the knife return to her back, but this time it cut her bonds.

"Lefty!" Ezmoria shouted.

"I'm going to have to start charging for saving you," Left Hand whispered in her ear.

Sarah's heart leapt with joy. She threw her arms around Left Hand's neck and kissed him.

"More time for that later. Stay low and keep up with the pack. They're our cover until we can reach the streets. After that, we'll go back to the sewers and meet up with Blade."

***

Rat watched in horror as Bal-eeb pointed his sword right at him and kicked his horse into a full gallop, breaking out ahead of the soldiers.

"No!" Rat shouted and raised his hands, teetering on the edge of panic as members of his gang rushed to and fro, slamming into him from every direction. "Stop! We got her, we'll give her to you."

Rat drew his knife and frantically looked about for Lucatta. And then he saw Blade.

He stood just inside the tunnel's mouth, sword in hand, as waves of children ran by him and into the darkness like water vanishing down the drain. "You shouldn't have betrayed me, Rat."

Rat dropped his jaw and his knife. "You're dead."

"No, Slug is dead. Turn around."

Numb, Rat turned just in time to see Bal-eeb's sword flash down upon his neck.

***

Bal-eeb pulled the reins hard to keep his steed from barreling into the tunnel. Rat's head bounced and rolled until it came to rest at Ezra's feet just outside the tunnel's darkness.

Ezra stared cooly at Bal-eeb with that royal cockiness Bal-eeb had come to hate. "Come get me," he taunted. "You can never truly be king as long as I live."

Bal-eeb dismounted as his men caught up with him. "Into the tunnel!" he commanded.

The soldiers hesitated, looking at one another.

"What are you waiting for? Bring me Ezra's head."

No one moved.

"We have no torches, my Prince," an older, more experience warrior said. "They'll cut us down in the dark."

"Perhaps." Bal-eeb turned his head and grimaced, considering the blackness just inside the tunnel entrance. Then, with lighting speed, he ran the soldier through with his sword. Wide eyed, the warrior slumped lifelessly to the ground.

Bal-eeb spit on the body. "And if you stay here, I will cut you down in the light." He turned his iron gaze to the remaining warriors. "Do I have any volunteers?"

Ten men advanced into the tunnel and, to the clank of armor and scuff of sandals, faded into blackness.

Silence gave way to shouts. Shouts gave way to screams. Screams surrendered to silence.

***

Left Hand led them into the city through several back street twists and turns, until they came to a deserted dead end alley. She stared at his back as they ran, squeezing his hand to make sure she wasn't imagining all of this.

"Slug said you were dead!" Sarah said between gulping breaths.

"Slug's the dead one. Me and Blade took care of him."

"Where's Blade?" Ezmoria asked.

Left Hand dropped to all fours at a narrow drain at the edge of the cobblestone. "Blade, you in there?"

No answer.

"We beat him here." Left Hand looked up and grinned at Sarah. "You ready, Princess?"

"When did you know?" Sarah asked, shocked.

"Always knew." He winked and held out his hand. "C'mon, no time to waste."

Sarah reached out to take his hand when she caught a whiff of strong animal-like stench, and felt bristly hair brush against her arm. She barely registered Ezmoria's scream when, an instant later, a large black shape flashed to her left and launched itself onto Left Hand. Sarah didn't grasp what had just happened until Ezmoria yanked her away from the snarling mass of hair and teeth.

A huge dog tore into Left Hand's throat; its flat, massive head violently shaking back and forth. Sarah could no longer see his face or body, only his arms and legs flailing wildly like a rag as the beast tore into his flesh.

Screaming, Sarah pulled away from Ezmoria and launched herself at the animal. She halted when the dog jumped between her and where Left Hand was being mauled.

Squat, broad, and with powerful dripping jaws, the snarling beast slowly advanced on Sarah and Ezmoria. Sarah could smell its foul breath, but didn't back down.

She *couldn't* back down.

Ezmoria wrapped her arms around Sarah and dragged her backward. "You can't help him."

"It's killing him!" Sarah cried.

A man's sandpaper voice echoed down the alley, "They're hungry! I haven't fed 'em for a day. Not sure I can control 'em, know what I mean?"

Small and bent, he advanced down the alley, partially pulled forward by a third massive dog. Swirling tattoos covered his naked torso and crawled up his face like tentacles until they encircled slitted eyes and extended over his bald head.

Sarah sobbed and pulled against Ezmoria. "Call off your beasts!"

"You're lucky they ain't killing you," the man snorted as he approached and casually considered the carnage. He slipped a noose over the snarling dog facing Sarah and Ezmoria and, with some effort, pulled it back. "Can't have your pretty face messed up. You're worth too much."

Sarah dropped to her knees at the man's feet. "Call it off, *I beg!*"

The dog man threw his head back and cackled. "It was too late when he caught your scent." He waved a piece of golden silk before tucking it into his belt. To her horror, Sarah recognized her headscarf.

He pulled a looped rope off his belt and whistled in a high tone. The dog released Left Hand's limp, bloody body and returned obediently to its master, who slipped a noose over his head. With an air of satisfaction, the dog man pulled nuggets of what looked like dried meat from a belt pouch and tossed them at the dog.

Sarah fell beside Left Hand. Blood bubbled up from a ragged gash in his neck. She placed her ear to his mouth and heard rasping, wet breaths.

"Don't try to run, sweeties, or I'll unleash my pets again." He turned and shouted toward the main street. "I got 'em!"

Sarah tore off her dress, exposing the tattered golden silk barely covering her body. She heard voices approach, but didn't look up or even care. She ripped the dress and stuffed strips around Left Hand's neck wound.

Ezmoria knelt beside her. "Sarah," she said tenderly. "He's gone."

"He's breathing."

"Not for long," the dog man chuckled.

"Shut up, bastard!" Ezmoria shouted through her tears.

Sarah lay her head on Left Hand's chest, holding him tightly, willing him to stay in this world, vowing to never let go.

"Jackal, once again you have come through for me!" A jovial voice called from down the alley.

Ezmoria glanced at where the voice came from, and turned pale. "Gods help us." She knelt and urgently whispered in Sarah's ear. "You have to let go,"

"I can't," she moaned and buried her face into Left Hand's chest. "It hurts...."

Ezmoria lifted Sarah to her bosom. "You have to be strong. If you give up, he died for nothing. Your brother and your mother will have died for nothing. You will die for nothing. We must think about survival now." Ezmoria glanced down the alley where several men approached, let by a short, bald man with furs heaped upon his shoulders. "We must be strong."

"Stand her up!" the short man shouted, arms wide as if greeting an old friend. "I want to see what all this fuss has been about."

Two of the men, who looked to Sarah like Sammujad barbarians, tore her away from Ezmoria and Left Hand. The small man paced around her with an appreciative eye, thumbs hooked into his belt.

Sarah glared defiantly through her tears.

"Oh, it's her. No doubt. The golden silk, her beauty." He blew out a soft whistle between his teeth and then locked his eyes on Sarah's. "Princess, you and I are going to spend a lot of time together. You are very valuable to me, but understand this will be the last time I ever use the term "princess" when referring to you, unless it is to a client, of course. By sunset you will be my property, and we will be begin the process of curing that defiant streak."

Sarah remained silent, but never lowered her stare.

"What about that one?" one of the Sammujad nodded to Ezmoria.

The small man turned, frowned and then smiled. "Ezmoria! Isn't this unexpected."

"Hello, Virag," she said drolly.

He looked her up and down. "It looks as if Hur-ar hasn't been too rough on you. I sold you, what, three years ago? I'd ask what you are doing here, but there will be time enough for that later." He looked about, and rubbed his hands full of self-satisfaction. "Boys, we still have lots of work to do and time is running short."

He quickly fired off orders. "Bolian, run ahead to the Master of the Block. Tell him I will be there shortly with the merchandise." He slapped several coins into the man's palm. "Tell him not to start until we arrive. I'm a good customer, and he would be wise to delay."

He turned to another of his warriors. "Wadim, send word to Bal-eeb we have her. Inform him I will personally deliver her to the Master of the Block, registered her under the House Azubehl, of course." He looked skyward at the dying day. "I don't have time for the prince to fetch her, and the dumb bastard would probably lose her again."

Virag knelt before Ezmoria like a man proposing. Removing a set of manacles from his shoulder, he clasped them around Ezmoria's ankles. "I'm keeping you as payment for doing Bal-eeb's dirty work. I still have customers in the Marshes that inquire about you."

Sarah saw the life drain from Ezmoria face. Her eyes closed and shoulders sagged as if suddenly under an enormous weight.

Virag stepped before Sarah. "I've been waiting a long time for this."

"No!" Sarah shouted. She shoved Virag aside and bolted for the drain only a few paces away. If she could reach it, she could escape.

A heavy blow knocked her to the cobblestones, she rolled over just as two heavy paws settled on her chest. Drool dripped from bare fangs a hair's breadth from her face as the dog strained against its leash.

"It's best you don't try that again." Virag leaned down. Sarah watched numbly as the metal, cold and heavy, encircled her ankle.

It locked with a dull click.

Virag stood and strode down the alley. "Let's go."

***

From just outside the alley the acolyte of Ba'al watched intently as the party made their way toward the Grand Market.

"Shellbaz will be pleased," he murmured and hurried away.

Part Five: Sunset

34. Goodbye

Surrounded by a handful of Untouchables, Ezra knelt before Left Hand. He no longer felt the sun on his back. It had sunk too low, bathing the eastern side of the city in shadow. A cold draft lingered in the alley as all light and warmth drained from his soul.

Ezra wanted to cry, but he couldn't. He wanted blood. He wanted vengeance.

"Is he dead?" the little one-armed girl asked. She stood with a small group of thieves who accompanied Ezra through the sewers to the rendezvous point in the alley. There, he found Left Hand's savaged body, and no sign of Sarah or Ezmoria.

Ezra removed the blood-drenched robe and examined the wounds. "Not yet," he whispered.

Left Hand's eyes fluttered open and looked about, as if he didn't know where he was.

"Left Hand, do you hear me?"

He rolled his head toward Ezra and then seemed to achieve lucidity. He smiled, blood oozing out the corner of his mouth. "Did I ever tell you I don't like dogs?" Each syllable sent blood bubbling from his neck wound.

"Never mentioned it."

"Well, now you know."

"I rushed here as fast as I could," Ezra blurted.

"You were…always a little…late," he wheezed and tried to catch his breath, but it wouldn't be caught. "Being fat…and all."

Ezra laughed, and the tears finally came, quiet and steady.

"We had a…great time, didn't we…Blade?"

Ezra nodded quickly, "I've got people here to help. I'm going to get you to the Wide. You can rest and get better there."

Left Hand grasped Ezra's arm tightly, as if holding on to the edge of a cliff. "Ain't happening." He sucked in shallow breaths, each more labored than the previous. "You know it."

"Gunna try, brother."

"No time…dummy. Save Sarah. They took her…the Block."

He looked up at Ezra with that impish grin, the way he did the first time from the cellar pipe. "Kissed…your sister. She's…crazy about me."

Left Hand's grip relaxed and his wound stopped bubbling.

"Let go, brother. Go home." Ezra closed his best friend's eyes.

35. The Block

In all his years of attending Hur-ar's great auctions, Virag had never beheld a spectacle such as this. It seemed the entire city packed into the Grand Market. Virag would be lying to himself if he didn't admit the raw power of it all slightly awed him.

The afternoon's minor auctions had concluded, and all waited for the Master of the Block to present the final three events, the two princesses and a throw away slave for the Dragon.

Virag called in a few loans and favors from around the city to substantially fatten his purse, just in case trouble reared its head. He could hire a small army with the gold he carried. In a few moments, he would purchase not one, but two slaves of royal blood from one of Hur-ar's most powerful houses. He would do so with the blessing, and assurance of one who would likely be the next king.

Already a respected slaver and merchant, after today he would be known as a feared power broker, both in the city and beyond.

Virag bit deeply into one of the delicious fruits he had come to enjoy during his time in the city. Now, however, he knew its name. Peach. He liked them, but they rotted too quickly to be a useful trade good.

"Boys, take a good look around." He gestured to the massive crowds pressing in from all sides. "You'll not see the like again."

"It's loud, master." Spako mumbled from the picket of bodyguards. "Hurts Spako's ears."

Why did I waste my breath? Virag thought.

Once again, his bodyguards kept the crush at arm's distance. Virag enjoyed breathing room and a perfect view: show-center and upfront before the Block.

He glanced at the low wall surrounding the sunken market, lined with warriors carrying heavy spears. Their function was both ceremonial and practical, and usually performed by the City Garrison. Today, they wore the colors of the Wall Guard. Virag spotted a well-groomed officer with a limp pacing the wall.

Virag nodded. Bal-eeb nodded back.

"He better have greased the right palms," Virag muttered and wondered how Bal-eeb acquired the limp.

Litters, belonging to Hur-ar's royalty, looked like boats floating atop the restless crowd.

The elites coming to witness the sacrifice of one of their own, he thought. Fitting.

A particularly ornate litter rested only a few paces away, reclining upon it was the feared Snake of Hur-ar herself. Dressed in a sheer, black gown dripping with gold, Virag instantly appreciated Ashtoreth's stunning beauty.

He rubbed his chin. He had no doubt that the woman defiantly acquired what she wanted, even a kingdom for her son.

The crowd erupted into deafening cheers as the Master of the Block made his appearance. Bedecked in the finest red robes, dangling golden jewelry, and flowing *kafya* headdress, the royal auctioneer's stroked a finely groomed beard as he waited for the noise to die down.

He raised his arms and shouted, "The event you've waited for has arrived!"

Thirsty for royal humiliation, the crowd roared again, even louder this time. Virag couldn't help but smile.

"We have none other than a wench of royal blood," the auctioneer continued. "Tazrech, former second daughter of the House Azubelh, graciously donated by the great house's new First Wife, the majestic Ashtoreth!"

Ashtoreth raised her goblet, and casually stroked the hair of a woman curled at her feet like a pet. In a gown similar, but even skimpier than Ashtoreth's, the woman's dull gaze betrayed a deep state of intoxication.

No visible brand, Virag thought. Probably a lover.

Chains rattled. The crowd roared, and two guards escorted the naked girl to the block.

"She's the real deal," Virag said. "Soft skin, soft hands."

He could tell she was screaming, but he couldn't hear her over the crowd.

"Surprisingly skinny for a royal. Nose is a bit big, if I must say," Virag remarked aloud once the crowd quieted down. "If she wasn't a royal, I wouldn't pay more than four silver stallions."

Several of the nearby slavers murmured to one another and nodded in approval.

"But she is a royal," he added. "It will be interesting to see what that's worth."

"Bidding starts at two silver stallions!" the auctioneer began.

Bidding started fast, and quickly escalated to two golden crowns; every bid placed by outlanders like him. Virag knew no royal family, or even a Hur merchant, would dare risk offending The Snake.

"She's a collector's item," someone said.

"What's she screaming?" asked another.

Virag quickly deduced what the girl screamed, and who she screamed it at.

"Mother!" Tazrech cried over and over at Ashtoreth's litter. Tears ran down the woman's face curled at Ashtoreth's feet like a dog. She wouldn't look at the princess on the block.

"Brutal," he whispered to himself, quickly realizing Ashtoreth had sold a fellow royal wife's daughter into slavery.

Bidding began to slow at 10 Golden Crowns. Virag took his cue. "Thirteen Golden Crowns!"

A few moments later, Tazrech was his for fifteen gold coins; he would have gone as high as twenty. He estimated it would take thirty Golden Crowns at most to secure Sarah for his stable. Virag brought seventy-five to the auction. He would take no chances.

They dragged Tazrech off the block, kicking and screaming and cursing her mother and Ashtoreth to damnation.

Virag blew out between his cheeks. "That horse will need swift breaking."

His men laughed.

The auctioneer raised his hands for the restless crowd to quiet down, but the excitement of the impending sale proved too much to control.

Black robes swiftly filed across the stage. The crowd noticed, too, and quickly hushed. He looked about, and saw more priests filtering through the crowd, many positioned unusually close to his men.

Too close.

"What is this treachery?" he said.

The auctioneer looked about nervously, wiping the sweat from his forehead. "And now, for the final auction of the day..."

The crowd erupted in boos and hisses.

Virag shot Bal-eeb a foul glance, but the Captain of the Wall's bewildered look told him everything.

Then he saw Shellbaz standing behind the Master of the Block like a grim shadow, brandishing a sinister grin directly at Virag.

"What's going on?" Wadim asked as the circle of priests inched closer.

"The Dragon wants the princess, that's what." Virag wanted to stomp and curse, but that would show weakness. He had some decisions to make, and fast.

A fearful hush fell upon the crowd and Virag could clearly hear a woman's laughter float above the deathly silence.

Ashtoreth is enjoying this, Virag fumed. And why not, this was Bal-eeb's deal, not hers.

Gasps rippled across the mob as Sarah stepped onto the platform. Head held high, back straight, her chains barely clanked. Fearless, she took the stage like a conqueror.

Like a queen.

Virag didn't know if they let her keep the tattered remnants of her golden gown on purpose, or they just didn't have time to strip her. He decided the latter more likely, as the thief's blood still streaked her hair and dress. Even in her bedraggled state, she was stunning in the golden sunlight. Even if she wasn't royalty, he'd pay a hefty sum for her.

"Men would kill for a woman such as that," he said aloud.

His statement met with grunts of approval from all around.

"The King's auction presents another donation from the House Azubelh, the most beautiful Princess Ashtoreth be praised!"

A smattering of cheers and then silence. After a few more awkward moments, the Master of the Block continued, trying to infuse excitement into the afternoon's main event. "Only yesterday she was the Golden Princess, a stunning beauty and certified virgin and, for the first time ever, seen without her veil. For your consideration, the Crown presents Sarah, former First Daughter of ..."

"Daughter of Meribeph!" Sarah interrupted, leaving the Master of the Block speechless.

She looked out over the packed market. "My mother loved this city, she loved its people, especially the weakest among us. She represents all that was still good about us. I am the daughter of the best of Hur-ar!"

She raised her manacled hands and pointed to the Black Fortress. "She followed the teachings of the Narim. She loved freeman and slave alike."

"Spare her!" someone in the distance shouted. Virag sensed a nervous, uncomfortable energy emanating from the mob like ripples of heat.

"We were once a good people!" Sarah pleaded, her voice carrying high and strong over the crowd. "Long ago, the Narim offered us a choice, follow the ways of righteousness, or suffer the consequences. That choice is before you again. If you follow the Black Dragon and the witch Ashtoreth, you choose evil. Is that truly what you want? *Decide, Hur-po!"*

A hush fell over the crowd as the weight of her words settled over the people of Hur-ar.

"Free her!" a smattering of voices meekly called out, but most remained silent.

Virag wasn't listening to Sarah. He watched the priests draw closer to his picket, curved crimson daggers just visible under their cloaks.

"It was my deal!" he said under his breath.

"We start the bidding at one Golden Crown," the auctioneer started.

"One Golden Crown," Shellbaz said, never taking his eyes off Virag, as if daring him to speak and seal his fate.

Prince Tuma won't be satisfied with Tazrech, Virag thought. No one would. If I don't bring back Sarah, the Scythians will roast me. If I challenge the Dragon, Shellbaz will roast me.

"What do we do, boss?" Wadim asked, eying the encircling black wall.

"Do I hear another bid?" The auctioneer licked his lips in anticipation of ending this uncomfortable situation.

Sarah lowered her head.

The Sammujad lowered their heavy sagar spears as one. It didn't matter if the heavy shafts were designed for running through Scythian horses, they would work just fine on priests of Ba'al.

"If one of those black bastards gets too close, skewer his ass." Virag cupped his hands around his mouth. "FIVE GOLDEN CROWNS!"

The market erupted. The crowd pulled away from where the Sammujad and Priest of Ba'al faced off against one another, eager to witness a bloody showdown.

"Thirty!" Shellbaz snarled.

Virag looked back for Bal-eeb, but he had vanished from the wall. "We just lost our underwriter."

He caught Ashtoreth staring at him, smokey eyes barely concealing hell fire.

"Thirty-five!" Virag called out.

"Forty," Shellbaz countered.

Virag knew the Dragon's purse was much deeper than his. He once promised himself he'd never get drawn into a no-win situation like this. Yet, here he was.

With every bid he placed challenging Shellbaz, the market roared in approval. Everyone knew what the priest had in store for the Princess. Virag knew the people loved her, or at least loved her mother.

Sarah held her head high, but Virag could see the defeat written across her face. The princess would lose either way, but damned if he didn't admire her. "FORTY!"

"Forty-five," Shellbaz countered.

A priest crept closer to Virag's men. Without warning, Spako slammed his fist down upon his head. The servant of Ba'al crumpled into a heap.

"Spako don't like the crow men. Scare Spako."

Wadim laughed. "I think you scare them."

The other priests backed off, but Virag knew they would eventually rush them. The crowd stumbled and shuffled into an even wider circle in anticipation of the coming battle between the priests and Virag's small band of warriors.

"Forty-seven!" Virag shouted. He knew he made a critical error, but he had no choice. By slowing the bid, Virag told his opponent he was approaching his limit.

"Fifty-five," the High priest countered cooly.

"Sixty." Virag cast his lot, and waited for Shellbaz to finish him off.

***

Shellbaz recited the Creed under his breath as he prepared for his victory over the outlander. "Blood begets Power. Power begets Wealth. Wealth begets Power. Power begets Blood. This is the way of death. This is the way of the Black Dragon."

In the wicked heart of the temple, where blood and fire and terror became one, the Black Dragon had spoken to Shellbaz.

"The Golden Princess must die," the Beast had roared from the inferno. *"Drive the obsidian dagger into her heart. Spill her blood upon my altar."*

Shellbaz vowed to obey, and now stood on the precipice of victory. He sensed the outlander quickly coming to the end of his gold. The outlander stood alone, and would be dead by sunset.

He opened his mouth to speak, to utter the price which would seal his victory, but no words came forth.

Something sharp pressed into the small of his back.

"Keep your eyes straight ahead and your mouth shut," an enemy whispered from behind.

"I don't know who you are, but you meddle in the affairs of the Dragon." Shellbaz smiled coldly toward the crowd.

"Make another bid, and you and every priest on this stage dies."

Shellbaz eyed the warriors only a few paces away on either side of the platform. Spears in hand, the warriors stood with their backs to the priests, vigilantly scanning the crowds.

"Signal the guards, and every priest on this stage dies."

Shellbaz glanced left and right. His priests stood in wide-eyed surprise as small cloaked figures hid behind each of them. Concealed from the crowd, the enemies held long knives at the acolytes' backs.

"Do I hear sixty-five?" the auctioneer said.

Shellbaz opened his mouth to speak, but the dagger penetrated his outer garment and pricked his skin.

"You have no idea how badly I want to kill you," the enemy whispered.

"If it honors the Black Dragon, my life is of no consequence. Blood is the first step to power. If you desire power, then do it."

"Do I hear sixty-five?" the Master of the Block repeated, looking back at Shellbaz with trepidation.

"I don't want power, I just want to kill someone. Might as well be you."

"You're trying to save the Princess."

"Sixty-five..." the auctioneer repeated, staring straight at Shellbaz.

"Close the bid!" someone shouted, and the cry was quickly repeated by others.

"If you open your mouth, raise your hand, nod, blink or even break wind I will slice open your bowels, and my men will slay your dogs. Or maybe your god would gladly accept your blood in place of the Princess? C'mon, let's tempt him and see what he says!"

"*Sixty...five...*" the auctioneer asked again, slowly, methodically.

Shellbaz inhaled deeply and winced as the knife began to sink into the skin.

"No bid!" Shellbaz blurted.

"No bid?" the auctioneer repeated, astonished.

The knife sank deeper, delivering serious pain. "No bid, you fool! Didn't you hear me?" Shellbaz shouted.

The Master of the Block shook his head and cleared his throat. "The slave goes to Virag! The Block is closed, enjoy Festival." The auctioneer retreated quickly from the platform and away from Shellbaz, not daring to look back. Guards escorting Sarah followed closely behind.

"So you *do* love your life more than your god," the stranger whispered. "Let the slaver and his caravan depart the city unmolested. Any black robes caught within sight will have their throats cut."

Shellbaz felt the bloodlust ripple from the stranger like heat off the street in the dead of summer. "What is your name?"

"I am the slayer of the Legless King. I rule the Narrows and the Wide, where warriors fear to tread. My palace is darkness, silence my cloak. I am Master of the Night, ruler of the Untouchables, Lord of the Underworld. I am your enemy."

The pressure abated and, after a moment, Shellbaz spun around to face an empty platform.

36. The Courtyard, Part 3

Following the kitchen uprising, Ashtoreth wasted no time issuing orders for the massacre of every remaining household slave.

She also issued instructions that Meribeph be forced to watch. The new palace captain, a warrior brought in from outside the household, had the bodies removed before sunset. They carted the dead away on the wagons Meribeph and Asul were to use for their escape and dumped the corpses in a ditch beyond the city wall.

The sunlight had all but almost vanished, and the night watch took their places along the wall. New slaves, ones hurriedly rented from other wealthy households, lit torches in the courtyard. In the courtyard center, beside the lion fountain, a lone figure in a tattered slave dress crouched on her knees.

Under the stern eyes of two sentries, the kitchen wife scrubbed the blood from each courtyard cobblestone. Her fingers bled and her knees throbbed in agony. Over and over, she dipped a shredded rag into the bucket of blood-black water.

She couldn't hear the Festival celebrations beyond the wall. Perhaps because the sound of dripping water from her rag made too much noise. Perhaps because the courtyard fountain's gentle gurgling taunted her, reminding the kitchen wife of what was, and will never be again. Perhaps because the deafening buzz of flies feasting on the blood of those she once cared for blocked all sounds of merriment. Perhaps the stares of the dead on spears along the wall drove away any revelers from the gates of Azubehl.

She only heard her own breathing, and wished it would stop.

Finally, she stood and dragged the heavy bucket to the courtyard drain. Before she could pour the filthy water into the hole, she saw a fresh sunflower resting beside the sewer grate. The flower had not been there minutes ago, of that she was certain. Other than her guards, no one else had entered the courtyard since Ashtoreth's litter departed several hours ago.

Meribeph dropped the bucket and fell to her knees. Freshly cut, this flower did not come from her garden. She cradled the flower close to her heart and began to sob silently, letting the tears of grief flow freely.

In the distance, she heard the faint echo of a child's laughter. Meribeph wiped her eyes and craned her head around, searching for the source. In a moment, she realized it did not come from beyond the wall, but from deep inside the drainpipe.

37. Sunset Over the City of Gold

The sun gave no warmth as the wind picked up cold and strong from the west. From a rooftop near the city wall, Ezra gazed at the crowds packed alongside the Avenue of Kings. There, he saw Sarah's small figure, along with Tazrech and Ezmoria, shuffling in chains at the head of the slaver's caravan. From here, he spotted his thieves mingling in the crowd, looking for any signs of Ba'al's agents.

If Shellbaz wanted to make a bid to stop Virag, he saw no sign of it.

Sarah and the slaver's caravan probably faced more danger from the raucous crowds than the Priest of Ba'al. Shellbaz would be hard pressed to mount an attack in such short order. They are priests, sometimes assassins, but not warriors. Asul once told him such men needed time to plot, and were averse to quick action. The sooner the slaver's procession departed the city, the better the chance they had of survival.

Ezra squinted, but could not get a good look at the slaver who had purchased Sarah and cursed himself. He knew without that slaver, his sister would be dead. That cold fact would weigh heavily on Ezra's decision to slay, or spare the man should they ever meet.

Far below, the gates opened, allowing the sunset to temporarily pour down the Avenue of Kings like a flood. The caravan vanished into the light, and the gates closed behind them with a dead thud he could hear over the wind even from this distance.

She was gone.

Ezra's heart fell, and he knew he was truly alone. He lifted his face to the dry, clean breeze and closed his eyes. "Hang on, sis. Somehow, someway I'll find you."

He replayed the events in the Market over and over in his mind. If he had snatched Sarah, the guards and Bal-eeb's men would have been on them well before they could have escaped to the sewers. Ezra knew he had no choice, but it didn't make it easier. Surrender Sarah to the slaver, or have her perish at the hands of the Dragon. Now Ezra had no idea how he was going to save Sarah, or his mother.

His mother concerned Ezra most. The slaver had invested a king's ransom in Sarah, and she would likely be safe for the immediate future. Ashtoreth would soon grow weary of humiliating Meribeph and arrange her convenient demise. Bal-eeb would make gaining entrance to the palace nearly impossible.

Time was running out. He needed options.

He took a cleansing breath and opened his eyes, before turning to face a dozen Untouchables waiting on the rooftop.

Squinting in the last embers of the ruddy sunset, filthy faces looked expectantly to the new Prince of the Underworld.

This is my kingdom now, Ezra thought. These are my soldiers.

Left Hand's voice echoed in his thoughts. *There are no half-thieves in the Narrow and Wide, only good ones or dead ones.*

"So boss, what's next?" A tall, gangly girl they called Stretch fidgeted, toying with the tip of the dagger.

"Yeah, Blade, what gives?" asked another, a wild haired freckled boy they called Ripper.

Ezra pushed through them and walked across the rooftop. "First off, my name is Ezra, not Blade," he said. "Make sure everyone knows it, especially our enemies. I want them to fear it, every bit as much they feared Slug."

The thieves looked at one another with confused expressions.

Ezra halted, and considered his long shadow stretching out before him until it melted with the darkness seeping across the city. Around them, lanterns began to twinkle on the rooftops.

Ezra looked to the east and the Cliff Wall painted blood red by sunset's last flames. For a moment, he thought of the token of hope he left for his mother, and prayed it was enough to keep her going just a little longer.

"Boss?" Stretched called from behind. "You okay?"

Ezra wasn't okay, but he would have to keep his grief bottled up and hidden from the pack of wolves he led. The Prince of the Underworld could not show weakness before the Untouchables.

Let go, or go home.

Ezra put on a mask of cocky confidence, turned and grinned. "Ping-ping to be grabbin' and wine to be a'drinkin'. What'cha waiting for? It's wilding time!"

38. At The City Gates

As the sun touched the top of the western wall and glared in Virag's face, he felt satisfied, but not yet safe. To either side of the avenue, soldiers of the City Wall kept the mob away from his men and merchandise.

At least Bal-eeb got that right, he thought.

Several hundred yards remained down the Avenue of Kings before they reached the city gate, and at least three hundred paces beyond the wall before they were out of bow range. He expected Shellbaz to unleash his assassins upon them before they reached the gate, but so far no black robes materialized among the crowd.

Virag wasn't sure what transpired to make the High Priest back down, but he wasn't about to argue with his stroke of fortune. One day, he would have to reckon with The Dragon. He'd figure something out then; he always did. Today, he would bask in victory.

Virag patted his nearly empty purse. He'd never make back the money he spent on Sarah, and resolved to merely pimp her services to the Scythian prince, and not sell her outright. Unfortunately, Virag knew the Scythians well. Eventually, they would want to claim a woman as beautiful as Sarah as their own. They would take her, and eventually destroy her. He'd sold plenty of wenches to the Scythians, and what they did to them was of no consequence to Virag.

But Sarah wasn't any woman. Where before it had been business, now it was a matter of pride.

Tuma can bed her as much as he pleases, Virag thought, but she's *my* trophy.

If and when the Scythian's threatened to steal his trophy, he'd figure a way to keep her safely hidden until he could reclaim her. Only two places in the world were safe from Scythian hooves - behind the walls of Hur-ar or deep within the impenetrable marshes surrounding the Great Sea.

The mob followed them into the avenue and mixed with Festival revelers. They cheered Virag like a conqueror.

"Look, here he comes!" he heard them say. *"That is the one who challenged the Dragon."*

"He's the one who bought the Golden Princess!" others said.

He could see how such adulation might be addictive, but unsuitable for a realist like himself. He watched as Bal-eeb limped quickly ahead of them to the wall, wearing a sour expression.

He hates that the cheers are not for him, Virag thought, amused. If this is the elixir of kings, then they can keep it. I want my yurt, my fire, and my wine. It will be good to smell the marshes again.

The crowd, full of wine and bloodlust, taunted his slave girls. They screamed and shouted a creative mix of profanities and insults, none of which concerned Virag. Then an old woman in peasant rags darted from the mob with surprising speed, and grabbed at Sarah before one of his men beat her back. Something flew through the air and struck his trophy in the face.

While Sarah didn't appear hurt, Virag shouted at the city guards lining the avenue, "Hey! Keep these people away from my merchandise!"

Some of Virag's tension eased as the gate loomed just ahead, and the crowd began to fall away.

"Boys, tonight we camp on the steppe!"

His men grunted in approval.

Virag bit once more into his last peach, leaving only the pit. "But I will miss these. Too bad." He looked around at the wild throngs of Festival revelers in disgust. "I've had it with this place."

He threw the peach pit into the crowd, where it was caught in a child's hand.

***

"You stupid bitch!" Wearing only her slave chains, Tazrech stumbled over the cobblestones and screamed at Sarah. "This is your fault, every bit of it." She shook her chains. "I didn't deserve this. Do you understand? I DIDN'T DESERVE THIS!"

Deserve? Sarah thought. What does that matter anymore?

Through tears, Tazrech searched the mocking crowd. "Mother!" she sobbed. "Where are you? Why have you forsaken me?"

The mob howled in laughter, and cruelly imitated Tazrech's pleas, but saved most of their vitriol for Sarah. They spit on her and hurled insults.

"Look at the Golden Princess! Not so high and mighty, now."
"Whore!"
"Slut!"
"The outlander will put her to good use!"

An old hag darted out from between the guards lining the avenue. She tried to rip away what remained of Sarah's golden silk before one of Virag's Sammujad beat her back.

Then something soft and putrid struck Sarah across the face. She looked down to see a dead rat lying on the cobblestones.

"Hey!" Virag shouted from behind her. "Keep these people away from my merchandise!"

"Don't worry," Ezmoria said as she walked stoically beside Sarah. "You won't have to endure their insults for long. You've never heard quiet until you spend a night on the steppe."

Sarah said nothing and kept her attention fixed on the gate, wondering if salvation or damnation waited for her on the other side.

"Listen, Sarah, I will teach you how to survive. I've been where we're going."

"I've lost everything. Everyone," Sarah said numbly.

"You haven't lost your life," Ezmoria chastised. "And you're not burning in the Dragon's belly."

"I've lost hope."

"My people say where there is beauty, there is always hope. And it can be beautiful out there." Ezmoria nudged her. "Wait until you see the sun rise and set without walls blocking the view. And the air, it's sweet. Sweet like you can't imagine. Everyday you wake up, you must look for hope. If you cannot find it, make it."

A piece of rotten fruit struck Ezmoria across the face, accompanied by an unintelligible insult likely meant for Sarah. Ezmoria took it in stride and looked over her shoulder at the city. "I've been trying to find a way out of Hur-ar since I bought my freedom." She spit onto the street. "If this is how it happens, so be it. That is hope enough for me today."

"Boys, tonight we camp on the steppe!" She heard Virag shout from behind her. His men responded with approving grunts. "But I will miss these. Too bad." He paused for a moment. "I've had it with this place."

Something, perhaps a small stone, went flying over her head and into the crowd to her left. A naked, filthy beggar child stepped unnoticed from between two guards and caught it.

Sarah caught her breath as she recognized the child as the one she gave bread to in the slums. This time, however, she appeared much different, captivating Sarah with intense eyes that glowed softly with a bluish light.

She turned and paralleled to the procession just inside the line of soldiers along the avenue. "Do not lose hope," the beggar child said clearly, looking right at Sarah. "You are not alone."

No one took notice as the child vanished behind several soldiers. Sarah drew a sharp breath as Leonus, not the little girl, emerged on the other side. Hand resting on sheathed sword hilt, the old Scythian strolled along with his trademark bowed-legged gait, as if on a casual walk through the courtyard. He smiled, his eyes glowing with the same blue light as the child's. "You've been brave, little girl. You must be braver yet."

Sarah reached for him. "Leonus!"

He stepped behind a pack of drunken young women wearing animal masks. Rashka, not Leonus, stepped from the other side.

Sarah sobbed, her heart bursting with joy and sadness. "Rashka, help me!"

"Who are you talking to?" Ezmoria looked over to where Sarah stared raptly at her handmaiden.

Rashka smiled warmly, with the same unearthly eyes as Leonus and the child. She, too, strolled among the throngs invisible to all but Sarah. "Carry nothing from this evil place except the love in your heart. It is because of love that the Emperor of Heaven chose you."

The procession entered the gate's chilly shadow. They had come to the wall.

"Halt!" Virag commanded from behind and strode to the head of the procession. He tucked his thumbs into his belt and shouted up to Bal-eeb, who had already made his way to the top of the wall.

"Captain of the Wall! I, Virag of the Marshes, have concluded my business in the City of Gold. Open the gates and let me pass."

Silhouetted against the dimming orange sky, Bal-eeb replied, "Your taxes are paid in full, trader. You may depart the city." He turned and shouted to his men, "Open the gates!"

Sarah looked around for Rashka, but she had vanished. *"Rashka!"*

"She's lost her mind." Tazrech laughed hysterically. "Leonus is dead, and so is Rashka, stupid fool. I saw Ashtoreth slice her head off myself."

Sarah put her head in her hands and sobbed, wondering if she had truly lost her mind.

"I've watched you for a long time." A woman's voice floated on the air like music. Sarah looked up to see the Golden Woman from her dreams standing before her, gazing down with opal eyes blazing blue with power and glory. Just as in her dream, she held out the seed pit in her open palm.

Around them, a hush fell on the world. It looked to Sarah as if time stood still. The crowds appeared frozen, grotesque expressions of lust and rage locked upon their faces. Ezmoria stared ahead, squinting into the sun. In this moment, only Sarah and the Golden Woman seemed to exist.

"You have been chosen," the Golden Woman said.

"For what?" Sarah whispered. "Who are you?"

The Golden Woman didn't answer, and continued to hold the pit in her outstretched hand. Sarah didn't know if she represented the promise of heaven or hell.

Maybe both.

Not knowing why, Sarah took the seed. Betraying no emotion, the Golden Woman dropped her eyes, turned around and glided away until she stood before the double gates.

Sarah looked down at the seed pit. It flashed into a dim ball of light before evaporating into gray ashes. A slight breeze announced the world had come to life again, and blew away all traces of the pit from her palm. The roar of the crowd filled Sarah's ears.

She looked up half expecting the Golden Woman to have vanished, but she remained standing before the enormous double gates. The guards took no notice of her as they parted to either side. The creak and clicks of pulleys and ropes filled the air, and the gates cracked open.

"Why did all this happen?" Sarah called to the Golden Woman. "Why did everyone I love have to die?"

"Sarah?" Ezmoria said, concern in her voice, looking about.

"She's mad!" Tazrech howled. "Mad! Mad! Mad!"

The gates began to swing open.

"You shall know love again," the Golden Woman said as sunlight began to pour through the gates and washed over her figure.

"I'm not strong enough," Sarah sobbed.

"These things shall come to pass before we meet again..."

"Move them out!" Virag shouted. "Lots of ground to cover before we make camp."

"You shall capture a good man's heart..."

To the crack of a whip and the rattle of chains, the three slave women shuffled toward the gate.

"Your lover's king shall set you free..."

The Golden Woman spread her arms, and her robe billowed out like wings. "And you shall know a father's love."

The gates opened to a blazing sunset that consumed the Golden Woman like a fiery halo. She transformed into a pillar of swirling mist and fire. Her eyes blazed forth like fiery lightning, her voice thunder. *"You shall be like a light burning on a midnight shore, leading the lost to a new age!"*

A blast of cool air washed over Sarah, drying her tears as she stepped through the gate and into the sunset. "I am not afraid."

The End

Sarah and Ezra's adventures continue in *Black Sea Gods*, the first novel in The Chronicles of Fu Xi series.

BLACK SEA GODS

The fish have disappeared from the sea. The animals have vanished from the land. All humanity, and even the gods, tremble under the specter of a pending cataclysm. The demigod, Fu Xi, races home from the edge of the world bringing news of a looming god war, but finds his land under attack by monsters he once called his children. He discovers a terrible curse has been cast, one intended to destroy the gods and all life. To his shock, Fu Xi learns that mankind's last hope rests solely on him, a simple fisherman, and a banished slave girl.

Beset on all sides by ancient foes, both immortal and mundane, Fu Xi knows he must act quickly and races west to rescue the saviors. Unaware of the real doom that awaits, Aizarg the fisherman and his party begin a perilous journey across a dangerous steppe. They seek the last of the Narim, the legendary Black Sea Gods, who hold the key to their salvation. Leading them is the rescued slave girl Sarah, the only one among them who knows the path to the land of the god-men.

Over seven days, the defining struggle of gods and humans begins under the onslaught of a powerful force whose true objective and origin remain a mystery. Fu Xi knows the secret to victory resides in the fisherman and the slave girl, whose lives he must protect, even if it means the rest of the world must perish!

***

Reviews are crucial to indie authors! Please leave a review on Amazon of Goodreads. Follow Brian L. Braden on Facebook, Twitter and check out his websites theillusionexotic.com, BlackSeaGods.com, and UndergroundBookReviews.org.

The Golden Princess

www.ingramcontent.com/pod-product-compliance
Lightning Source LLC
Chambersburg PA
CBHW072206170626
46813CB00003B/821